KU-490-569

Praise for Christina Hopkinson

'Utter genius.' Lisa Jewell

'A razor-sharp dissection of the madness of modern fame'

Sandwell
Metropolitan Borough Council

Please return this item to any Sandwell Library on or before the return date.

You may renew the item unless it has been reserved by another borrower.

You can renew your library items by using the 24/7 renewal hotline number - 0845 352 4949 or FREE online at opac-lib.sandwell.gov.uk

X

19·3·16 THANK YOU FOR USING YOUR LIBRARY H T

...sekeeping

...onally very
...arie Claire

...bed as the
The Times

Daily Mail

...ly *Express*

Red

...emands of
...paced and
Image

...funny.'
**** *Red*

...that make
...everyone
Fabulous

...pped into
...ng mother

...f *Blondes*

...ervational
Spectator

humour and sharp one-liners.

'A hugely witty read, which will appeal to almost everyone.' *Lady*

'Immensely en... ...kfans.co.uk

I2710271

Also by Christina Hopkinson

The A-List Family
Just Like Proper Grown-Ups
The Pile of Stuff at the Bottom of the Stairs
Izobel Brannigan.com

About the author

Christina Hopkinson is an author and journalist whose work has appeared in the *Daily Telegraph*, *Guardian*, *The Times*, *Grazia* and *Red*. She lives in London with her husband and three children.

Visit Christina's website at www.christinahopkinson.com and follow her on Twitter @Xtinahopkinson.

The Weekend Wives

Christina Hopkinson

HODDER

First published in Great Britain in 2016 by Hodder & Stoughton
An Hachette UK Company

1

Copyright © Christina Hopkinson 2016

The right of Christina Hopkinson to be identified as
the Author of the Work has been asserted by her in accordance
with the Copyright, Designs and Patents Act 1988.

All rights reserved.
No part of this publication may be reproduced,
stored in a retrieval system, or transmitted, in any form
or by any means without the prior written permission of the publisher,
nor be otherwise circulated in any form of binding or cover other
than that in which it is published and without a similar condition
being imposed on the subsequent purchaser.

All characters in this publication are fictitious
and any resemblance to real persons, living or dead,
is purely coincidental.

A CIP catalogue record for this title is available
from the British Library.

Trade Paperback ISBN 978 1 473 63027 7
Ebook ISBN 978 1 444 78531 9

Typeset in Sabon MT by Palimpsest Book Production Limited,
Falkirk, Stirlingshire

Printed and bound by Clays Ltd, St Ives plc

Hodder & Stoughton policy is to use papers that are natural,
renewable and recyclable products and made from wood grown
in sustainable forests. The logging and manufacturing processes
are expected to conform to the environmental regulations
of the country of origin.

Hodder & Stoughton Ltd
Carmelite House
50 Victoria Embankment
London
EC4Y 0DZ

www.hodder.co.uk

Alex, William, Celia and Lydia – sharper,
funnier and truer than anything I could ever write.

I

First-World Problems

'Welcome to the weekend wives' club,' Sasha Rayburn said to Emily Dawlish.

They were standing at a midday drinks party to celebrate – or commiserate over – what the host, Tania, referred to as 'back to normal', that mid-January feeling of new resolutions and beginnings.

'What do you mean?' asked Emily. 'Weekend wives?'

Sasha smiled. Emily felt as intimidated as ever by her. She'd had this fantasy – yet another of her fantasies – that life in the country was going to liberate her from fashion and caring what she wore. She'd be like her mother-in-law, whose woollen jumpers were flecked like mohair with dog fur, and who wore shoes that were comfortable to the point of orthopaedic. And yet here was Sasha, as exquisitely dressed, yet at the same time as quirky, as any fashion blogger Emily had ever seen on the streets of East London. She had a worldliness about her, too, that contradicted all the folk stories about charmingly simple country mice and their vainglorious city cousins.

'I hear you've been abandoned by Matt,' Sasha explained.

'Oh, that. Not abandoned. He's just going to be working in London.'

'For how long?'

'Only a few months. It's a really interesting project for a company he's always wanted to work for. They're restructuring their whole corporate communications set-up.' And in the process paying Matt more in a month than he'd earned in a whole winter of freelancing here. 'He couldn't really say no, but it's just a temporary thing.'

'That's what they all say,' said Sasha. 'But it's always for ages and ages. When we moved back from Los Angeles, Ned was supposed to follow in a few months. It's been nearly five years.'

'I'm sorry. That must be really hard for you.'

Sasha shrugged. 'We all want the country life and the city money, don't we?'

'Not me.' This was not strictly true. Emily didn't think of herself as materialistic, but that first winter had taught her that she had never known cold in the city, with its houses huddled together for warmth, like that which had assailed the cottage. She had always thought she was a put-on-another-jumper-and-put-up-with-it type, but she had been savaged by the cold, and even more so by the bills that came in its wake. She felt as though she'd moved not just to the country, but to another country completely, one with a different currency to explain why the utility bills were so much higher than they had ever been in the city. London was only a hundred miles away (or 'just 99.7 miles', as she and Matt told themselves), and yet the weather reports would mock her with its extra five degrees of warmth throughout the year. Her new neighbours said the local wind came straight from the Urals, and it certainly felt Siberian. 'Anyway, Matt's not going for longer than four months. Six at most. And it's only London. It's not like it's the other side of the world.' Emily realised what she'd said. 'I'm sorry, I didn't mean that it would be worse to be on the other side of the world.'

'Well it is,' said Sasha. 'It's so hard to find a moment when Ned and I are both awake and available. When he's working on a film, his hours are punishing, and family life over here sort of closes around that small window.'

'Do you actually have a weekend wives' club?'

Sasha laughed. 'If we formed a club, when would we ever hold the meetings? During the week, we've no other half to pick up the babysitting, and when they're back at home, we have to cherish their return, don't we?'

Emily sighed with disappointment. She wanted to join a club, any club.

'But I tell you, it would be heavily oversubscribed if we did have one. I don't think I know of a single couple here who actually live together all the time. Well, the ones like us.' Sasha seemed to capitalise the 'like us' bit, and Emily knew what she meant. There were some well-paid jobs here, of course, old-fashioned ones: the teacher, the local solicitor and the doctor; those stalwarts of village life in period dramas. But if you wanted something a bit more new-fangled, maybe with a job title incorporating the word 'digital', then you had to commute. Emily and Matt had believed what they'd read in the features pages of newspapers about how the Internet enabled people to work remotely, and while she sometimes felt *very* remote since the move, he'd been unable to work from home after all. 'Everyone's in London during the week, or in Dubai two weeks on two weeks off, like posh oil rig workers, don't you think?' continued Sasha. 'It's the modern way.'

'I suppose,' said Emily, though it didn't seem very modern given that it was based on an assumption that some-body would be tending the home front – and that somebody mostly seemed to be the women. The modern way had become so modern as to have become positively retro, like those hip young men who wore Victorian beards.

'Are you finding it OK?' asked Sasha, with unexpected warmth.

Emily thought she might cry at this sympathy. She wasn't OK really, but she hadn't been able to admit this to those she'd left behind in London, the people she still thought of as her real friends. Instead she told them how amazing it was to see stars in the sky instead of police helicopters, in this place where the ground was covered in daisies rather than the steaming shits of muscular dogs, and where white T-shirts stayed white all day. 'I don't know,' she sighed. 'It's quite hard, isn't it?'

'You get used to it,' said Sasha. 'Too used to it. You start off missing your husband so much that it hurts, then after about a year you start missing his absence when he's actually there. A bit like when you give up sugar.'

'I wouldn't know about that,' said Emily, looking down at the stomach that had borne three children.

'Wouldn't know about what?' asked their host, Tania, who could throw a party with the ruthless efficiency with

4

which she held down a demanding job in Brussels and brought up four high-achieving children.

'I was just welcoming Emily into the world of the weekend wives,' said Sasha. 'When the husband is away working all week and only back on Fridays.'

'Interesting. I suppose I'm a weekend wife too,' said Tania.

'No,' said Sasha. 'You've got to be the one left behind. To man – wrong word – the barricades at home.'

'Why?' asked Tania. 'Who says those are the rules? That's sexist.'

'No,' said Sasha. 'What's sexist is a capitalist global economy increasingly predicated on a free labour market that is dependent on one partner fucking up their career and that person almost invariably being the woman. Your husband, Tania, being the exception to this just proves the rule. Am I right, Emily?'

'I suppose.' Emily was taken aback by the unexpected ferocity of Sasha's speech. She had wrongly thought that somehow her cloud of blonde curls meant that Sasha had an equally fluffy personality. 'Though to be honest, I was the one who wanted to give up my job.'

She'd earned more than Matt, too, something that had never given her as much satisfaction as it caused her pain now that those days were over.

'Yes, well, whatever,' said Tania. 'It's a first-world problem.' She did that professional wave-and-walk thing to leave them as abruptly as she had arrived.

'I hate it when people say that. Of course it's a bloody first-world problem. Other than starvation, they're all first-world problems, aren't they? Tania is *so* not in our club,' said Sasha, leaning in conspiratorially. 'Ben can be, though.' She glanced in the direction of Tania's husband and made a little purring sound, which Emily assumed to be ironic. Objectively, though, she could see that Ben was an attractive man, if you liked the fisherman's-jumper, bearded, soulful look that belonged in the sort of niche catalogue that sold misshapen Welsh pottery and trousers made from mattress ticking to urban people dreaming of escape. People like her.

'What is the world, then, of the weekend wife?' she asked.

Sasha considered. 'Secrets, there will be secrets. Not necessarily serious ones, but the triviality of them almost makes them worse. Someone will start smoking. One of you will see an ex and for some unknown reason decide not to tell your other half, and before long it's become a *thing*.' She sighed. 'None of it really matters, I know, when I say it like that, but it all chips away at your relationship.'

'Still, those sorts of secrets, like you say, they're not anything serious, not like . . .' Emily paused, unable to say the word out loud.

'Like an affair?' said Sasha. 'This set-up is a recipe for adultery, don't you think? Look, there's little Tamsin, another one of our number. Oi, Tamsin, come over here!'

In fact there was nothing particularly little about Tamsin, who was tall and slim and another of the women in the village who dressed both beautifully and expensively. It was only as Emily looked at her more closely that she could see how young she was, like a girl dressing up in grown-ups' clothes. Tamsin glanced around her nervously, but then did as she was told and flitted towards them.

'Tamsin, I was just telling Emily here how we should form a weekend wives' club. John's always off working away, isn't he?'

'Yes, he's got this big project in Kent at the moment. He's building three houses – executive homes, they're called.' Her voice was so quiet that Emily had to lean in to catch what she was saying. 'They're going to be amazing.'

'So he stays down south when he's working, leaving you up here?' said Sasha. 'Then you're another weekend wife. As I thought. It could be a proper movement, like the scouts,' she continued. 'We could have our own motto.'

'What would that be?' asked Emily.

Sasha thought for a moment. 'There's only one thing worse than missing them. Not missing them.'

'That's awful,' said Tamsin, wide-eyed.

'Or: part-time wife, full-time whinger.' Sasha laughed. 'What is the divorce rate these days? One in three, is it? It's so got to be higher than that for weekend wives. I'm guessing at least two in three.' She nodded her head, counting the three women as she spoke. 'Oh dear.'

'You're painting quite a depressing picture,' said Emily, glad that her weekend wifery was to be only temporary, but equally pleased that Sasha seemed to be seriously suggesting starting a club. She was lonely, very lonely. 'So when shall we meet?'

Sasha laughed. 'I was only joking. We can't seriously start a club.'

'Oh, of course.' Emily forced a laugh. 'No, that would be mad.'

'I don't think John would like it anyway,' said Tamsin. 'I'd better go and find him. He's here somewhere and he'll be wondering where I am.'

With that she was off towards the kitchen, followed by Sasha, and Emily was once more alone. She didn't get invited to many parties these days, but she couldn't say that she particularly enjoyed those she did attend. She never quite got the form. It was as though everyone else in the village had received a memo attached to the invitation that outlined the dress code in precise detail, what the timings really meant and how much sustenance would be served. The parties seemed like plane journeys where you never quite knew when the food would arrive and whether it might be surprisingly palatable. This one was a drinks thing starting at twelve on a Sunday. Pre-lunch, she supposed, which kind of presumed you had someone back home cooking a roast for you. Or to at least switch the oven on to warm the pizzas.

Back in London, she knew what to expect. There would be birthdays in upstairs rooms in pubs, the occasional house party where you'd end up drinking the disgusting wine that people had been waiting to offload for years, or lunches with friends-with-kids where a DVD would be put on while the adults used the freedom of those ninety-five minutes to get more drunk than they had intended. At least Matt was here, though he too seemed to understand what was expected of him in a way that she felt she never would. Matt, Sasha and Tamsin had all grown up here. They were returning home, while Emily was embarking on life in a foreign land.

She used the time instead to observe and write little notes in her head on the oddities she could see. When people had asked her what she was going to do once they'd moved, she'd shut them up with the magic words 'I'm going to write a blog.' This was to an underemployed mother what 'I'm working on my script' was to anyone at a loose end in Hollywood.

She had been overjoyed to give up her job. As she had said, in a cliché to rival the one about first-world problems, 'It's not like I'm working on a cure for cancer.' But it turned out writing a blog wasn't so easy, and even if it were, who'd want to read it? 'Woman with children writes about the hilarious little things that happen to her each day and the funny things kids say.' Emily was herself shamefully addicted to similar sorts of blogs. Some – those that dealt with the challenges of bringing up an ill or autistic child – moved her to tears of sympathy tinged with relief that these were not problems she faced. Others, where women with tiny bodies and large families posted pictures of the fun crafts project they'd just completed while wearing matching outfits of pale grey and chambray, made her feel a failure.

Perhaps she could broaden her blog to include all of village life. Then again, she was learning that nothing ever happened around here. And if she did, the people she was writing about might read it and she'd have to give them coy little nicknames, like 'Power Woman' for Tania or 'Quirky One' for Sasha.

Tania's house was the biggest in the village, and that gave her a gravitas above that of being an MEP. Her own achievements were nothing in comparison to having a boot room off the hallway. Society was so strictly stratified by acreage and square footage that it made Emily gasp with the transparency of its snobbery. It was almost feudal.

All her friends had lived in identikit houses and flats back in the city, Victorian terraced places in a concentric ring that circled the more expensive centre. The flats were pretty identical, just in bigger houses with those funny shared gardens that nobody ever ended up using. It was as if they'd bought the same Lego kit to build their homes but some had managed to get a few extra pieces – the attic conversion, the extra metre of width, the longer garden, the side extension. And once inside, she had known her way around without ever having been shown – the narrow hallway with the bikes and scooters to trip over, the kitchen at the back that wasn't quite big enough for the expansive family table they had all bought with dreams of rustic Italian-style banquets, the IKEA plastic storage units for the toys.

Emily and Matt's house had looked exactly the same as all the others, but was just that bit smaller as it had been a much later post-war infill, between two Victorians. Only a few feet here and there, but when the houses were quite small to begin with, it made the difference between being able to get past the bicycle in the hallway or not.

Funny how twenty-four inches of missing space had led to their journey of a hundred miles.

'You all right?' Matt asked as he sidled up to her. 'Don't listen to Sasha, she's always been a bit sharp.'

'I'm fine.' She mustn't blame him. Her friends thought he'd kidnapped her and made her come to live up here, but that was far from the truth. He'd not been the one who'd wanted to come back to the place where he'd grown up. The whole thing had been powered by her and her lifelong affliction of believing that something better was just around the corner.

She thought of Sasha's dark hints about infidelity. Matt smelt weird when he came home on a Friday evening. Not bad, just different, of an unfamiliar washing powder, the cinnamon chewing gum he only seemed to buy when he was away and the stew of bodies on the train home, all accompanied by a base note of an unidentifiable spice. He smelled disgustingly and deliciously of the city. She had taken to burying her head in his shirt and inhaling the stench like a grieving wife going through her dead husband's wardrobe.

He gave her arm a squeeze. 'Mum thought you looked a bit bereft.'

'That's very sweet of her, but I'm fine. I quite like just watching sometimes.' She had never known that of herself, that she was one of life's observers rather than partakers. Or perhaps she had no choice. 'Sasha was just telling me about how you're going to have an affair.' If you say these things out loud then they won't come true, she thought. She loved him so much, even though she had to keep reminding herself of this fact now that he wasn't around enough to remind her in person.

Sasha, hearing her name, rejoined them.

'What was that?' she asked.

'My wife tells me you've been talking nonsense,' said Matt, but with good humour, since he'd known and liked Sasha ever since they were children.

'I wouldn't say that necessarily.'

Emily looked petulant. 'She was telling me I was now a weekend wife and how it's a recipe for adultery.'

'Yes, but it could be yours as much as mine, couldn't it?' said Matt. This suggested to Emily it was something he'd already been thinking about. 'Like I say, don't listen to her.' He gave Sasha a playful punch on the arm. 'It's not as if I'm working away for long.'

'Just a few months.'

'Exactly.'

'You two will be fine,' said Sasha. 'He's right, don't mind me.' She smiled reassuringly at Emily.

'You mean our marriage will be the one in three that survives,' said Emily, belatedly realising that she'd drunk too much Prosecco.

'Are those the odds?' said Matt. 'I'll definitely put a bet on that.'

Sasha waved as if by agreement and melted back into the party.

'And that you've got secrets,' Emily said to Matt. 'That's what she says. Well, that we've both got secrets. Have you?'

He exhaled. 'Yes, I do.' A dramatic pause. 'Sometimes,

down in London, I go to work not having eaten a proper breakfast.' He smiled. 'What's yours?'

'That I miss you so much when you're away.'

'I should hope so. Not much of a secret. Anything else?' he asked.

'No, of course not.' She turned away, hoping that he wouldn't see any signs that she was lying. She did have a secret, one she couldn't tell him, tell anyone. It was shameful.

Rafa was her secret, her quite literally filthy secret. The way she felt about him and the way he seemed to feel about her was something that had to remain hidden and yet in plain sight. If she ever told anyone how she really felt, they'd tell her she was mad, jokingly, because they wouldn't believe her. But it was true: evil lurked and only she could see it.

'Let's go,' she said, with the feeling she got every Sunday afternoon of being faced with a giant egg timer reminding her that his leaving was once again imminent. Going home with Matt meant she wouldn't be alone with Rafa, at least not until he got the dawn train the next morning. She tried to stop herself from shivering with fear.

It was a bit of a lie anyway. Sasha wasn't a weekend wife. She was a monthly one. Emily had seemed touchingly devastated about the prospect of Matt going all of three hours away down to London, but that time would only get Ned to the beginning of his plane ride to Los Angeles. City of Angels, literally, the ones who modelled for Victoria's Secret. They probably wore their wings in bed.

His bed, possibly, for Ned was an attractive man with a successful and well-paid career as a director of photography in a city of gay men and beautiful, ambitious women.

A bit like parents of a newborn arguing about who was more tired, these spouses of absent workers could get quite competitive about who had it tougher. Ned didn't travel to the same country. He didn't even go to the same continent. He was what they called a supercommuter, though there was nothing super about it in reality.

Sasha had lived out there in Los Angeles with him and the children for a few years, and it had been great, really it had, but they had both winced every time the children had said poop, braid and cell instead of poo, plait and mobile. Los Angeles was one of those rare places where the reality was exactly like the cliché. It was all swimming pools, valet parking and movie conversation. There were palm trees and roller bladers, impossibly good-looking restaurant staff and traffic-logged highways.

Ned was deemed by US immigration to be a person of extraordinary ability and so could work freely, but Sasha's own proficiency as a script editor on TV dramas was considered rather more ordinary, and she'd been unable to do anything other than look after their home life. She'd yearned for a job when they'd lived out there in that ultimate industry city, and yet when she and the children had moved back to the UK, she'd rejected employment in favour of starting her own business, sourcing and selling twentieth-century ceramics over the Internet, something she turned out to be rather good at. Clarice Cliff, Susie

Cooper, Jessie Tait . . . all the best ceramists of the time had been women, a fact that seemed to Sasha fitting for her now female-dominated life.

They had moved back with the knowledge that Ned would be working all over the place but the belief it would be mostly in Britain. The UK film industry was booming, or so they'd thought. But then one job after another followed back in Los Angeles, and it seemed as if he had become employable only over there, at least at the rates he was charging.

She'd better get home to the children. It wasn't that she didn't trust Bailey to look after Spike – almost the opposite: she was so earnest she might lead him into good behaviour rather than astray. She didn't want Bailey to do that big hair and fake tan thing that seemed fashionable now, but she wished her daughter wouldn't cower behind the baggy clothes and the veil of her too-long fringe. Every time Sasha said, 'But you've got a lovely face, I don't know why you hide it,' she realised that she sounded exactly like her own mother, except the issue then had been the eyeliner she'd etched across her eyelids in the eighties.

She tried to concentrate on the short drive back home, but was distracted by thoughts of her fourteen-, almost fifteen-year-old daughter. She was worried about her, but she couldn't quite work out why. Bailey's schoolwork was excellent, she was always polite, she never stayed out late (or indeed went out at all). Sasha had nothing to worry about, and that was what worried her. Bailey had been fine over the holidays, but a week before going back to school she'd become withdrawn. The unhappier she became, the politer and more perfect was her behaviour.

As Sasha neared the turn-off to their house, she felt the steering wheel pull away as if by some force in her hands.

Her. That woman.

What was she doing walking up and down, up and down outside Sasha's home once again? The first time Sasha had seen her ambling along the pavement of the road that bisected the village and ran past their small turning, she'd been mildly curious. She might have been able to ignore the woman in the city, but not here, where strangers really were strange. The second time, curiosity curdled into disquiet. And now for a third time here she was, circling purposelessly like a teenage fan outside a boy band's house, just about to leave a teddy-bear tribute.

Coincidences, as Sasha used to say in script meetings, weren't plausible. The woman was her age, maybe a few years older, as Ned was, and well dressed. Nothing flashy, but sensibly heeled boots, well-cut jeans and a pull-the-look-together blazer. The first and third times she'd worn a scarf, expensive-looking too.

Sasha had ignored her initially, but on the second occasion she'd stared and the woman, unembarrassed, had stared back, forcing her to look away in the game of chicken. She had that feeling she got at the top of tall buildings, of being afraid that some force would compel her to jump off, but this time it was that an unseen spirit would make her turn the steering wheel towards the woman to mow her down. Whoever she was, Sasha somehow knew that she could be bringing no good to her family.

She braked suddenly and climbed out unsteadily from the car. It was obvious, wasn't it? Ned was an attractive man who lived a whole ocean away; how had they ever been so deluded as to think this wouldn't happen? She'd often wondered what the 'other woman' might look like, but she'd never thought she'd be like this, older than her, nothing fancy. In her imagination, she'd pictured someone younger, more glamorous, an upgrade, almost certainly American. That was what always happened: people ended up with someone so much like the one they'd left, you wondered why they'd bothered.

The woman didn't show any sign of surprise that Sasha should be marching up to her like this. Instead she smiled, as if they were guests being introduced to each other for the first time at one of Tania's stupid drinks parties.

'Who are you?' Sasha felt her words slurring, though she'd only had a couple of glasses of Prosecco.

'Why don't you ask Eddie?' The woman smiled and then walked briskly away towards the village's one remaining pub.

Sasha saw her disappear behind the pub towards its car park. She knew she ought to run after her, demand more information, but at that moment she found she really didn't want to know.

Tamsin got into the passenger seat of John's car. She couldn't drive, and anyway, she lived in the passenger seat of life.

'What were you talking to Sasha about?' John asked her, patting her knee as he did so.

'She was talking about a weekend wives' club for people like us. Ones who are on their own during the week.'

'You're not on your own, sweetheart,' he said. 'Even when I'm not there, I'm with you. I know what you're doing all the time because I care about you, you know that.'

'Yes, I do. I'm so lucky to have you.'

'And I'm lucky to have you, Tamsin. I looked around the room and there was no one even half as beautiful as you. You're so much slimmer and better dressed than all of them put together. I'm proud of you.'

'Thank you,' said Tamsin. 'I'm proud of you too.'

'We're both so lucky,' he said as they pulled into the carriage driveway of their new – in all senses – home. 'Our lives are perfect.'

Sasha decided that she would follow the woman's instructions; she would ask her husband to explain. Her husband, the man she and everyone else called Ned, not Eddie. Ned not Ed – it sounded like a line from a picture book, but somehow she sensed that this was a story with an adult theme.

'Hi, guys,' she said, coming into the house. Bailey was in the kitchen on her laptop. Sasha didn't even have to glance at the screen to know that there would be nothing inappropriate on it – it would be homework, or earnest chats with fellow feminists. 'Where's Spike?'

Bailey shrugged.

'Don't scowl, darling, you'll get frown lines.'

Her daughter scrunched up her face still further.

'You are supposed to be looking after him. Thanks for doing that, by the way.'

'How was the party?'

'I wouldn't really call it a party. That implies a good time.' Sasha glanced at the clock in the kitchen. Two o'clock here, ungodly o'clock in Los Angeles. Her brain was like a smart hotel in which a wall of clocks was set with the times of transatlantic cities. She always knew what time it was in LA. Only an hour to wait until seven their time, which was really too early as well. She was always woken up by Spike, their nine-year-old son, at that time on Sunday mornings, but Ned usually got a lie-in. He deserved it, of course, working so hard like that, that was what everyone said. The injustice never failed to rankle.

She made the kids some late lunch and watched Spike accompany his chicken with a slurp of the pool of snot that always seemed moustached to his upper lip. She loved him, obviously she did, it went without saying (although it was said a lot, all the time, as was the modern way), but what was it with the nose? She enjoyed the brief distraction from thoughts of the woman, before they invaded her again with impatience. 'Oh, it's no matter,' she'd tell people. 'What with Skype and FaceTime, it's like he's not even away.' What crap that was. 'It's like he's in the same room,' she'd say, as if being in the same room with someone meant that they'd be at a strange angle and constantly at risk of cutting out. There seemed to be no middle ground between ignoring the computer and carrying on with life as normal, and having very stilted, overly self-conscious conversations in front of it.

She felt her heart thud as the connection went through. Answer, answer, oh God, don't answer. 'All right?' Ned said on picking up, clearing his throat of nocturnal huskiness. He was looking tanned, well rested, handsome. The women in LA would love him, a less dithery version of the posh Englishman from romantic comedies. The slight fuzz of the screen just pixelated out any wrinkles, like Vaseline smeared on the lenses of cameras filming the Hollywood divas of yore.

'Yes, fine,' Sasha snapped. She hadn't realised until now how rattled she had been by her encounter with the woman.

'Good. Where are the kids? Aren't you in the kitchen?'

They had a routine with the daily call. At first, five years ago when this arrangement had started, they'd had those awkward, forced conversations, like a technologically assisted transatlantic version of the one that all parents have with their children after school. 'How was your day?' 'Fine.' 'What did you do?' 'Nothing.' 'Who did you play with?' 'No one.'

Now, they just popped Ned into the corner while they got on with their business around him, an immobile Cyclops, a detached brain on a screen. Occasionally they'd forget he was there. And vice versa – Sasha would see him playing with his phone, disappearing off screen or, once, casually cupping himself until she reminded him that he was in front of the children. Sometimes they used to buy two copies of the same children's book so that he could read it out to Spike across the Atlantic in a bid to be a good father.

But not today. Today she needed to talk to him.

'You can speak to them later. I want to have a word.' She shuffled him into the sitting room and closed the door carefully behind her.

'What's up?' He had definitely developed an American hue to his accent. These days he said hey instead of hello. He claimed it was East London meets South Central, despite the fact that he'd lived in neither place. His voice was another way in which he was the odd one out in their family quadrangle.

'Nothing. Well, I don't think so. I just . . . there's this woman.'

'What woman?'

'Well, that's what I want to know. I keep seeing her around and I finally spoke to her today, and she said I should ask you.'

'Ask me what?'

'Who she was.'

'You're not really helping me here, Sasha. How do I know who she is if I haven't seen her. Have you got a photo?'

'No.' Sasha was indignant. 'That would be stalking.' She felt her stomach constrict. She hadn't used the word until then, but that was what this woman was, surely: a stalker.

'Well, what can you tell me about her?'

Sasha stared at the screen to see if she could detect any

nervousness behind the pixels. It wasn't a high-definition interrogation.

'She's blonde. A bit generic, highlights, nice clothes, not from round here, I'd say. Posh voice. Older than me, about your age.'

'You're describing almost every woman I've ever known.' The irritation was more evident now.

'I don't know what more to say. I've seen her around, three times – I think she's deliberately hovering on the pavement before the turning to our house – but today was the first time I actually spoke to her. Not that I got much out of her. She just said you'd know. Well, not you. Eddie. She called you Eddie.'

Was there a flicker of something across his face, or was it just the dodgy connection?

'I don't know,' he said after a moment's hesitation. 'Look, if you see her again, ask her for her name or something. Ask her what it's about. No, tell her to contact me directly – give her my email – and to leave you alone. It sounds a bit weird.'

It is, thought Sasha. It is.

2

Where Things Are Done Differently

Tamsin – or little Tamsin, as Sasha still insisted on refer-
ring to her all these years since Sasha had been her family's
babysitter – woke up in her immaculate house and
proceeded to have immaculate sex, as she did every
morning that John was there.

'There, right there,' he instructed. 'No, don't move.
Still.' Even in the midst of abandon, John's commands
had the precision of a PowerPoint presentation. She knew
that the next slide would be him coming with a neat gasp
and her taking the clean towel that lived by the bed to
make sure that nothing spilled out of her. Not that it
mattered anyway, since she washed their sheets daily on
these occasions.

She lay with her hair fanned on the pillow, just the way
he liked it, and remained rigid. Sometimes he liked her
to pretend to be asleep, but this time she'd been told to
keep her eyes open.

'Soon.' He closed his eyes. 'Five, four, three, two . . .'
the last stretched out, 'one.' He came, and she grabbed the
towel, put it between her legs and went to the bathroom, careful not to lock the door although she always
wanted to.

An hour later, he had left her with the sheets spinning in the washing machine and two whole days alone. She felt shaky at the prospect of him going like this, but it was something she'd learnt to accept, since he was the breadwinner and brought home the bacon. Other food metaphors included the fact that, financially speaking, she was an empty biscuit tin. She was so lucky that most of the time she had him to look after her; a few days of solitude was a small price to pay.

She put on the fancy digital pedometer bracelet he'd bought her and set off to get an early march on the 15,000 steps she did each day. The bracelet connected to her phone and then on to a website, which he checked regularly to keep tabs on her progress. He'd be pleased she was making such a positive start towards her total. He liked the fact that she had what he called the hottest body in the village.

As she stretched her legs in their running tights (the ones that promised to wick sweat, which made it sound like somehow it could be woven, a tapestry of perspiration), she looked ahead so as not to get distracted. Women were returning from dropping their children off at the village school, and she didn't want to get into a conversation. She waved at Emily, who had that stressed look that all mothers wore along with their comfortable shoes. Emily's dog, some sort of poodle-type creature, was running yapping circles around its mistress, and Tamsin wondered what would happen if she attached her pedometer to its hind legs. Then she could hole herself up in the house for two days and let the dog do the walking for her.

A car slowed down to kerb-crawl her. 'Hello, sexy lady, do you want a ride?' Sasha shouted at her from within.

'That's very kind, Sasha, but I'm trying to get some exercise.'

'As if you need it. Go on, I want to go to that new farm shop place down the road. Apparently it has great coffee.' Sasha laughed. 'Yes, I'm going to drive five miles for some caffeine, but if I take you too, I'll feel less bad about it.'

Tamsin patted her smooth thighs. 'But I don't have my wallet with me.'

'Don't be daft, I'm buying. It's the least I can do if I'm making you slog across the county in search of a decent coffee.'

Tamsin never has her wallet, thought Sasha. I'm not even sure she owns one. It was the source of some bitching from others in the village, that the woman with the expensive shoes never put money in charity boxes or contributed to the summer fete. If anyone else had been so slow to reach in their pocket, it might have bothered Sasha, but there would be a part of her that always saw little Tamsin as the cute youngest child and then the lippy teen she later became. She spoke up for Tamsin whenever she was criticised, but had never actually thought to speak *to* her about why she never had money with her.

'How are things?' she asked. Sasha was like the coolest girl in school who showed an unexpected tenderness to the vulnerable. And vulnerable was how she always saw Tamsin, however sophisticated she had become.

'Great, thanks. The house is done now.'

'That must be lovely, to have got rid of the builders and to have a home at last.'

Tamsin shrugged, and Sasha got a glimpse of the girl she had once been. 'I think John wants to put it on the market straight away and begin the next project.'

'Really? Is that what you call homes these days? Projects?'

'I'm lucky, we've lived in some beautiful places.' Tamsin said it in a way that suggested that she'd used the phrase many times before, or at least had heard it told to her a lot.

'Does that mean you're not going to stay here in the village?'

'I don't know. Depends on John.'

'It would be a shame for me if you moved. Do you find it odd living here, though? Back in the village where we grew up?'

'A bit. Do you?'

'Yes, crazy. I've lived in London, New York, Los Angeles, and yet here I am, back where I started. I can't quite work out why it's happened. Well I do know. I wanted us all to be near my parents as they're getting older. I couldn't bear for anything to happen to them and for me not to be around to help. And God, I missed the weather here.'

'Really?' asked Tamsin, looking out to the grey-stained landscape.

'Yes. I'm like a mushroom. I need damp to make me grow. I felt parched out there in the sunshine. I know my clothes may be colourful, but I've got a dark heart.' That was the wrong expression, but there was a part of her that felt comfortable with the melancholia of the climate here. She'd found LA's weather exhausting, since she'd never shed that British impulse constantly to make the most of the sunshine. Middle age had made her want to retreat into the bubble of her children and her parents, while it seemed to cause Ned to go further and further into the bright world away from it.

They were interrupted as Tamsin's phone beeped with a text. 'It's John. Wondering where I am. He worries about me when he's away. Smile, Sasha.' Tamsin then proceeded to take a selfie of the two of them. Sasha was irritated, as though she'd seen a photo of one of her children on a website without having signed the permission slip allowing the reproduction of their image. She glanced over to see Tamsin texting the photo of them. She was unnerved to have been co-opted into someone else's marital habits.

'Do you often take selfies to send to John?'

'He likes to know where I am, to know that I'm safe. Like I said, he worries about me.'

'And do you worry about him?' Sasha asked.

'What do you mean?'

'When I was talking to Emily about our husbands being away, I was telling her how we all end up with secrets. Silly things, maybe, like drinking too much or bumping into an old boyfriend or something, but we can't share everything with our other halves when we don't see them every day.'

'I've no secrets from John. You just saw me send that selfie. He knows exactly what I'm doing and where I am. He could write the book on me. Not that anyone would buy it, I'm so boring.'

'Yeah, that would be one very weird coffee table book,' said Sasha. And she wouldn't put it past John to self-publish it with a run of just one. 'But yes, sure, I can see he keeps a remote eye on you. But do you do the same back? Do you have any idea where he is now?'

'Kent. Well, on the way down there. On the new development.'

'Yes, well, somewhere between here and Kent. Doesn't exactly narrow it down.' Sasha sighed. 'Sorry, I'm not trying to infect you with my paranoia. It's just that I've been thinking a lot about this recently.'

'Because of the whole weekend wives thing you were talking about the other day?'

Because of the woman, thought Sasha, the woman who calls Ned Eddie. 'I suppose.'

'Can I ask you something?' said Tamsin, looking out of the window, away from Sasha.

'Fire away.'

'I was wondering if you ever needed a babysitter.'

'Less now Bailey's old enough to be left in charge of Spike.'

'Oh right, I see.'

'Why? Are you interested?'

'Yes. I just thought, sometimes when John is away, I've got nothing to do and maybe it would be nice, only if you want, to babysit your children like you used to babysit me. You've always said it's difficult to go out. But if you've got Bailey, don't worry about it.'

Sasha couldn't bear to see the disappointment on Tamsin's face. 'It would be lovely for me to take Bailey out, just the two of us. I could book a table at the Red Lion. Could you look after Spike tonight?' Maybe she'd manage to find out what was bothering her daughter. She was definitely weird. Not, of course, the sort of weirdness that was a rite of passage. Bailey's was a blank sort of strangeness.

Tamsin grinned and again became recognisable as that gobby girl who used to hoick up her school skirt and whom Sasha had seen on many an occasion at the bus stop vigorously snogging that rough-looking boy she had once gone out with. 'It's a date.'

Emily saw Tamsin leap into Sasha's car and felt a surge of envy. She remembered when Clem had first been born, how she had stared at other mothers in the park with a yearning that she hadn't felt since she'd been fourteen and mooning after boys. She'd fantasise that she and these new friends would share confidences about the secret malevolence they felt towards their newborns and just how much time they spent ignoring them in favour of browsing celebrity gossip sites.

Then, without even realising it, she'd made friends, one in a baby group, another in a singing class. Returning to work four days a week meant that she no longer had the gaping need for these friends, and at that point she found she had more than she could cope with, along with a few new ones made once Clem and then Zanna had started school. Little had she known what she was giving up when she came here.

If she had been invited into Sasha's car, then she would have been able to avoid being home alone with Rafa. Oh

God, how she dreaded those hours she had to spend with him.

The house they had moved so far to live in was the last of a trio of cottages on the edge of the village, right on the main road, without even a pavement to buffer them against the lorries that seemed to screech along. The kitchen, the only room they'd so far been able to decorate, was perfection of sorts. It looked like a stage set of the ideal cottage kitchen, the sort of porn she'd salivated over for years in magazines called things like *Country Idyll*. If she built the set, she had reasoned, then she would be able to act the part and eventually inhabit the role completely. On the windowsill there sat a Roberts radio, and beside it Kilner jars filled with wooden spoons. Her huge ceramic butler's sink overlooked another windowsill with its vase of wild flowers, and beyond that the garden, where her Enid Blyton fantasies of children treehouse-making and collecting sticklebacks met the metal reality of a trampoline.

In one corner shone her expensive coffee machine, the one that had been a leaving gift from work and which she used every morning. It never tasted the same as those expensive ones in plastic lidded cups, seemingly missing the grime of the city.

On the opposite wall, a giant iron symbol of her life, was what she called 'the not-Aga Aga', an ancient stove that was supposed to warm both their hearth and their hearts. The fact that it was some unknown brand that relied on ugly gas canisters, rather than an oil-burning stove, seemed to sum up the gap between her dreams of country living and the reality. She felt that the coffee machine and the not-Aga Aga were in a stand-off against one another, each representing the different stages of her life.

And there, in another corner, was the final thread in her tapestry of the perfect country family – the dog. Sometimes that was how she referred to him, as The Dog rather than Rafa. It made her feel happier somehow.

'What are you staring at?' she said out loud to him.

He did that thing he always did, that snarling baring of teeth with a faint throaty growl. The children would get very excited when he did this, and coo, 'Oooh look, Rafa is smiling at you, Mummy.' She wanted to tell them that dogs didn't smile, that he was expressing something very different, and that it was always directed at her.

'Stop it, stop staring at me.'

His eyes followed her round the room like a creepy portrait in a horror film. She went to lock herself in the toilet. Yes, they'd moved here for the extra space and she was holed up in the bunker they called the guest cloakroom.

She couldn't even blame Matt for this. She'd been the one most keen on getting Rafa. She'd thought that having a dog would turn them into a dog-owning family, by which she meant the sort of people who enjoyed long walks and throwing autumn leaves at each other, before coming back to eat the casserole that was bubbling away in the slow cooker. People whose children didn't whine at the prospect of leaving their screens and eating food with unidentifiable ingredients, but who would willingly wrestle their pooch amid mud that would miraculously not follow them into the house. The city greyness would drain from their faces in favour of apple-cheeked wholesomeness. All because of the dog.

The whole moving to the country and getting a dog thing was either a mid-life crisis or a railing against the realisation that she would have no more children, Emily wasn't sure which. Or maybe it was both. How cruel that they should coincide. She saw it in her friends, too. As their youngests went to school full time, they left their husbands, became obsessive gym bunnies or decided to retrain as psychotherapists.

'Fur child' was what a dog was known as in upscale gay communities. She'd found the expression cute when she'd first heard it, but now it sounded grotesque. A hairy monster of a baby, the sort you had nightmares about birthing when you were first pregnant, the doctor pulling the yapping ball of black out of you and declaring, 'Ms Dawlish, you've got a lovely baby Jack-a-poo.' A child born with teeth and a precocious desire to hump adult legs and sniff bottoms – what could be more disgusting and frightening? Fairy tales were written about such creatures, a fur changeling rather than a fur child.

She hadn't grown up with dogs and so hadn't been indoctrinated into the belief that they were man's best friend. Matt had come from a family where dogs slept in your bed and licked the plates before they went into the dishwasher. When she had fallen in love with Matt, she'd also fallen in love with his family. If, like her, you'd grown up near a roundabout on the way out of London with only your mother to keep you company, a warm, bear-hugging family with a rambling house seemed like very heaven.

Matt hadn't even been fazed when, soon after the arrival of Rafa, the whole family had begun to complain of itchy bottoms. 'Worms,' he'd said, all matter-of-fact, as if this was as normal as a childhood cold. Which, to him, it was, as he waxed nostalgically about the revolting raspberry-flavoured medicine he'd had to drink on the many occasions that his arse had been filled with tiny wriggling maggot-like creatures. Worms, real-life worms, inside you, she'd wanted to scream at him, wondering why he wasn't plagued by visions of the swarming, swirling mass of tiny white aliens as she was. She was reminded of the photo of the world's longest intestinal worm, pulled out of a poor man in Africa, that had so fascinated her school friends in their biology textbook.

Dogs were revolting. This was obvious to her now. It was like having a farmyard animal living in your house, sleeping in your bed. Why hadn't she realised that before getting one? Rafa was a cross between a poodle and a Jack Russell, with all that was bad in both breeds – the whininess of the former and the feral inability to be trained of the latter. Hybrid was what they called such a splicing. Hybrid: even the name sounded fearsome, as created by a mad scientist in a laboratory and about to take over the world, a dog produced by a child's game of consequences.

When they'd got Rafa, they'd even made a joke about how at least they'd been able to find a hybrid to replace their Prius, sadly swapped for a diesel people carrier on the arrival of their environmentally unfriendly third child. They had been so smug back then, but now she felt they had far less to be pleased with themselves about.

She thought she could hear his low-level growling from the other side of the door. The longer she barricaded herself in the toilet, the more afraid she became. It was crazy, she knew, but during the hours when Clem and Zanna were at school and Nate at the nursery, she couldn't help it.

'Emily,' she heard a voice bark from the kitchen. It was husky and posh, which was exactly the way that Rafa would speak if he could. For a mad moment, she thought it was him.

'Sue,' she said with relief, and hurried out to greet her mother-in-law. She couldn't get used to the way that people walked into each other's houses in the country. It was another thing she'd found impossibly alluring before they'd moved there. Much like her mother-in-law herself.

'What were you doing?' Sue asked.

'I was in the toilet. Loo,' she corrected herself. 'Cup of tea?'

'A quick one, yes. I was just wondering how you were. I don't know, you seemed a bit sad at the party.'

Emily felt like someone who'd been pounced upon by well-meaning strangers after falling over in a public place – it was nice of them, really, you knew it was, but oh, the humiliation. 'I'm fine, great. It's so beautiful here, I couldn't be anything other than happy.' She gestured towards the window, the garden and the fields beyond.

'I'm sorry that Matt's not here during the week to enjoy it,' said Sue, her head tilting in sympathy.

'Not your fault.'

'I didn't say it was. Just that it must be hard for you. How's your computer diary thing going?'

Emily felt that Sue knew full well that it was called a blog, but she was one of those people who referred to the Internet as the Interweb to express their disdain. 'I haven't launched it. I'm still working on a beta version in order to have a good archive when it goes live.' She hoped this lingo would baffle Sue. It certainly baffled her.

'I'm taking Bono for a walk – can I take Rafa along too?' Sue knelt down to put her face near to the fangs of Satan, who happily licked her. 'So sweet, you're such a sweet boy, who's a sweet boy?'

'That would be brilliant, thank you. I could get on with my blog plans.'

'Good.' Sue paused. 'I know it must be hard. Giving up your jazzy London life.' Sue often used words like ritzy and snazzy, and talked about 'the fashion', asking, 'Is that what *people* are wearing these days?'

'It didn't feel like a sacrifice, honestly, Sue. I was the one pushing for the move by the end.'

'Well, just know that you can talk to me if you need to.'

'Thank you.' Emily felt the need to hole herself up again, but this time she was tearfully touched at her mother-in-law's kindness.

Tamsin waved Sasha off for her dinner with Bailey with a surprising feeling of excitement. She loved Sasha's house, had done ever since Sasha had returned to live here. It was a converted chapel, with high ceilings. Where once people had felt the divine through singing hymns, Tamsin now felt it in the way that Sasha's life oozed through the walls and surfaces. Every bit of the place seemed to have been designed to make you feel alive, from the bright broad-stroked modern art that splashed across every wall to the patchwork cushions that appeared wherever you wanted to sit. The sofas were low and lolling to encourage visitors to do the same, and there always seemed to be something baking or boiling that warmed the house with a fug of spice and steam.

Colourful was a word that people used to describe the rackety lives of others. Sasha and her home were colourful in the true sense, though; they were like the Technicolor blazing into Dorothy's black and white Kansas. Tamsin's retinas still burned with the image of Sasha leaving to go to the pub with her daughter, shining in her gold-threaded jumper and purple skirt. Tamsin's own home was black and white; or more specifically, it was painted grey, a fashionable pale shade that was as magnolia had been to walls in the eighties. It was the only colour that John wanted, since it was the one that most potential buyers liked. It was the new neutral, he explained.

Everywhere she looked in Sasha's house, she was assailed by the ways in which it differed from her own. There were all the paintings to begin with. Tamsin wasn't allowed to put nails in her walls. There were a few pieces of artwork that hung off the picture rail, but the canvas had to be near weightless so as not to chip any paint. A new lot of pictures were bought every time they moved, from a company that specialised in the sort of work that was as much about decor as art, the paintings you found in anonymous hotel rooms.

Then there was Sasha's door frame, scored with the heights of the children. Tamsin didn't have children, which was another story, but if she had, she knew she'd never have been allowed to do this. John had all sorts of rules, the kind that landlords imposed on tenants, so that she sometimes felt as if she were renting her own house, or worse, squatting in it until someone came to evict her for living such a fraudulent life. She fought a desire to stick Blu Tack on the walls and fight over getting her deposit back.

She was very lucky, she reminded herself, to have John to look after her. Her house, well, houses, she supposed, were amazing. Everyone said so.

'Your mum said I should read to you,' Tamsin said to Spike, her charge for the night. He was a freckle-faced, old-fashioned-looking boy who seemed as though he should have permanently dirty knees and a schoolboy's cap. 'But you can read yourself already, can't you?'

'School says we should read with parents for fifteen minutes every night, either us reading out loud or them reading to us.'

'Really? But why?'

He shrugged. 'It's part of my success criteria.'

'Your what?'

'We're always supposed to be questioning our success

criteria to see if our learning is competent, accomplished or exceptional.'

She frowned. He looked at her as though she were stupid. Which, admittedly, she probably was. 'It's all a bit different to when I was at school.'

'That's what my mum says.'

'Hang on, she's loads older than me. She used to be *my* babysitter. And I don't think she ever read to me.'

Tamsin tried to remember if her parents had read to her as a small child, let alone when she'd been as old as Spike. She'd been the fourth and the least bright, or so she'd always been told, and had pretty much been left to bring herself up, despite the affluence and status of her parents. It was as though having had three high-achieving children already, they could afford for one to be the dunce. Since her birth, so long after her older sister, had been an accident, they might as well bring her up without purpose or design. Her mother always boasted of her belief in the benign neglect school of parenting, but, wondered Tamsin sadly, how could you tell if neglect was benign or malign? Surely the two were indistinguishable from the outside. Especially when viewed by a child.

'So what shall we read, then?' There was a pile of books on the floor of the open-plan family room. That would never happen at her house, partly because neither she nor John was a big reader, but mostly because every-thing had a place. John was a genius with cupboards; it was one of his trademarks, and he would always specify that there was a special compartment for phone chargers and other things that normal people might not think of.

She picked up the slimmest of the volumes, a book called *Text Back Time*. 'Is this one of yours?' She read the back out loud. '"Dark and funny, and darkly funny, Jake V. Bond takes his readers on a voyage through life and love that will remind us all of what it is to be young." Whatever that means. What's it about, anyway?'

'Dunno, I haven't started it yet. We got given it at school, everyone did. I don't know why. The author gave lots of copies to my teacher or something.'

'You hardly need more books,' said Tamsin, looking at his groaning shelves.

'Mum's always buying me books and making me read them.'

Spike looked disparagingly at the cover of the book, which showed three young people of indeterminate age in bright red hoodies wandering down a wooded road, their backs turned. 'It sounds like it might be a bit,' he stumbled on the words, 'kind of PSHE.'

'What's that?'

He giggled. 'Personal, Social and Health Education. We're doing puberty this term.'

Not literally, thought Tamsin, as she looked at his skinny little body in its pyjamas. I think it will be a fair few years until that hits you. A delayed adolescence had not been a luxury afforded to Tamsin, who had been slow to learn to read but quick to develop breasts and exploratory fingers.

She continued with the description of the book on the

back cover. "'Kez Farnham is an ordinary boy living life being ferried by his protective parents from school to after-school activities in the city. But then one day he finds himself transported to a world where everything is done differently and children can roam the woods alone. Luckily he finds two new friends who are his guides as they are plunged into a past mystery that he will need to solve if he is ever to understand his present.'" She paused. 'Shall we give it a go?' She had glanced inside and seen the reassuringly large print. 'You start.'

This is nice, thought Tamsin, as she let his monotone drift over her. He read with almost no expression and a fair few errors, like an audio book with the world's worst actor, but the plot of the book was surprisingly engaging. She'd found even the Harry Potter books a bit slow going, but already in chapter one, Kez had discovered a magic mobile phone that allowed its user to text back to a specific time and place as easily as messaging your mum.

'Your turn,' said Spike, as in the book Kez found himself split into a million pieces to whizz up through a satellite and back down to earth towards the end of the previous century.

'I'm not very good at reading,' she said. He looked at her as if she were mad. She was an *adult*, wasn't she? 'OK, here goes. "Chapter 2, Where Things Are Done Differently."'

At first, she had to concentrate so hard on reading the words correctly that she found she wasn't absorbing the content. But after a while, she got into the different voices – Kez with his London accent (or her approximation of one, based on soap operas, which was about as authentic as Dick Van Dyke's in *Mary Poppins*), and the people he met in the rural past with accents not dissimilar to the locals round here. Tamsin's own voice was a combination of placeless posh and the flat vowels that reflected the area's location halfway between East Anglia and that glorious swathe of the country that Londoners always referred to as 'the North'.

It made her laugh, though, that the dim and distant past where kids didn't own mobiles and had a more relaxed attitude to stranger danger was so recent. To Spike it must seem like the seventies did to her and the sixties or even fifties to Sasha: a land that existed before he was born.

She hadn't read much children's fiction, not even when she was a child. There wasn't a lot of this sort of stuff back then – it was straight from Enid Blyton and Jacqueline Wilson to Judy Blume and the rude bits in their mothers' Jilly Coopers.

'Shall I stop now?' she asked Spike.

'No, it's quite good, isn't it?' Spike was curled up against her in a way she found endearing in a nine-year-old, whom she had thought would be too old for such sweetness.

Yes, it was rather good. Well, really readable for a non-reader like her. She dreaded to think what her father or John would make of the fact that the only book she'd opened this year was one aimed at pre-teens.

She carried on as Kez took his cod London accent back through his magic mobile to an unspecified place in rural

England in the late nineties. There he met a thirteen-year-old girl, Issi, and her wild friend Monkey, who had just arrived at the local comprehensive after yet another move with his single mother. The three of them formed an immediate bond, especially when Kez was unable to return to the present on account of there not being a phone charger to fit his magic mobile (otherwise known as an iPhone).

Tamsin had a vague feeling of déjà vu, as if she'd read it before. Maybe it was a bit derivative after all, but of what she didn't know.

She continued reading. "'You're all right,' said Monkey to Kez. "You can hang out wiv me and Issi. You can even come down to the Nell wiv us . . .'"

The words came out as she concentrated on Monkey's yokel accent, but a second after she'd said 'Nell', she found herself unable to go on. Her face flushed and she felt her whole body lurch as if on the downward spree of a fairground ride, as if she were herself, like Kez, travelling back in time. A time when she was different – a wild, unparented child who was afraid of no one.

Her mind was filled with images of two teens, almost the same age as the characters in the book – children, just children – and the hours they'd spent in an abandoned agricultural storage building, one that she still passed as she walked and walked to achieve her 15,000 steps. There they would fool around, finally discovering a sport in which they both excelled and a place where they were valued. Her stomach flipped and she felt a heat between her thighs at the memory, one she only called up when she was very sure that John wouldn't see inside her filthy mind.

'The Nell . . .' she repeated.

'What's a Nell?' asked Spike.

'It's not a proper word. We . . . they've got it wrong. They've got it mixed up with dell, which is a valley or special place or something. Most people don't use the word Nell at all. It's a special word.'

'Like a secret code?'

'Yes, exactly, a secret code.'

The agricultural shed that she and Mickey had called the Nell. Mickey, who had arrived at her school as if by magic to save her from her loneliness and low self-esteem. Mickey, who had made her, for that brief time, into a person who stopped caring about whether others liked her or what they thought of her and who as a consequence valued herself for the first and only time in her life. Mickey, with whom she'd spent so many hours exploring each other's bodies.

The shed that only they had called the Nell. That as far as they knew only they ever visited, apart from whoever had purchased the ancient porn mags that they'd enjoyed stumbling across, their pages glued together by age or something worse.

'Go on,' said Spike.

She blushed some more at the thoughts that were rushing through her head in front of this child. 'I . . . I think it's late. Your mum said you should be in bed by now.'

'No she didn't. I'm allowed up until eight thirty.'

She wanted him gone; she wanted to read on alone, to find out whether this book was what she thought it was. 'Please go to bed now.'

His shoulders sloped. 'All right, but I'm allowed to read in bed for as long as I like.'

'Fine,' she said, and then watched with wretched disappointment as he picked up the book and took it up to bed with him.

'I had a lovely time last night,' Sasha said to Bailey at breakfast, with the desperate air of a woman trying to convince a potential boyfriend that their first date had been a success. Daughter-date was what she had called it, appropriately, since it was as awkward and forced as the worst dates that she'd been on two decades ago when she'd been single. Other women went shopping with their daughters and giggled with them in the changing rooms, then sat on bar stools laughing over a salad. Other women didn't feel the need to jot down a list of ten conversational openers on their phones in preparation for going to the pub for a meal. Other women didn't feel that their own child had somehow been replaced by a random, unknowable sort of girl-child with whom she made polite conversation.

How she longed to be one of those women who had big blow-out rows with their daughters. She must be the only mother in the world who had encouraged her underage daughter to have a glass of wine, only to be rebuffed.

Other women might even confide in their daughters

that there was a strange woman from Dad's past vaguely stalking them.

'Yes, it was nice,' Bailey said. 'I liked the risotto.'

'Delicious, you did choose well.' And here they were again. Like two strangers in a kitchen, except one loved the other with a ferocity that she was unable to express. Sasha had tried to talk to Ned once about Bailey's behaviour, and he'd laughed at her, saying, 'You're the only mother in the world to complain that your daughter is too polite.'

They were interrupted by a shriek. 'She stole it!' shouted Spike from his bedroom, which, like the others, was off the balcony that ran around the double-height main living area, above the kitchen where Bailey and Sasha were awkwardly chatting.

'Who stole what?' asked Sasha. Spike would never become unknowable, surely, not even when he was taller than her, hairy and monosyllabic.

'Tamsin. She stole my book.'

'Which book?'

'The one about texting. Mum, can I get a phone? Everyone in my class has got one.'

'No, of course not. So this book . . . ?'

'She definitely took it from me,' he wailed.

'Don't be silly. You know how I hate the way you always accuse people of stealing stuff that you yourself have lost. Remember the shin pads?'

'She did, she must have done. It was by my bed.'

'Where it probably still is.' Sometimes Sasha felt as though she were a doll with a certain number of pre-programmed speeches that would vomit out at the touch of a button.

The one that was most frequently used was 'I don't know, probably where you left it.' It was hard being a lone parent, which was how she thought of herself.

'It's not.'

'OK, I'll come and look, but if I find it within two minutes, you owe me a pound.' She stomped upstairs, sure that it would be under his bed or a pile of clothes and that she'd locate it within seconds.

Five minutes later and Spike's pound was safely still his. 'Are you sure you took it up to bed with you?'

'Yes, I definitely did,' he said with a nine-year-old's oversized sense of injustice. 'I was reading it last night. She read me some and then she went all funny and said I had to go to bed.'

'Good for her, you did have to. It was a school night.'

'And I took the book, the one with the boy who goes back in time, and I was reading it in bed, I read up to chapter nine, which was page seventy-three, so I did loads. But then she stole it from me.'

'Why would she want to do that? It's a kids' book, and have you seen her house? I expect she could buy her own copy, she's got loads of money.' Sasha stopped, remembering something from last night with a flush of embarrassment. When she had returned, there had been an awkward moment when she'd been saying goodbye to Tamsin, who had hovered in the hallway in a way that Sasha couldn't quite read. Now she realised that it was exactly the way that tour guides and luggage carriers in American hotels took too long to say goodbye, hanging around in expectation of a tip.

Tamsin had been expecting to get paid.

Sasha had assumed, naturally, that she was just wanting to reverse the roles they'd had when she herself had been the babysitter. If she had stopped to think about it, she might have thought that perhaps Tamsin looked back with nostalgia at that time: she had been so vital, so wild, so full of life. How could a woman with shoes that Sasha knew cost upwards of £300 be wanting to engage in the grubby transaction that drunk parents across the country did with their babysitters at the end of the evening: 'You came at seven thirty, didn't you, and it's now, what, eleven, that's four and a half hours – no it's not, it's like eleven minus seven, oh, that's five, but it was half past, OK, so four times six is thirty-two . . . Have you got any change? Oh, it's not, well, shall we just call it thirty quid? No, twenty.'

And even if for some bizarre reason the wife of a millionaire property developer was short of cash, what was she doing nicking children's books? She wouldn't cover the cost of post and packaging on eBay if she tried to flog it (and Sasha should know, such margins being the very stuff of her income from the ceramics). And she'd hardly want to read it, would she?

She heard Bailey slam the front door on her way to get the bus to her private school on the other side of the nearest town from the comprehensive where the rest of her diaspora of friends from primary had gone. Sasha smarted at the rejection – she'd offered to take Bailey this morning by car, leaving Spike at his primary school's breakfast club, but then she'd been derailed by this business of the missing book.

'It'll turn up, Spike, I'll have a good look for it today, I promise.'

'It's just that I really want to know what happens. There's a secret, you see.'

There always is, thought Sasha, there always is.

3

Homecoming Kings

By the time Friday came around, Emily felt as if she had become crazed with boredom and loneliness. Her three children were gorgeous, obviously – she loved them dearly, wouldn't be without them and all that – but there were only so many conversations about poo she could have without feeling an urge for greater intellectual stimulation.

Lately, she had begun to feel a perverse nostalgia about all those things people left the city to get away from. She wanted to see bare-legged old women pushing shopping trolleys full of newspapers, threatening-looking boys in hoodies doing wheelies on their bikes, hear the *innits* and *bluds* that made up their speech; she wanted to be squashed against the smelly bodies of strangers on the tube.

When Matt came home, she didn't know which she was more excited about – his return, or the way he brought the city with him, the smells and the tales.

She heard his key in the lock. The excitement and relief was always tinged with nervousness, the way that each week they became strangers to each other, despite knowing him better than anyone in her life.

She heard his voice and then saw him, so familiar and yet strange in the low doorway of this home. 'Hello, boy, I've missed you.' He crouched down to let Rafa lick his face, which the dog did with an almost sexual enthusiasm. Do you kiss your wife with that mouth? she thought, as she saw Rafa give him a full-frontal slurp.

'Only Rafa?' She tried to inject some coquettishness into her voice. She felt compelled to make the weekends perfect, since that was all her marriage now consisted of. One of her friends had warned her that returning husbands tended to greet the children first. Here it was the bloody dog, then the children, and finally the wife.

'Course not,' said Matt. He came over to her and they had a slightly awkward kiss, with her trying to take in the heady scent of commuter sweat and building works while at the same time wondering if she were getting second-hand Rafa spittle. They were interrupted by five-year-old Zanna.

'Hello, gorgeous,' Matt said, embracing her and receiving a static shock from the polyester of her red school fleece. Zanna was stiff in receipt of the hug. The children's reunions with their father, a bit like their mother's, never quite matched up to the cinematic fantasy of running into open arms that they had envisaged. 'Where are your brothers?' he asked.

'Clem's on the computer,' said Zanna. 'Nate's got his telly time 'cos he doesn't want to watch the same as me. He still watches CBeebies. What a baby.'

'What are they doing looking at screens on a lovely day like this?' Matt turned to Emily, glancing through the window towards the chilly drizzle. 'They should be out playing football.'

'Nate's got to go to bed in less than an hour, and who's Clem supposed to play football with?' said Emily. It was all very well buying a garden big enough for sports, but that was no good without a whole team of kids to play with. Back in London, there had been a scary-looking five-a-side pitch near their house, where it was rumoured a boy had been stabbed and which was known as 'the cage'. It now seemed quite appealing.

'Or making a den, then,' said Matt.

Den-making, blackberrying, crabbing, butterfly-collecting . . . like so many of their friends, they had a remarkably old-fashioned view of what made the perfect childhood. They had all devoured a list produced by the National Trust called '50 things to do before you're 11¾'. It was their oracle, promising an arcadia of animal-tracking and apple-picking, of muddy puddles, ponies and picnics that was unachievable in the city. Combined with this aspic-preserved view of what childhood was supposed to be like was paranoia about the dangers of screen time. This despite the fact that the grown-ups themselves spent hours gazing lovingly at their phones and laptops without getting ADHD. If they had ever stopped to question the gospel of barefoot children in the meadows, they might have realised that their offspring would more likely grow up to work with screens than streams.

Emily had swallowed the doctrine wholeheartedly back in the city, but moving to the country had made her agnostic about its truths. 'Funnily enough, Clem finds building a complex cityscape on Minecraft a bit more satisfying,' she said. She resented the politicians and celebrities who boasted that their children weren't allowed screens. Who decided, she wondered, this hierarchy of shameful parenting, that put this awe-inspiring technology alongside drinking Coke from a baby bottle and being pushed in a buggy too long?

'You need to limit his screen time.'

'I do.' Emily sighed. Three minutes in and they were already arguing about the best way to bring up children. When they'd been together every day, they had made decisions about the children jointly. Now it felt as though Matt had become the manager who'd flit by for critical appraisals, while she was the assistant coach, brought in to do the grunt work and blamed for anything that went wrong. Be nice, she thought. This is the precious weekend. I love him, I really love him, we are happily married, I've missed him. She repeated the mantras to herself. 'How are you?'

'Tired,' he said. 'I couldn't get a seat on the train.'

'Me too. Tired, I mean.'

'Well, at least you get to relax while they're at school.'

Here we go, thought Emily, the ridiculous who's-more-tired conversation, the one that she thought they'd left behind with the baby years. When she'd worked, they'd both been aggrieved at the loss of what they called the 'decompression drink' – that half an hour of slumping on the sofa on returning from the office. Now she felt as though Matt wanted a decompression weekend – since he worked away all week, he reasoned that he needed longer to make that transition from professional to family man. But she felt that after a week away from the children – and from her, she supposed – he ought to be straight into the tiring yet unstimulating job of looking after three children under the age of eight.

Be nice, she told herself again. We only have the weekend. It was the same every Friday. She longed for his return, and yet they bickered almost immediately, ruining everything. 'I've made pork belly. Your favourite,' she added, in case he needed reminding.

'Lovely.'

Why did it seem as if they were only natural when they were arguing over something, but polite like strangers when they were being pleasant to each other? The grumpy stuff seemed so much more real.

He went upstairs to remonstrate with Clem on the computer and to change out of his grimy clothes. He'd once joked that he should have proper country clothes to mark his return: herringbone plus fours or something. Rafa followed him up, giving every impression of being the lovable pooch they'd planned to have and, as Matt often complained, the only one to really seem glad that he was back.

It was often true that the whole mood of the weekend would be set by these initial interactions, like that old trope about first impressions counting. Emily followed him up the stairs, determined to give him a proper hug and to tell him how much she'd missed him, but to make it sound affectionate rather than resentful.

As he saw her coming into the bedroom, he stuffed an unfamiliar-looking mobile into his jacket pocket and then smiled with forced jollity.

'What was that?'

'What?'

'Have you got a new mobile?'

'That? Work's just given it to me. They give one to everyone working on contract. I think it's so they can contact us at any time. Own the mobile, own the person sort of thing.'

'I think the children aren't the only ones that need to restrict their screen time,' she said, trying to eliminate the bitchiness in her voice.

'It's work,' he insisted. Oh yes, 'work', the word that shut down any argument now that she could no longer use it as her own excuse.

His hand stayed protectively over the pocket containing the phone.

What was it Sasha had said about weekend wives? That the whole set-up was some sort of Petri dish of secrets and affairs.

She put on her best face. 'It's so lovely to have you home. I've missed you.'

Rafa was sitting on the bed, *their* bed, and she could have sworn he gave her a smug face, one that said, *ha, you fool*. She looked again and he'd turned on his back and was now having his tummy vigorously tickled by Matt.

She thought of Rafa as so clever and manipulative, but here he was liking nothing more sophisticated than having his tummy rubbed.

He was just a dog after all, just a dog.

The expression 'like stealing candy from a baby' would have been apt to describe the lifting of the book from Spike's bedside table. Tamsin knew she should feel guilty, but Spike's shelves were groaning with books, plus he had a Kindle. And anyway, she was only borrowing it.

She'd forgotten how great nicking stuff was. It had left her giddy. These days she never machine-washed items whose label told her they were delicate. She never cut a corner that took her off the public footpath across privately owned land. Yet there had been a time when she'd not only broken the law but enjoyed doing it. She'd been entirely without conscience. She and Mickey had gone on the bus (without paying, natch) to the nearest town and helped themselves to sweets and clothes. It was pretty easy when you were as buxom and winsome as she had been and you made sure you only targeted the shops patrolled by men.

It was as if, like Kez in the book, she too was now able to time-travel to a place where she was the sort of person who nicked stuff and was lippy to authority figures.

It was annoying that Sasha hadn't paid her for baby-sitting; it would have been lovely to have a bit of money of her own. Still, she couldn't regret having been at Sasha's house that night, for without it she'd never have chanced upon the book.

She could have dismissed the mention of the Nell as a coincidence, but she'd known, she'd known straight away, that it was anything but. In fact, she now realised that she'd known all along, and the mention of the Nell only made explicit the nagging sense of familiarity she'd had as she and Spike had looked at the book together. She'd thought somehow that she'd read it before, but now she knew that she hadn't read it, she had *lived* it.

She'd raced through *Text Back Time* as soon as she'd got home from Sasha's, devouring it in a way that would have surprised anyone who knew her as 'the pretty one', as opposed to her sister's role as 'the clever one'.

Every so often, she'd put the book down to breathe deeply. When she did, she could smell the dust, the sun-tanned skin and the sweat that had been the perfume of that summer. She could smell it over the fabric-conditioned sheets, fresh paint and scented candles that had become the stench of her new life.

She was Kez, travelling back in time, and she was also Issi, the girl in the story. Not that the book told the whole truth of those underage fumblings. It was categorised as 'young adult'. If it had described what she and Mickey had really got up to in the Nell, it would definitely have been in the adult section of the library. In the story, Issi and Monkey were innocent best friends, while she and Mickey had been so much more.

When Mickey had arrived midway through the first term of Year 10, Tamsin had not been discontent so much as disconnected. She'd been the last of four children, but the first of them to go to the local comprehensive. Her brothers had gone to boarding school from the age of eight, while her sister attended a private girls' school further away – the one that Sasha had gone to and which Bailey now attended – leaving Tamsin marooned alone at home, a sort of only child with none of the perks such as undivided parental attention. Her father used to joke, in her earshot, that it wasn't worth spending money on her education, not with that pretty little empty head of hers.

She was never quite sure why her mother had had so many children, when she gave every indication of not liking them very much. She was a brilliant wife but a fairly mediocre mother, given to disappearing for days at a time to meet up with their father at overseas conferences, leaving the girls alone with Sasha and a tin-opener. If they'd been poor, Tamsin was sure social services would have got involved.

If Sasha was unavailable, their mum would go off anyway. (The tin-opener, Tamsin remembered now, was a particularly rubbish one too, one time slicing off the top of her finger so that Mum returned to a kitchen that looked like a crime scene in a TV drama.)

They never ate together as a family; the kids would have whatever they could rustle up early evening, while their parents had a proper meal later on. Her mother told her it was important to keep a man happy. Now Tamsin realised she was talking about sex, but then it seemed to be all about having a separate adults' supper with things like chicken Kiev and, latterly, meat with a complicated jus smeared across the plate.

It was in the middle of October, just an ordinary school day, when into her monochrome world walked Mickey in full Technicolor. Corny, but that was how it seemed. The rest of the class wore badly fitting black polyester blazers and looked like teenagers on their way to a job interview at a call centre, while Mickey wore bright yellow jeans and a royal blue shirt instead of the school uniform. Even his hair was a brilliant red (and Tamsin knew immediately that nobody would be calling him a ginger whinger, Duracell or Carrot Top, as was the case with every other child with even the merest hint of auburn. No, on Mickey, red hair was the coolest thing any of them had seen, ever).

'Ah, welcome, Michael,' said Ms Downing, their teacher, as he came in. 'Are you intending to wear uniform or do the school rules not apply to you?'

He grinned apologetically, and that seemed absolutely acceptable to Ms Downing. She must have felt it too, the way he glowed with sex like no one Tamsin had ever met before. He was burnished with it.

He sat down at the desk across from her and winked. That was that, she was hooked. Still was, she now realised.

Monkey in the book had red hair too, and according to the text it was the best colour. By the time Kez came into their world, Issi and Monkey, the neglected posh girl and the boy who'd moved house eleven times, were as interwoven as strands of DNA. Kez was the narrator and observer, and through him, Tamsin felt as though she were being allowed to watch a DVD of her own adolescence (smutty bits erased). The book made much of the contrast between the freedom of their world and the modern one that Kez had left behind, but Tamsin didn't care about all that.

There were boring descriptions of the woods and the landscape, and some irrelevant plot stuff too. Monkey, Issi and Kez found a knife in the Nell and so spent a lot of the book trying to find out who it belonged to and what it had been used for (skinning cats, rather revoltingly – the baddie was a bitter and twisted barman who wanted revenge on his mad cat-lady of an ex-girlfriend. Tamsin was surprised by how unashamedly gory and brutal the story was).

This was of no interest to her. She was reading and rereading the book to find out what it meant to her and *for* her. What it meant to Monkey and Issi, to Mickey and Tammy. And to Kez, the boy who was as old as her memories of that time. What it meant now, today, as grown-ups. Mickey had written this for her, for surely it had been Mickey; it couldn't be that he'd told someone else, this Jake V. Bond author person, because there were things that only she and Mickey could know about, little phrases they had shared, in-jokes, their made-up language and names for local landmarks.

She looked again at the place where the author photo should be, but there was just a squiggly line drawing of a bearded man and the words 'Jake V. Bond lives alone in his imagination' as the only biography supplied. It was hard to tell if the drawing was of Mickey, since she hadn't seen him in sixteen years, and truth be told, it was a bit rubbish as drawings went.

'I can see your lips moving,' said John when he returned from his trip to Kent. Tamsin had been so engrossed in trying to decipher the message of the book that she hadn't heard him come in.

'I'm so sorry, I thought you were coming back later,' she said, flustered. 'Let me take your bag. Do you want a drink? I'll go and change, too. Sorry, it wasn't meant to be like this.'

'I don't know what's more shocking, you in your sports mufti or you reading a book! It really doesn't suit you. You don't want to muddle yourself with books.'

'I know, I know. It's silly.' What could she do with it? She wanted to hide it as effectively as any man with porn on his laptop. It was hers, all hers; he couldn't have the book, in the same way he could never take that time with Mickey away from her. Go, she willed him, go to the bedroom to change, or the bathroom; just go, and please don't take my book.

Thank you, God, she thought, as he went upstairs to the bedroom. She ran into the kitchen and hid the book in the 'cheap cupboard', where she kept the food she ate when John was away: items from the basics range at the supermarket, in contrast to the organic and finest stuff reserved for him. It would be safe there.

Then she went to the utility room and found the lingerie she'd hand-washed that morning, and went upstairs to greet John in the way a good wife should.

Sasha was ready for the return of her hunter-gatherer. Since he only came back for a five-day stint once a month, and sometimes even less frequently than that, it was important that she should be chipper. She would try to banish any thoughts of how much easier it could feel when he wasn't there.

The airport was unglamorous. Most airports were these days, as was plane travel generally, but this one was particularly so, filled as it was with disobedient parents taking their school-age children on cheap term-time package holidays to somewhere hot.

They, or more accurately she, had been back living here for over four years. The first year, she'd made an effort by standing at arrivals brandishing a placard as though she were a driver or tour rep. On it would be emblazoned his surname, Rayburn, spelt a variety of wrong but witty ways: Rat Burn, Ray Burp, Rap Bro, et al. To be honest, it was only funny the first time, but somehow the act of preparing the board made her feel as if she were making herself, the house and the children ready for him.

The second year, she'd always made sure she wore her best outfits. 'I'm going commando,' she'd once whispered in his ear on the drive back, and they'd pulled over into an unromantic A-road lay-by and had sex that satisfied them if not physically, then at the very least cinematically – get them with their rough in-car coupling! Yes, they were still hot for each other after all these years and two kids.

By the third and fourth years, the outfits were less impressive, but her hair was done and make-up on.

Now they were on to the fifth year. There had been some long stints in the UK between jobs for Ned, and even occasional movies filmed in Europe (obscure bits of Estonia for the wintry ones, Cyprus or Morocco for the hot ones). But mostly they had got into the habit of him taking the well-paid work in LA and not even looking too closely for an alternative.

By the sixth year, Sasha thought to herself, she probably wouldn't be picking him up from the airport at all. The misspelt placards of a driver for whom English was not a first language would at last become real.

For the moment, though, she liked the way the two-hour car journey home from either Stansted or Birmingham airport gave her something to do while their relationship unbent from their estrangement. She could concentrate on driving, he on swapping from his LA to his UK phone.

She glanced over at him. Damn, he was good-looking, and he knew it. Talented and handsome as well as charming and well paid. He was a catch, that was what everyone said, even now. What about me, she'd wanted to wail, aren't I a catch too? Women weren't though, she'd come to realise; they were just the bait.

'Ned,' she said, but in her mind the name 'Eddie' kept ringing. He looked ridiculously well, as he always did. The permanent tan of Los Angeles had not yet given way to leathery premature ageing, and he carefully offset all the sitting in cars with regular air-conditioned trips to the gym for extreme cardio sessions. She wished she could luxuriate in his well-maintained good looks, but instead she questioned whether she, acknowledged as the fashion superstar of the village, could compare with the porn stars who did the Xtreem Squatz class with him.

'It's lovely to have you back,' she continued, trying to rinse out the stiffness from her voice with a swig of tepid bottled water. It wasn't true, of course. It was hard not to feel that life was just that little bit easier – well, a whole lot easier – when it was just her and the children. Over the time they'd been back in England, it was as if the family had gone from being a four-legged chair to a three-legged stool. Ned's absence no longer tipped them over. In fact his presence now knocked them out of balance.

'It's lovely to be back, darling. Can't wait to see the kids. I'm starving,' he added. 'What's for supper?'

'That beef and anchovy dish you like so much, and some mash and roasted vegetables. It's slow-cooking as we speak.' Yes, she hadn't put on her special underwear, but she had made him a special meal. This was less to do with wifely devotion than the fact that Sasha loved to feed people, especially with a steaming hot piece of Le Creuset in the centre of the table.

'I love you,' he said in a jovial, jokey sort of way, meaning *I love the way you cook for me*. Do you? she wondered. Enough to tell me the truth about this woman? I haven't forgotten her, you see, despite the fact that your Skype always seems to conveniently cut out every time I've tried to talk to you about her.

'So . . .' she said, concentrating on the road.

'So?' Everything was a question with him now that he'd picked up the Californian intonation.

'You never did tell me who you think this woman is.'

'What woman?'

She wished she could look at him, but this was a notoriously accident-ridden stretch of the motorway.

'The one I've tried to talk to you about every time we've spoken recently. The one who calls you Eddie.'

'I don't know. Probably no one.'

'She's certainly someone,' snapped Sasha. 'I've seen her four or five times now, and it's not my imagination.'

'I didn't mean that. I meant nobody important. I wasn't suggesting she doesn't exist.'

'Well what does she want from you? From us?'

'I don't know.' He was exasperated now. 'I've no idea. Look, I've been working hard and I just want to enjoy some quality time with my family. Is that too much to ask for?'

'Well, she must be someone who knows you from university.'

He sighed. 'What makes you say that?'

'She calls you Eddie. People from way back call you Edward, people now call you Ned. You're weird the way you have to have a new name to go with each of your reinventions.'

He scoffed. I bet you're calling yourself something else entirely now your family has left Los Angeles, Sasha realised with sudden clarity. What are you now? Something androgynous, one of those trendy surnamey names that they'd chosen for their own daughter. Probably something like 'Ward'.

'OK, I can see it's a bit vague, but she told me that you'd know, that I should ask you, and that's what I'm doing.'

'Like I said, tell her to get in touch with me directly, whoever she is, and to stop bothering my family.' He puffed out as he said the last two words, all proud protector. Which is all very well, thought Sasha, but how can you protect us if you're never here? It's like putting out the bins; you have to be here to do it.

When they got back, Ned gave Bailey a hug that filled Sasha with jealousy, not for Bailey, but for her husband and his ease with their daughter. Not fair, she wanted to whine. Bailey doesn't recoil from you, while she is rod-like when I try to hug her. Then he beckoned Sasha over to join them with the words 'My two favourite girls'.

'Girls?' scoffed Bailey, but she didn't move away from his embrace.

'Ladies, then.' He laughed. He was good at making sure that his sexism was ironic in front of Bailey.

'Yes,' said Sasha, keen to side with her daughter, 'women will do.'

'Hark at her,' said Ned, 'the great feminist.'

Bailey giggled, and Sasha realised that he had successfully realigned the teams again so that she was out on her own.

'What's that supposed to mean?' she said.

'You're hardly my feminist role model,' said Bailey, serious now.

'I look after everyone, I work . . .'

Bailey and Ned laughed again.

'You sell pottery on eBay,' said Bailey.

'Which is great,' added Ned with the full weight of the patriarchy in his voice.

'Actually, it is. I earn really not a bad wage, and I'm not "selling pottery", as you put it; I'm sourcing early- and mid-century ceramics and selling them on through my global business.'

'Global business,' said her daughter and husband with one voice.

'Yes, global business. I have a web presence, therefore it's global. At least half my customers live overseas. And even if I didn't have my own business that earns really quite well, I could still be a feminist.'

'You're obsessed with cooking and clothes,' said Bailey. She talked so much more when Ned was around, but it was only then that Sasha wished she'd talk a little less.

'Which is my right. It might surprise you to know, Bailey, that feminism wasn't invented by Twitter. I was in the women's group at university and everything.'

To Bailey, this must seem like ancient history, like women trying to get the vote or the right to education, but Sasha was desperate to position herself with her daughter, to prove that although the man of the house was off hunting and gathering overseas, she could still be an emancipated woman.

'So what did you do in your women's group?' asked Bailey, and Sasha could hear the inverted commas around the last two words.

'We campaigned for better street lighting by going on Reclaim the Night marches, and . . .' God, what did we do? she panicked. She did remember whining a lot about boys who didn't call. 'And we campaigned about date rape.'

'Date rape?' asked Bailey.

'Yes, date rape was really big in those days. That sounds wrong, like it was fashionable, like raves or oversized T-shirts. What I mean is that it was a big issue for us. Back then, marital rape wasn't even illegal and it was people like my women's group that changed all that. A husband could rape his own wife with no consequence.'

Ned slunk off looking awkward at this point. Sasha had won, perhaps with her citing of marital rape – not that this was an issue for them, but it certainly seemed to make her husband escape upstairs to peel off his jet-lagged clothes.

4

Texting Back Time

The weekend had dragged for Tamsin, as she yearned to get back to reading the book she'd stolen from Spike. When John was at home, she spent every minute with him. No wonder she'd never had a job.

She wanted to eat up *Text Back Time*'s words and scour it for clues, but this was denied to her over the weekend. She was sure that within the book, Mickey was talking to her directly across the years. If she could decipher his message, then they would meet again. She didn't dare to think what such a meeting would mean for the life she was now leading.

On the Monday, John had revealed that, ta-da, he was working from home that day. When he did that, he liked her to sit in his office with him. Not reading or writing or tidying or doing anything, just being. It made her feel all fidgety, like a model in a life-drawing class – an analogy that was particularly apt, since sometimes he preferred it when she was wearing only her underwear. Other times he liked her to change her clothes every hour or so, a very slow catwalk show with only one model and one front-row seat. He always cooed appreciatively at her outfits, unsurprisingly really since he'd chosen and paid for them all.

She was lucky like that. He had exquisite taste and she was as a consequence the most expensively dressed woman in the village, only rivalled by Sasha and her bold tastes.

Tuesday came, and with it her chance to get the book out from beneath the tins of basics-range chickpeas. 'Come wiv us to the Nell,' Monkey had said in its pages. And so it seemed to her that the real Nell would be as good a place as any to start. She would go there with Monkey/Mickey as her spiritual guide.

She slipped the fancy pedometer on to her wrist and allowed herself a flicker of rebellious satisfaction that she would be both totting up her steps, just as John liked, but also visiting a place from her past, which she knew he would not.

She walked through the woods scattered with spent cartridges, over the fields of now scored crops, past the medieval burial mound, until the traffic noises faded and she was almost a mile away from the village.

It hadn't changed much, the Nell, not in comparison to the changes that had been wrought on her in that time. When something was crumbling and disintegrating in the first place, the years didn't do as much damage.

Had she really not been back in all these years? She'd lived in various places across the county with John but had now at last ended up back where she had started, in the village of her parents. They were no longer there, of course, since they'd moved to be 'nearer the children' – the ones that mattered, that is, the ones who had produced grandchildren and now lived in commuting distance of London. It was John who had brought her back here – well, a great investment opportunity by way of the undeveloped land on which to build a house – but not once had she returned to the Nell.

It hadn't changed, but she had. She was sixteen years older, but she wondered whether she was any wiser. Her knees buckled like those of a fifteen-year-old in love as she gazed at the Nell through those eyes. It was special, a sanctuary, a place of nature where she'd done things that had felt more natural than anything she'd done since.

Like most fifteen-year-olds, Tamsin had lacked curiosity about anything that didn't affect her directly, and so had never questioned what the purpose of the building was other than to provide a haven for her and Mickey. In many ways, her development was so arrested by the traumatic ending of that love affair and a youthful marriage to an older man that she didn't show much more curiosity now. It was, if she thought about it, some sort of abandoned agricultural storage building, but as far as she was concerned it served only as a portal to her past. She and Mickey used to call it theirs, and so it seemed still today. She barely saw the way it looked; it was blurred through the lens of nostalgia and the memory of lust. Half hidden by brambles, it was like something from a fairy tale, a secret place that only she knew.

She fought back the thorns and wondered, momentarily, how she would explain the scratches to John.

When she finally reached the door, she found that it was locked with a padlock. She shook it angrily only to find that it fell open in her hands. It was either broken or had never worked. As it opened, a cloud of dust was thrown up, and it seemed to Tamsin as if it were a magical puff of smoke; as if her coming back here was ordained. Muscle memory from way back told her that the door opened out rather than inwards, and she braced her foot against the wall to tug at it. Each inch was an effort, leaving her breathless with both exertion and excitement.

At last there was enough of a crack for her daily-shrinking body to squeeze through, and she found herself standing in the gloom, only illuminated by what light could fight its way through the weeds and dust that coated the windows.

She didn't know what she had expected. Well, she did, but it was too crazy to admit. She had expected Mickey, standing there waiting for her with a couple of bottles of Hooper's Hooch and some roll-ups. Yes, I am stupid, she told herself. She'd thought she was being all cool and rebellious coming back to the place where she had been both those things, but in fact she was as stupid as everyone had ever told her.

Mickey wouldn't be here waiting for her, preserved as a gorgeous skinny-limbed youth. He was somewhere else, writing his books, if it was even him who wrote them. He might have lost all his auburn hair or become fat; he might be married with children or even dead. Maybe it was all a coincidence; perhaps the book wasn't a love letter to a golden teenage affair but a work of complete fiction by a stranger. Had Mickey ever really existed? How could she know, since she had no proof of him, no photos, no reminders?

She sat on an old plastic cement bag in the corner of

the room, coughing as she dislodged the dust that had gathered over the years. She and Mickey had cleaned the Nell – well, sort of; it hadn't exactly been worthy of a spread in an interiors magazine, but it had been less dusty back then. Something about the smell of it, like rotting mushrooms, helped to take her back in time. This was the corner where they had always sat, and then later lain. She traced the wall with her finger, wishing that they'd made some mark or carving for her to feel, not daring to look to see whether her last, solitary visit had left its stain.

She got out the book and began to read it yet again, flicking straight to references to the Nell. She found the bit where Monkey was explaining to Kez what it was. 'It's a place where we can be ourselves, me and Issi. Where we do stuff.'

Where we do stuff.

To each other, with each other, all over each other, thought Tamsin. An innocent line in a children's book brought back a heap of memories that had no place in pre-teen fiction. People always talked about teenage boys being sex-obsessed, but she remembered a time when she could think of nothing else. She'd been permanently sex-dazed. She'd been like a rutting animal, wanting to touch herself all the time, diving into toilets to do so. No wonder she'd left school with scant GSCEs.

They used to lie down on a makeshift bed – not an old cement bag like this one, but a foam mattress shaped like egg cartons that she'd taken from the generous supplies in her parents' airing cupboard. At first they'd just lain next to each other, talking about their lives and dreams, with the lack of self-consciousness of teenagers. Mickey's first ambition was to not move house again. 'I don't want to leave here. I don't want to leave everything.' He'd paused and then turned to her. 'I don't want to leave you.' Tamsin had felt happier than she'd ever felt in her life.

Then they'd moved on to kissing, spending hours on all that snogging, pointless and delicious. In the cold, they'd kept their clothes on, but just by rubbing themselves against each other through their woollen and denim contraception, they'd both come. They came so easily, remembered Tamsin. It was like leapfrog or PlayStation; young people could do it with such agility and instinct. Not for them the hours of foreplay, but instead a bit of kissing, a bit of rubbing, done, over and over.

Of course, that wasn't enough, but as luck would have it, the days warmed as their lust heated. By the Easter holidays, they were licking each other all over, and by the summer term, full sex had occurred. Her mother had vaguely warned her about the dangers of pregnancy (the same mother who now vaguely warned her of the dangers of leaving pregnancy too late), but her parents were of course best friends and drinks-party buddies with the local GP, so she and Mickey had relied on an arbitrary mix of condoms, counting and withdrawal methods. She'd known that she was, officially, under the age of consent, but she'd given her consent oh so willingly and with no moral qualms. She didn't feel a trace of guilt. She was someone who was usually susceptible to the opinions of others, but what she did with Mickey was so obviously beautiful, so obviously right, that she couldn't feel bad about it.

On the contrary, she felt so good. Oh God, so very good. Even when she wasn't with him, she'd dream of him, waking up with a need to put one of her vast collection of Beanie Babies between her legs to calm herself down.

It seemed to her that sex with Mickey was a totally different concept to anything she'd experienced since, with the six boys and men she'd slept with in the six months after Mickey had left, when she'd been hungry for solace, and then for the last twelve years with John. Just John. It was as if sex with Mickey was the World Cup, while everything else was just a Sunday afternoon kickabout with amateurs.

Despite the dingy dustiness of the Nell in which she found herself now, all these years later, something stirred between her thighs. She breathed in, and the smell of the room was the same, of damp straw and spore. She slid her fingers behind the barrier of her running tights and down into her pants. And to her surprise, it turned out to be just as easy as it had been back with Mickey. He had been speaking to her through the book; now he was touching her as well. She too was using her fingers to go back in time.

'You think you're so clever, don't you, behaving one way with me and another with everyone else.' Emily leavened her loneliness with long conversations with Rafa. It was a classic abusive relationship, she thought, and she wished she knew how to quit him. Hating him at least gave her something to do. 'You little fucker.'

She looked around and saw one of her mother-in-law's friends walking towards her. 'My lovely boy, who's a lovely boy, yes you are,' she added in a loud voice that seemed to belong to someone else.

In the empty hours between school drop-off and the pre-school finishing at noon, walking Rafa gave her some exercise too. Everyone's a winner with a dog, she thought ruefully.

She used to say how much she hated walking in London because of all the pedestrians and cars. Now she realised how much more interesting it was to look into people's houses and at shop windows than the monotony of open fields and countryside. She'd been suffering from a literal case of the grass being greener in the country, while now she wanted her grass tarmacked over and flanked by pop-up coffee shops.

Changing seasons, different birds, cloud formations, she told herself just as she would her children, with that desperation to make sure they were not disconnected from the natural world. Autumn, it's lovely, it's so wonderful to really see the seasons changing, she'd tried to chirrup to herself as she would to those friends she'd left behind.

The country made her feel like she sometimes did in front of modern art – everyone else seemed to find it beautiful, but she didn't understand it. The landscape was like a beautiful man who you knew to be gay. While she could just about appreciate its aesthetic splendour, she knew that she'd never really get it.

'Lovely mists,' she said out loud to persuade herself, before walking across the empty field and through the woods until they came to Rafa's favourite spot for rabbiting. Yes, it was messed up, her relationship with the dog – she hated him and yet she was keen to make him happy too.

'All right, all right, you can come off the lead now.'

She stood looking soulfully into the distance for a few minutes, pretending she was on the cover of some folk revival album, and then got bored and starting faffing around on her phone. It was important, she believed, to leaven some of this nature with a bit of screen time, just as her children did. Damn the country, she thought – no signal as ever. She jabbed at it, turning it off and on with no luck. Her vague plans to write a blog were constantly thwarted by the fact that the village seemed to be located in the centre of a broadband black hole.

When she looked up, Rafa was nowhere to be seen. She shouted uselessly for a few minutes, her voice becoming increasingly hoarse and then fraught. He's doing it on purpose just to annoy me, she thought. She sometimes had fantasies of Rafa being run over and how everyone would feel sorry for her losing her beloved dog, but she knew that actually the children *would* be devastated if anything happened to him, especially if it was her fault.

'Come on, Rafa!' she shouted again, rustling the bag of doggy treats as noisily as she could.

She heard what sounded like a brief yelp coming from

the abandoned concrete bunker-like building at the edge of the field and ran towards it. It didn't sound exactly like Rafa, but it didn't sound particularly human either.

'Bloody dog,' she said out loud as she grappled with the thick brambles that covered the way to an ugly corrugated-iron door. Her ancient but favourite cashmere jumper snagged on the thorns and she struggled to disentangle herself.

Finally, she successfully fought her way to the door, where a rusty old padlock hung impotently. The building, with its grey pebble-dashing and menacing air, was the architectural equivalent of the animal excrement that Rafa always seemed to want to roll in. God, he's a revolting creature, she thought as she shivered at the idea of entering this building with its walls the colour and texture of uncooked mince beyond its sell-by date. When people thought about the country, they thought of picturesque cottages with roses round the door, not the far more prevalent industrial prefabs that farmers threw up to litter the landscape.

She heard the sound of movement from within and felt an angry relief that Rafa was OK. She pulled open the door ready to admonish him.

'Oh!' she said on seeing 'little Tamsin', as Sasha always called her, flushed and manically brushing dust off her shiny running tights.

'Hello, how are you?' Tamsin said, extending her hand for a handshake and then hurriedly retracting it. They both seemed as embarrassed as two businessmen caught in a porn shop in 1960s Soho.

Emily laughed at the absurdity of the situation, and to her relief, Tamsin joined in. 'What are you doing here?'

Tamsin shrugged. 'You?'

'Looking for my bloody dog.' Her body slumped as she realised that the presence of Tamsin indicated the absence of Rafa. What would she say to the rest of her family? They'd know, wouldn't they, that she had wanted him gone, and now he was.

At that moment, they both turned at a scurrying sound, and in burst Rafa as if arriving on to the stage through the French windows in a farce. 'Rafa, you bastard!' said Emily, and he rushed towards her. She felt a surprising warmth and gratitude that he could be so affectionate towards her outside of mealtimes. As he got closer, though, she couldn't stop herself retching at his pungency.

Tamsin looked at her with amusement. 'I think he must have rolled in a fox set.'

'That's all right, then. This revolting stench of death is all *natural*, so I should embrace it. Get away from me, Raf, you smell like medieval London.' He did that teeth-baring thing at her again, as if displeased by her criticism of his personal hygiene. She stopped herself from saying something to him. She was crazy when it came to Rafa, but not so much that she wasn't aware of just how crazy others would think her. 'So what does bring you to a place like this?' she asked Tamsin.

'I felt like getting away.'

'Chose a nice spot for it.'

Tamsin smiled. 'Yes, it is, isn't it.' She was glowing and

looked more alive than the pallid, skinny, well-dressed person Emily usually saw around the village.

'I was being sarcastic.' Emily looked at Tamsin's questioning face and felt guilty, as if she'd told one of her children that Santa didn't exist. 'Although I suppose you could say that it does have a certain charm.'

'More than that for me.' A dreamy look came upon Tamsin's face. 'The thing is,' she began, 'I used to come here when I was younger, a teenager. Something made me want to come back.'

Emily looked at her with interest. 'Really? What did you do here? Were you one of these rural teens that sniffed shedloads of glue? And what's made you come back? You're too young to be having a mid-life crisis.'

'What do you mean?'

'Everyone my age is having one.' Emily laughed bitterly. 'It's what brought me to live here. But the men are the worst. They're all contacting their exes from back then with badly poetic emails about how they feel that nothing has changed, despite the fact that they themselves have aged so terribly. It's a thing when you hit a certain age: you want to go back to your youth. Is that what's brought you on your trip down memory lane?'

Tamsin picked up the book that had been lying beside her on the cement sack. She never would have thought she'd tell anybody about it, but something about Emily's enthusiastic curiosity and her desperation to make sense of it all led her to want to share. 'You're going to think I'm mad.'

Emily laughed. 'I won't. I promise you I won't.'

'I started reading this book, a children's book I guess. It belongs to Spike, Sasha's son.'

'Right.'

'And I think it's about a time in my life.'

'The love of your life?'

'Yes. No, I mean obviously John is the love of my life. My first love, I suppose. I think it's the story of that time when we used to come here. We called it the Nell, and as far as I know, nobody else does; we made it up because we thought it sounded romantic. I think that somehow the person who wrote the book is trying to talk to me. Maybe it's him, the boy from back then. Though he's a man now, obviously. Oh, that does sound mad, doesn't it?'

'No, not at all. Is that the book?' Emily looked over to the slim volume that Tamsin was clutching and saw a rather generic young-adult cover of the sort of thing her children were too young to read. They were still in the phase where a story became more, rather than less, interesting to them on being repeated for the seventy-fifth time. 'Let's have a look.'

She glanced at the blurb on the back and then immediately looked at the line drawing that represented the author's image. 'Is this him, your lover boy?'

Tamsin blushed, which made her look younger, as young perhaps as the girl who used to come to this place she called the Nell. 'It could be, but then it could be anyone really.'

'You know, when I'm reading or watching a thriller about a woman haunted by some person from her secret past, I always find myself shouting, "Just bloody google them!"' said Emily.

Tamsin looked blank. 'What do you mean?'

'I presume you've searched for this Jake V. Bond on the Internet?' said Emily. 'To see if he's your friend?'

'Oh right. No, I haven't.'

'Why not?'

Tamsin looked sheepish. 'I don't actually have the Internet.'

Emily looked with astonishment at this woman in her expensive sportswear and high-end trainers. 'What do you mean, you don't have the Internet? It's not something you have, it's just there.'

'I never look at it. Why would I need to? It's not like I have a job or anything.'

'Give me your phone.' Tamsin got out a phone that was as up-to-date as her footwear and handed it to Emily. 'Well, this has got the Internet on it, and Bluetooth and all that. You've got one of those fancy wristbands that checks how much exercise you do, haven't you?'

'Yes, and somehow it links to the Internet, I think, because John likes to know how much I've done at the end of each day, so I plug it into his computer. But I don't really understand technical stuff like that. I'm a bit stupid, you see.'

'I'm sure you're not,' said Emily, staring and jabbing at the phone. 'Bloody hell, you're right. You don't have Internet access, although you do have the web on your phone. It's weird.' She shook her head in disbelief. 'There are parental controls on this phone. Why would you have those? Your mum and dad are hardly going to be worried about you searching for "naked willies" and "big boobies" like my eldest does.'

'John bought it for me and set it up. I just charge the batteries every night and take photos and text him. Basic stuff.'

'And that's another thing that really irritates me in those thrillers. When the battery on a phone is, for reasons convenient to the plot, flat. But annoyingly, I can't check for you because my phone doesn't have any connection here and I've got to rush back and pick up Nate from pre-school anyway.' Emily looked thoughtful for a second. 'Listen, do you remember how Sasha said we should have a weekend wives' club as therapy?'

'Yes, it was at Tania's party.'

'I know she was joking and everything, but why don't we start it? Come round to mine any time after nine the day after tomorrow and I'll get Sasha to come along too. We'll get to the bottom of your mysterious boy lover and this book. It'll be fun. What's your number? I'll text you mine.'

Tamsin shrugged apologetically.

'You don't know your own *telephone number*?'

'I've never needed to, I suppose.'

Emily tried to hide her astonishment and tapped a text to herself on Tamsin's phone, noticing as she did so that there was only one number saved into it. 'Here, you've got my number now. It's the last cottage on the left as you come out of the village, just by the postbox. See you then. Rafa, you gorgeous sweet-smelling boy, let's go.'

*

Emily felt happier than she had in months. She had a purpose, at last. She was going to find this ex of Tamsin's, reunite them and live vicariously through their drama. It was to be her job. She had something to do.

That was her other secret from Matt, you see. She was lazy. She'd always known it, but a busy office job and a natural quickness had hidden it from others all her life. She'd known just how much more she could achieve if she'd properly applied herself. It had been like that at school, and university too; that if only she'd done even half of the revision or research she'd intended, she'd have got better marks. Every time she'd tried to admit her weakness, people would dismiss her fears by pointing to all that she was achieving. But she knew the truth.

She'd been sick of her job as a patent attorney, working hard to trademark other people's creativity while feeling that she was thwarting her own. She used to joke that she'd lost patience with patents. That had been part of the reason for the move. Perhaps the whole reason, something she'd only ever admit to herself.

But now she yearned for the reassurance of an office job to save her from the shapelessness of her own indolence. The idea of writing a blog was a delusion. She was never going to be self-motivated enough to do that, nor could she lose her inhibitions to write in a way that would be honest and interesting. Her second defining characteristic, in addition to laziness, was self-consciousness. All her life she'd stopped herself from doing things because of a fear of mortification, the embarrassment of others knowing that she'd tried and failed. She also worried constantly about what people thought of her, so it would be impossible to write about her experiences of moving to the country without the anxiety of causing offence. She hadn't even been able to keep a secret diary as a teenager because she always read it through the cringing eyes of others.

So instead she was cleaning that stupid fake Aga until it gleamed, as a symbol of her wasted life, and bingeing for hours on celebrity websites until she felt sick with self-loathing. Every day she swore that tomorrow would be different and that she would start working out what to do with the rest of her life, but every day she would fall back into the rabbit hole of the Internet. She'd never thought she'd look with envy at commuters, but now she did, yearning for that scaffold of an office day.

The other advantage of Tamsin's revelation was that it gave her an excuse to approach Sasha. The same diffidence that had prevented Emily from setting herself up for failure had led her to passivity with regard to relationships. Her friends weren't necessarily the ones she would have liked best, but the ones who had been there and shown an interest in becoming friends with her. She didn't like to think that this extended to her choice of husband, but if pressed, the fact that she and Matt had both been single in a random house share in their mid-twenties had played as much of a part as any sense that they were soulmates.

But now she had Tamsin and that book. She wrote herself a pleasing list full of the initials AP for 'action point' circled in red, and got to work on this Jake V. Bond character. And with each point ticked off on her A4 sheet of paper, she felt a little percentage-point increase in self-satisfaction. Even Rafa, asleep by her feet, seemed almost cuddly now.

Sasha was so distracted by Emily's intriguing invitation to a post-drop-off coffee that she almost missed seeing the woman.

She was racking up the miles in her people carrier, as happened when she insisted on driving Bailey to school, although her daughter said that she preferred taking the bus that went from outside the garage. Poor Spike had to go along for the ride and suffer the embarrassment of his mother parking illegally on the zigzags outside the village primary.

Was Spike getting a tiny belly on his skinny body? Sasha wondered as she parked as near as possible to the school gates so that he only had ten paces to walk. Maybe she should make him take some exercise. They could run together, perhaps, or even go to that Zumba class that mad Maggie ran in the village hall.

As she rounded the corner near her house on the way to Emily's, she glanced at the former chapel, with its high arched windows, looking to it for reassurance as she always did. But instead of feeling happy at the sight of it, there *she* was, the woman, at last. Sasha had both wished and feared that she would never return. She was pacing the pavement just as she had before, her brisk march almost hypnotising.

Sasha screeched to a halt and jumped out of the car.

'Wait, you . . . you . . .' You what? You mad stalker person, you innocent random who happens to have once known my husband, you evil-wisher? She ran up to her. 'Hello.' Hello? Like this was a vague acquaintance she was bumping into at the supermarket?

'Hello to you.' Her voice was so calm, far calmer than Sasha's, which was breathless, and not just because she'd sprinted towards her.

'Yes, well. So, I've spoken to Ned.' Ned, his name is Ned now, not Eddie, do you understand? 'As you suggested.'

'Good,' said the woman, and Sasha felt an irrational urge to smack her in her politely smiling face. 'And?'

'You should email him directly, that's what he says,' Sasha said. 'I'll give you his email address.' She scrabbled in her bag for a pen and an old receipt on which to write it, embarrassed to find that her hands were shaking as she did so, especially on noticing that the woman's hands, on receiving the scrap of paper, were not. 'Whatever issue you've got is with him, not me. And I don't even know your name.'

'Don't you? Oh, how rude of me. It's Rosie. And of course I know yours, Sasha. You're partly right, it is Eddie's issue. Well, mine and his.'

Sasha hated the way Rosie was aligning herself with her husband, putting her outside the circle of their knowledge. 'Yes, your issue. But,' she was breathless again, 'what is the issue anyway?'

'I really don't think it's my job to tell you. Just ask him about Rosie on the night of the poll tax riots. He'll

know exactly what I'm talking about. It's been nice properly meeting you, Sasha, you seem like a lovely person.'

'Thank you,' she stammered, fighting a strange desire
to shake hands. She was aware that she was reacting in
a very strange way, but she wasn't sure anyone would
know how to act normally in this odd situation. 'Well,
I'm expected at a friend's house.'

'You must go. I should really be off too.'

'Do you live round here?' Sasha asked.

The woman shook her head. 'Just visiting.' She smiled
and walked away.

Sasha watched the figure recede, and with it her chance
to find out what this business was all about. She felt as
though she'd received an envelope containing exam results
for a test she knew she had flunked. Although she was
curious, there was part of her that didn't want to find
out what was going on, overwhelmed as she was by a
sense that it might change her world.

She was still disconcerted when she arrived at Emily's
cottage at the end of the village. As she entered, she was
assailed by the strong smell of coffee and croissants being
warmed. A jar of wild flowers had been placed on the
kitchen table, and Emily was gabbling manically in
welcome.

'I'm very intrigued by your text,' Sasha said, hoping
to take her mind off the woman named Rosie. 'What's
this about little Tamsin? Quick, explain before she comes.
We don't want to scare her away like a delicate woodland
creature.' Tamsin always seemed to be on the point of
being startled by a sudden noise these days.

Emily looked happy to be the source of local news. Gosh, she was so perky and keen that it felt overwhelming to Sasha, who enjoyed her mostly solitary life, having moved back to put protective walls around her immediate family. 'Well, I bumped into her yesterday in that horrible agricultural shed thing, the grey one past the woods that looks like someone's eaten Farrow & Ball Elephant's Breath paint and then been sick over it. Creepy place.'

'Yeah, I know the one. What was she doing there? More to the point, what were you doing there?'

'Nothing,' said Emily quickly. 'Just walking the dog, you know, Rafa. Anyway, she was there because she'd borrowed some book of Spike's—'

'So she did steal it! It's called *Text to the Future* or something. Spike was adamant she had, but I'm afraid I told him he had to be wrong. How very strange.'

'She'd started reading it at your house and now she thinks this book is talking to her, that the author is giving her some sort of message. Which I know sounds a bit mad, like one of those schizophrenics who believe that people are talking to them through the TV, but she's really convinced.'

'OK, but what is it to do with you?'

'Well, nothing really, it's just that we can help her, you see. It's all very mysterious and intriguing for her, so I suggested she just google the author and contact him through the publishers.'

Of course, thought Sasha, *she* should google this Rosie person and the poll tax riots, though, damn, she didn't get Rosie's surname.

'You know,' carried on Emily, 'the writer could be a her rather than a him, I suppose. Tamsin might be wrong about it being about her and her life, and maybe a quick google would make that clear. But it turns out she doesn't have Internet access.'

'What? Is she Amish?' said Sasha. 'Nobody doesn't have Internet access. Especially not people who are way younger than me. And I've seen her phone, it's a smart one, why doesn't she just look online on that if she doesn't have the Internet at home?'

'That's the weird thing. I took a look at the browser on her phone and it's got parental controls.'

Sasha laughed, relieved to be talking about anything other than Rosie. 'Her parents exerted absolutely no control over her when she was a teenager, so I doubt they do now. It must be John.'

'Which is weirder, right?'

Sasha nodded, feeling a sudden cold fear on Tamsin's behalf. There had always been something that disconcerted her about Tamsin and John as a couple, and it wasn't just the age difference. There was a wrongness to them, and this news only seemed to confirm it. 'So you've done the research for her?'

'Yes, I have.' Emily looked proud. 'I don't know, I thought it might be nice for the weekend wives' club to have a project to get us going.'

'Weekend wives?'

'You said we should form a club, all of us with absent husbands. At Tania's party. It was your idea.'

Sasha felt bad when she saw Emily's stricken face, so

decided not to point out that she wasn't to be taken so literally. 'Yes, great, of course. The weekend wives' club.'

'So I thought we could help her and see if she can find this boy she was so into back then, as it sounds like unfinished business. She thinks the book is about what went on between them all those years ago. His name is Mickey.'

'Mickey? He must have been the one she used to hang around with when she was a teenager. She thinks it's him, does she?'

'You know him?' Emily spoke with such awe, it was as if Sasha had casually mentioned she was personally acquainted with Jesus.

'Not know him, really. I used to babysit Tamsin when she was way younger, long before Mickey, but I spent a few months back here when my mother was ill. It was just before Ned and I got married and before Bailey. In fact, Tamsin must have been about Bailey's age. I've always been really fond of Tamsin – somebody had to be, since her parents clearly weren't – so I used to see her occasionally. But most of the time she was too busy with this skanky boy; I'd forgotten his name was Mickey. I think they had a proper sex thing. Not boyfriend and girlfriend exactly – her parents would never have allowed that – but she always used to disappear off with him and return looking very flushed and dreamy. She kind of reeked of sex, like you could almost smell it on her.'

'How old was she?'

'Too young.' Sasha looked at Emily's shocked face. 'Sorry, you're very much mistaken if you think you're avoiding underage sex and drugs by moving out of London.'

There was a knock at the door. 'That must be her now. I haven't told you all this, OK?' said Emily.

Tamsin was, as ever, confidently dressed and diffidently deported. 'I'm so sorry,' she opened. 'I can't stay long.' She looked towards the door nervously.

'That's a shame,' said Emily. 'Why not?'

'Just that John . . . well, I've been out a lot recently and he says he prefers it if I'm at home. In case of emergency.'

'Well, we'll be quick,' said Emily. 'Grab a coffee and a croissant and sit yourself down. I haven't got much to show you, but it's a start.'

'Do you know about all this, Sasha?' Tamsin asked.

'A bit.'

'I've got Spike's book. I'm really sorry about that, but I was only borrowing it.'

'You could just buy it on Amazon,' said Sasha, feeling vaguely ashamed at her goading. 'On the Internet.' As she looked at Tamsin's face, she realised that it might not be just the lack of Internet that was preventing her, but also a lack of money. 'Seriously, forget about it, it's fine, I didn't buy it anyway, and Spike has more books than he'll ever read. He doesn't care any more as he's busy now with some boy spy or dystopian series.'

Emily got out her laptop, where she'd opened various web pages. 'So here's what I've got from a cursory look through. Firstly, the author's site.' She clicked on a page with a banner reading 'The World of Jake V. Bond', filled with the same squiggly half-charming, half-wildly irritating childish scribbles as the picture of the author in the book. 'It's got a biography bit.' She clicked. '"Jake was born a while ago in a place not far from here and now lives by his wits (though he would rather live by the sea)." It's not completely useful.'

'But it *is* incredibly annoying,' said Sasha. 'It's so twee it makes me want to hurl.'

Tamsin was frowning at the screen. 'That could be Mickey.'

'Obviously,' said Sasha, 'but it could also be Barack Obama. Or Emily's dog. Is there anything else on this site?'

Tamsin was staring at the screen as though it were the Oracle of Delphi, occasionally touching it as if it were allowing her to hold on to the past. Emily flicked through the pages.

'Not really. Tamsin, keep looking and tell me to stop if there is anything useful. Mostly it's stuff about where to buy the book, some fan reviews, extracts . . . It's odd, because I looked at some other children's authors' sites for comparison, and they all do book readings and work with schools and that sort of thing. There's no evidence here of the author being an actual person. My son Clem reads books that have clearly been computer-generated as there are so many of them, but Jake V. Bond has only this one.'

'Maybe he only needs to write the one,' said Tamsin.

'The only thing of any use,' continued Emily, 'is the contact-the-author link on the website.'

'I can talk to him?' said Tamsin, her hand shaking slightly as she twiddled her hair.

'Email him,' corrected Emily. 'Or her. Well, fill in a box thing. There doesn't seem to be a direct email address.'

'What would I say?' Tamsin's face seemed to alternate between flushed and pale, while her hand was ever more manically twisting locks of hair.

Emily clicked and began to type. 'Well, hello might be a start. "Dear Mr Bond" – oh no, that's all wrong, we'll stick with hello. "I really enjoyed your book and wonder if we might once have known one another." You happy with that?'

'I think so, but don't send it yet.' Tamsin stared at the screen.

Emily carried on filling in the boxes. 'I presume you don't have an email address. And,' she looked over at Tamsin, 'I'm guessing you don't want to use John's. Do you want to use mine?'

Tamsin nodded. 'But can you change what you've written? Can you say, "Hello, Mickey, it's me, Tammy."'

'That's all?' asked Emily.

'That's all.'

5

As a Family

'Wait, wait. Five, four, three, two, one . . . that's it. Yes.' The tone of John's voice was no more animated than when he spoke on the phone to clients or architects. He rolled off her with the barest trace of a satisfied sigh.

Tamsin lay still as she had been taught to do, with her hips raised to a forty-five-degree angle. It was, John insisted, part of their efforts to get her pregnant, though a little suppressed part of her brain suspected that he just liked to keep her impassive after sex, with her hair fanned around her face ('If you ever cut your hair, I'll cut your throat,' he liked to joke). She was, as he was fond of telling her, his 'living doll'. Little Tamsin, silly girl, still a teenager when they had met, empty-headed, don't you worry your pretty head about a thing. Her pretty head, though, was filled with thoughts that had nothing to do with John.

'It's the right time, isn't it,' he said. Said, not asked, because he tracked her periods as assiduously as he did the temperatures she would record on getting up each morning. He was in control even when he was not in the house. He knew how many calories she consumed, how many steps she took, where she went. Smart technology had been used on his dumb wife, just as he had installed the device that allowed the washing machine to be switched on remotely. That was what she was, remote-controlled, as well as a doll, like the sort of toy that would top the most-wanted lists at Christmas.

'Yes,' she answered. 'Day twelve.'

'We'll do it again this evening, too.'

'Great.' She forced a smile.

'It's been two years. Are you sure the doctor says there's nothing wrong with you?'

I know there's nothing wrong with me, thought Tamsin. 'Nothing as far as she can see. Which means it's either unexplained, or . . .'

He frowned. She didn't finish her sentence. John didn't like the suggestion that perhaps he should get his sperm checked out. He was really good at stuff, always had been, and was competitive even with his ten-year-old nephew in a game of penalty shoot-out. Luckily Tamsin had not provided him with competition in any field. Ever since she'd been born she was used to arriving last in all life's races.

He got up to allow her to strip the bed. If they had sex again tonight, that would be yet more sheets to wash. An image of the grubby old mattress that had been at the Nell flashed into her brain. It had been good enough for her and Mickey.

'Good girl,' he said.

She liked praise, she craved it. And yet something had changed, and it was no longer enough for her to be praised

for her housekeeping skills, her trim figure or her unde-
manding nature. She wanted more.

'And do get that referral from that idiot GP for further
tests,' he went on. 'You need to get it sorted. Don't worry,
I can drive you to the hospital.'

'Thanks,' said Tamsin.

When Sasha was younger, back in the olden days, as Spike
referred to them, having a connection with someone
meant something very different. 'I felt we had a connection,' female friends would wail about some undeserving
man who hadn't called them back after they'd connected
physically like two interlocking Lego bricks.

Now it wasn't that your minds were in harmony, but
that your technology was working well. Sasha stared into
the screen, filled with relief that for once the satellites
between here and Los Angeles had aligned to bring Ned
into focus, and with his face, her thoughts. It was six in
the morning there and he would be leaving shortly to go
on set. She had to concede that when he was filming, he
worked harder than she did back at home with the children, a thought that should have consoled her but which
somehow made her resent their set-up even more.

He shuffled in his office chair, ready for their daily
conversation.

'I saw her again. The woman who used to know you,
the woman called Rosie,' she said.

The face on the screen was defined enough for her to
see him flinch and pale behind the Californian tan. 'Oh,
right,' he said.

'She said I should ask you about the night of the poll tax riots.'

'You want my thoughts about the significance of the poll tax riots in British politics of the late twentieth century.' He gave a nervous laugh. He'd gone to the sort of boys' school where emotions could always be bundled into a bag of banter.

'No, obviously not.' You shall not derail me, Ned Rayburn. 'She said I should ask you about that night and that would make things clear. March 1990, I've looked it up. Year after you graduated.'

'I know, I know,' said the face on the screen. Sasha thought back to 1990. She'd been in the sixth form. The poll tax riots had been both thrilling and terrifying to a bolshie seventeen-year-old girl. She'd got off with a boy in her history A-level class purely as a reward for the fact that he'd been down to London to attend them and, apparently, 'thrown a rock at a pig'. Even at the time, she'd been sceptical about where he'd found this handy missile.

'So what happened?'

'Let's think.' He frowned in an apparent effort to remember. 'Dom had a party at his parents' place that night, after we'd been at the protests all day. They were away so we had the run of this amazing place in Kensington. We were all pretty high on the adrenalin of the day. It was exhilarating. It had been really sunny and there were hundreds of thousands of people in Trafalgar Square and it was just . . . wow, I felt so alive. Football hooliganism for the middle classes, someone called it, the freedom to shout and get angry and even fight.' He sighed, wistfully. 'I sometimes wonder whether we need to do that, whether something's wrong for men if they can't let off steam, if it's some sort of primal instinct.'

'Oh God, don't give me those caveman clichés,' she snapped.

'Well actually, if you must know, we attacked String-fellows nightclub with bottles, smashed the windows and everything, as a feminist gesture, so we were being manly and sensitive all at the same time.' He grinned winningly, expecting her to laugh or admire him.

'Enough with the nostalgia.' She felt her nose running a bit and wished she could just wipe it with her sleeve as you would back in the old days, when you couldn't be seen while you were making a call, but would wear pyjamas while talking in a sultry voice to a boy you fancied. She touched her hair nervously and noticed that Ned did the same, mirroring her across the Atlantic. 'What happened at Dom's place?'

'We drank a lot,' he said. 'We were playing a drinking bingo game, a shot for every cliché while we watched the news on TV and tried to spot ourselves in the crowds. A vodka shot every time a politician said "senseless rioting" or "the actions of a violent minority".'

'Go on.'

'As you can imagine, we ended up drinking a lot of shots, what with the way every bloody politician was saying the same old rubbish.' He laughed.

'So you were very drunk at the end of the evening, but what happened with Rosie?' It felt odd to be calling her by her name without the prefix 'that woman' or 'this Rosie person'. It humanised her with its familiarity. Sasha stared at the screen like an interrogator, looking for clues in her husband's face.

'I don't know,' he said. She stared at the pixels. He seemed to be telling the truth.

'What do you mean, you don't know? How can you not know when something happened that means she's stalking me and your children?'

'Come on, Sasha, stalking seems to be overstating it.'

'What would you know? You're not here to suffer it. There is something very odd about it, and I don't feel entirely happy sleeping alone at night knowing that there's a woman who feels strongly enough to travel up here from wherever she normally skulks to leave strange little hints about some event that you claim not to even know about.' Her voice was rising now. She hadn't been able to admit to herself just how disconcerted, disturbed even, she had been by this woman's interventions. 'What fucking happened?'

He flinched. She rarely swore, but when she did, its rarity made it effective. 'I slept with her.'

Sasha felt herself giggle in a hysterical high pitch. 'I do know you weren't a virgin when we got together. You slept with her. You slept with everyone, as far as I can tell. What was different about this one?'

'I was really drunk. Really, really drunk.'

'Again not narrowing it down much. Could you not get it up or something?' Her voice was scornful as it was lifted up into the sky and dropped back down into a two-bedroom house with a pool in the Los Feliz neighbourhood of Los Angeles, chosen because it was the most European district of the city, whatever that meant.

'No.' He seemed indignant. Sasha was losing her patience.

'Well what then?'

'I don't remember.'

'Oh come off it, Ned, is that what she's annoyed about? That you don't remember her night of love a quarter of a century ago?'

'It wasn't a night. It was at the party.' He dipped his head so she could no longer see his face. 'We were drunk, we went upstairs. Then I was sick.' He paused. 'And then . . . Oh God, it was such a long time ago, I couldn't even remember at the time.'

'Then what?'

'She disappeared, ran off into the streets, crying. She didn't take her coat but I don't think it was that cold. It had been so sunny during the day.'

Meteorological detail? His memory seems a lot better than he's admitting, thought Sasha. 'I don't believe she's angry about losing her coat, Ned.' She felt herself shiver, partly in sympathy for a young, coatless, drunk girl on the streets of London and partly because she had some sense of what he might be about to say.

'She went back to the flat she was staying in. The next day, she told her friends that I'd . . .' He sighed.

'You'd what?' whispered Sasha.

He grimaced. 'Forced it to happen.'

'She said that you'd raped her?' As the words came out of her mouth, he recoiled as if she'd reached through the screen to slap him. Ned appearing to her only on a screen increased her sense that she was watching a bad TV drama of somebody else's life. 'And had you?' she said, in an even quieter voice.

'What?' he asked.

'I said, did you rape her?' Loudly now.

She waited for him to say no. It might be a lie, but she just wanted him to say it.

'I don't know.'

'Oh for Christ's sake, Ned, how can you not know whether you raped someone or not?'

Ned's handsome face now appeared on the computer screen as if it were CCTV footage of a man wanted by the police in connection with their inquiries. 'I was really drunk . . .'

'Come on, that's no excuse.' For what – rape or for not remembering?

'Look, we had sex, I know that for sure. But she wanted it. God . . . Rape, that's such a terrible word.'

'It's a pretty shit thing to happen, too.'

'I know, I know, which is why I don't think it was rape. Honestly, she was all over me that night, ask anyone.'

Sasha shook her head. How crass those words sounded. She wanted it, she was up for it, she was wearing a miniskirt and no knickers, she'd drunk too much, she was a bad girl. 'Come on, you must know.'

'I've replayed that night so many times, tried to see it from someone else's point of view, but I can't, Sasha, I can't. I just don't know. I was drunk, we had sex, I know she fancied me, everyone knew that.'

Of course she fancied you. Everyone fancied you, didn't they? Do they still, while you're away from us, surrounded by the world's most beautiful women? 'And you really don't remember whether you might have pushed too hard, whether she might have said no and you ignored her and carried on?'

As soon as the words left her lips, Sasha felt memories invade the mind she was trying to keep logical and clear. The time when she'd said no, but too quietly, and then thought, oh well, might as well get it over with. Another time when she'd woken up in the middle of the night to find a boyfriend having sex with her without ever having wondered or asked whether she'd wanted it in her sleeping state. A few years later, that evening when she'd changed her mind about inviting a boy back to hers but thought it would be rude to say no since he'd paid for dinner and everything. All those occasions when she'd valued herself so little, but calling it regrettable sex rather than anything else had meant that she had been able to forget about it or turn it into a funny story to be shared with her friends. It all seemed fine at the time, but how different it would be if Bailey were the one to regale her with such tales, how clear she would be now that those times, all those times, were wrong.

None of those ambiguous times had happened with Ned, though. Her experiences of him were clean. He had never forced her or woken her up with his unwanted jabbings. No, not Ned, he wasn't like that, or so she'd always thought.

She stared at the screen, waiting for his reply.

He paused. 'I really didn't, I don't think so. And neither did anybody else.'

'What do you mean?'

Now he had the good grace to look embarrassed.

'Well, at the time, she told everybody that I'd done this, and nobody believed her. Everybody said it couldn't be true because . . . well, why would I? I could have had pretty much anybody, and she wasn't a somebody – she was no looker, particularly, even back then.'

'I see,' said Sasha. 'Only pretty girls get raped.'

'No, no. God, it's really hard to explain without coming across as awful.'

'That's an accusation of rape for you.'

He blanched at the word. 'False accusation.'

'That's not what you said earlier. You said you don't know what happened.'

'Look, everyone else thought it was a false accusation, in the circumstances. Even the girls she was staying with. I've gone over it so many times, trying to play it back, hoping that I could work out the truth, but I can't. I just can't remember. Sorry.'

Sorry for what? That he'd raped someone, or that it had been so unmemorable he couldn't even recall it? She continued to stare at the screen.

'Sasha, darling. Nobody thinks I raped her. Nobody at the time even questioned me like you're doing now. You're my wife. You above everyone else should believe me.'

'But things were different back then, weren't they?' she said sadly. 'I expect I wouldn't have questioned you back then. We barely even knew date rape existed.'

'Please stop calling it that.'

'I just don't understand why, if it was only dodgy sex, she'd be so obsessed with that night that she'd be coming here to tell me about it twenty-five years later.' Damn, she thought, what were the chances that he'd used protection? 'Is she . . . did she . . . could there be a baby? I mean, adult, it would be now.'

'No, there was definitely no pregnancy. I remember using a condom; I always did in those days.'

'Right, so you remember using a condom, but you don't remember whether you raped her or not.'

'I didn't rape her. Look, I don't know what her problem is. You'll have to ask her. It changed her life, I think. Nobody believed her, everybody believed me, so she ended up dropping out of university. I don't know what happened to her after that. Everyone thought she was a liar.'

'Poor girl.'

'Poor me, too, Sasha. She might have felt like she was telling the truth, but so was I. It's the one "crime"' – he irritated her by doing little bunny quote signs around the word – 'where everyone can be telling the truth. I didn't rape her, I really didn't, but maybe she's genuinely convinced herself that I did. She dropped out of university, big deal. If she'd gone to the police and I'd been prosecuted, my life would have been over, dead, before it had begun. Even though I'd have been proved innocent, everyone would have known my name – though she would have stayed anonymous. And you know how mud sticks. Jesus, even my wife doesn't believe me. How would any employers? This' – he waved towards the screen, and she felt herself obediently looking around at their beautiful kitchen – 'our lives, our home, our children . . . it would never have happened.'

She glanced at the last school photo of Bailey and Spike together, the one taken when Bailey was in Year 6 at the local primary school, soon after they'd moved back here. She was filled with fierce love for her children – the unselfish love that meant you would sacrifice yourself to save your child; the selfish love that meant you would also sacrifice somebody else's child to save them.

'OK.' She made a sentence out of the two letters. 'Just sort it out, Ned. I don't want to see her ever again.'

Here we go again, thought Emily. The jangling nerves of Friday afternoon had begun, the overwhelming desire for everything to be perfect coupled with the certain knowledge that it would not be. She'd changed out of the unflattering stretch jeans of the week into a dress; made supper so that they could eat together as a family ('Do we have to?' moaned Clem, especially when he saw that it was a stew 'with bits in'); and shaved her armpits. Not her legs, mind you, she wasn't going that far. Surely the whole joy of being in a long-term relationship was that you could forego the pre-date rituals, but weekend wifery had returned her to that state of nerves without any of the attendant excitement.

She heard his key in the door and felt a thud of disappointment that scared her. What was it that Sasha had said: it wasn't the missing them that was the problem, it was the not missing them? Everything had become easier when he wasn't there. She didn't have to juggle the conversational and nutritional needs of an adult with those of the children. When it was just her and the kids, she consumed a bland diet of bowls of cereal and toilet humour.

'Hello, darling,' she said with a smile that felt as plastered on as the tinted moisturiser and blusher she'd applied for the occasion. Darling? She had turned into a 1950s wife all of a sudden, befitting their recent reversal in breadwinning capacities. But he *was* her darling, she reminded herself, the funniest, kindest, most sensible man she'd ever met.

'Hi.' He kissed her on the cheek, which was strange, and seemed immediately distracted by Rafa. He'd once told her that having a dog was a wonderful thing because it gave the whole family a blame magnet when someone farted. It also, she had since discovered, provided a distraction from any meaningful interaction between a husband and wife. Soon they'd be like her parents-in-law, who spoke entirely through the dog. 'It would be nice,' she'd once heard Sue say distractedly, 'if Bono or Mr Mungo would empty the dishwasher sometimes.'

'So how are you?' she said, brightly.

'Fine, fine.'

She tried to give him a hug, but it was as awkward as those moments when you saw an acquaintance with whom you didn't know if you were on kissing terms. He presented a shoulder to her and she spent a few stiff seconds clutching the side of his body. They had always fitted together so well, their heights perfectly matched to spoon the night away, but now she felt as if she were trying to cuddle a suit of armour.

She moved away. 'The children have missed you.' But they haven't really; our lives just close like sand around the hole of your absence.

'Me too.' He made no move to try to find them. 'Listen, I've just got to check something online.'

She hated that, the way he would stand in the middle of the kitchen when he was back, staring open-mouthed into his phone. To be physically there but mentally absent seemed so much worse than not being there at all. He'd claim it was work, but half the time she'd glance over his shoulder and see that it was sports reports.

'Fine. Supper will be ready in five minutes.'

He grunted by way of a reply, but it was as if he'd already gone. He was frowning at the phone as he backed out of the room to go upstairs, to be alone with whatever was so important that the reunion could wait. She resisted the temptation to admonish him about screen time.

Her children were plugged into the television, her husband the Internet. Only she toiled away from the screens, laying the table so that they could bond as a family over supper. *As a family* – it was one of those phrases that was always being trotted out and italicised by those with lifestyles superior to her own. We like to go paddle-boarding *as a family*. We eat together every evening *as a family*. We walk our adorable dogs for miles *as a family*. Yes, thought Emily to herself, we bicker *as a family*. We live our weeks not *as a family*. We sit in separate rooms *as a family*.

As if reading her mind, Clem came into the kitchen with the words, 'Are we eating together as a family? I hate that.'

'Yes we are. Studies show that there's a really strong link between sitting down enjoying a meal with your parents and doing well at school.'

'I'm going to be a footballer, and they leave school at twelve.'

'No they don't. Come on, help me lay the table.'

He looked at her blankly, as the children always did when she asked them to do something simple and normal and wholesome like mild help with household chores. I love you, she thought, so very much, and everything I do I do for you, but sometimes, just sometimes, I don't necessarily like you very much. If you were my boss, I'd have resigned by now; as a friend, you'd have been long defriended.

'Don't worry, I'll do it. Get your brother and sister. Now.' It would be nice if Matt would help me, or at the very least chat while savouring the smells of lovingly slow-cooked food, she thought as she stomped up the stairs to retrieve him from the spare room that they used as an office.

She put her head around the door and saw that, yet again, he was looking at a sports website. 'For God's sake, Matt, can't you just engage with us for the brief time you're here?'

He jumped as she spoke and then quickly shut down the browser, as guiltily as if he'd been caught with child porn. 'Don't sneak up on me like that!' he shouted, in a way that seemed utterly disproportionate to her supposed crime.

She counted to three in her head. Don't ruin things, don't ruin things, she told herself, and painted the smile back on her face. 'Supper's ready. You must be starving after that long journey.'

Over the meal, she felt as though she were a UN interpreter between the domestic and foreign worlds that collided only at weekends. 'Clem,' she said, 'tell Daddy all about the project you're doing on the Romans at school at the moment.'

'It's all right,' said Clem.

'Good,' said Matt, holding his phone through his pocket, looking as though he yearned to sneak a peek at it.

'It's funny, isn't it,' she said, rhetorically, as she knew nobody would find it in the least bit amusing or even interesting, 'all history at school seems to be just Romans, Tudors and Nazis, with nothing in between. Please eat something, Zanna. Maybe the rice.'

Matt got up.

'Where are you going?' she snapped.

'To the loo.'

This was a cue for all the children to jump out of their chairs – Nate to moon his still squidgy toddler bottom, Zanna to wander off out of the kitchen and Clem to start kicking the indoor foam football against the not-Aga Aga.

Well, thought Emily, looking at her watch, that segment of *as a family* time lasted precisely twelve minutes.

*

They met, as had been arranged, outside Emily's cottage just after school drop-off.

'Any message? From him?' asked Tamsin.

Emily shook her head. 'Sorry. I'm really disappointed for you.' In truth, she was also disappointed for herself. In the bleakness of her weekend reunion with Matt, she had begun to check her phone for messages as often as he checked his for whatever it was that so enthralled him. But there had been nothing. 'Do you want me to email him' – she corrected herself with a gender-neutral '*them* again? What do you want me to say?'

Tamsin shook her head, but Emily saw that there were tears in her eyes.

'I'll keep checking, I promise. I've got your number now, so I can phone you as soon as I hear anything.'

Tamsin looked alarmed. 'Please don't call my phone, really don't. I can come here, every day, until there's news. Thank you.'

Her voice was so grateful that Emily wished even more that she could bring her word of this Mickey person. Of how he'd always loved her and wanted to find her, and now he had and they'd reunite and it would all be lovely, and faith in romance and true love would be restored throughout the land.

Rafa was chewing the fur on one of his paws, worsening the bald patch that this habit had already developed. 'Look, I'd better take the beast for a walk, but I promise I'll keep checking.'

She began to stride out of the village, feeling as though she might just go on walking for ever, pointing south until she arrived in London, anything to put off the moment when she'd get home and find she had nothing to do until it was time to fetch Nate from nursery. She longed for noon with all the yearning of a woman waiting for a date, and yet as soon as she picked him up, she became guiltily bored of all his toddler inanities and his obsessive interest in snail-counting on the way home.

She breathed in deeply, trying to taste the freshness of the air and appreciate the countryside with all her senses, then stopped to look across the fields towards the wooded copse, making a concerted effort to enjoy the gift of being able to stretch her eyes to the horizon.

As she did so, she saw a figure in the distance. She had watched too many crime dramas where a dog-walker got brutally stabbed for no obvious reason to feel entirely comfortable with the prospect of a stranger on the horizon. She realised that her soul must be formed from asphalt, because she never felt these nerves when she walked down city streets in the dead of night, yet the emptiness of the countryside, its great selling point, unnerved her.

As she dithered over whether to turn back, the figure came nearer and she recognised Ben, husband of Tania, the scarily high-powered village superstar, who was walking a pair of catalogue-handsome Labradors, one golden, one chocolate-coloured.

'Hello, Emily,' he shouted over to her.

She felt pleased that he had remembered her name as the recent incomer. How long do you have to live in a place before you're not the newbie, she wondered? Or do you have to be at least second-generation? 'Hello, nice day, isn't it?' she called back. Oh that was interesting, wasn't it? Weather and the word 'nice' in one sentence. She'd have expected more from one of the sentences Clem was forced to write for his spelling homework.

The Labradors approached Rafa, keen to sniff his bottom, which made him yelp in alarm. He started running in circles and then gnawing away at the bald patch with even greater enthusiasm than usual, his underbite working overtime.

'Rafa, stop that!' Her dog was so odd. It was like having a child that didn't behave like other children at the soft-play centre. She was embarrassed, especially in front of the elegant blonde dog she was comparing him with. Rafa didn't stop, of course, so she grabbed his collar and picked him up. She wondered whether dogs could be autistic. All middle-class parents fretted over what they saw as their children's Asperger's tendencies – obsessiveness, adherence to strict routines, meltdowns – before realising that for the vast majority, the line between the syndrome and normal self-centredness could be quite a narrow one. And now here she was wondering the same about her dog.

Ben was looking rather alarmed. He'd be one of those handsome country types, Emily thought, who loved his dogs as much as his children (and there were a lot of them, as she remembered, as many as four). He was some sort of gardener, at least that was what Sasha had told her.

'Is he all right?' he asked, pointing at Rafa, who was now licking the self-inflicted wounds around his balding patch of fur.

'He's great, aren't you, my boy?' She leant down to ruffle his curly fur. 'Who's my lovely boy?' She was sure that Ben would be able to see through her protestations of love for Rafa. He'd be horrified if he really knew what went on in her head. 'Are you starting or finishing your walk?' she asked, and then felt as if that might be shamefully inappropriate, the dog-walking equivalent of asking a man up for a cup of coffee.

'In the middle of it. Shall we?' He gestured in the direction of the hill that lay between them and the Nell.

This felt rather daring to Emily. Back in London, she'd been a twenty-first-century woman, working as an equal and in many ways superior to the men in her office. Here she seemed to have been thrust back fifty years, where she might need a chaperone out of doors and the only male she ever interacted with was the bloke who delivered the gas canisters for the fake Aga. While the London primary school her kids had attended had been full of improbably handsome and hip bearded teaching assistants, the village school currently had only a grumpy caretaker as a male role model for the impressionable seven-year-old boys.

She made sure she put at least a metre's gap between them as they walked up the hill, her dragging Rafa by the lead while the Labradors gambolled picturesquely.

'So, how long have you lived here, Ben?' This was at least a little more interesting than the weather comment.

'Only ten years.' *Only ten years*, thought Emily, who couldn't imagine another nine winters. 'It made sense to move here when Tania became the MEP for the area, and I'd always wanted to work in the great outdoors.'

'What were you before you became a gardener?'

'Landscape gardener,' he corrected, though Emily couldn't see what other sort you could be – a portrait gardener? 'I worked in financial PR.'

Emily quickly had to try to redraw Ben as a namby-pamby office worker, in public relations of all things, rather than the horny-handed Hardy character she had thought he was. 'Oh right, quite different.'

'I'd always hated living in the city, so it all came together quite well. It means Tania can commute to Brussels each week, but one of us is around for the children.'

'I see. Ideal, I suppose.' Emily hesitated for a few seconds and then plunged in. 'But not all the time, or is it? Ideal, I mean. I'm still getting used to it – you know, not working, and living here, and Matt being away during the week. I guess I'm looking for tips on how to make it work.'

Ben nodded – sagely, Emily thought. He had the sort of wisdom that could only come from working with your hands. 'It's all right. Works well for us and the kids.'

'But don't you find it really hard when Tania comes back at weekends and it's just been you and the children during the week? Sasha calls that bit when you all have to adjust to one another again "re-entry".' It was only then that Emily realised the innuendo contained within that phrase. 'You know, like when astronauts come back into the earth's atmosphere.'

'No, it's fine. We just get on with it.'

He's got that serenity thing, thought Emily, the ability to accept what he can't change. I need to get me some of that, but I just can't. She'd never been able to accept that there even *were* things she couldn't change, but instead railed uselessly against them, yearning for the better life around the corner – school, university, job, boyfriend and now whole new lifestyle.

Ben looked round at Rafa with a frown. 'Are you sure he's OK?'

'Yes, really. How about your Labradors?' Labs, that was what she should have called them, then she'd have sounded like a doggy person, someone who belonged and didn't mind their face being licked by a creature that liked eating rabbit droppings. Ben stopped staring at Rafa and started staring at her with an unreadable expression. She thanked the bitter wind for cooling down her flushed cheeks and let Rafa off his lead as a way of hiding her face still further.

'Oh look, we're going towards that disused farm building,' she said. She stopped herself from calling it the Nell. That was sacrosanct.

'That thing. Grim, isn't it?'

'I know what you mean, it has the air of a place where you'd hide a dead body.' He frowned at her remark. 'Not that I'd know about that, obviously. But then again, I can also imagine it having a certain sort of charm. If you were a teenager, for example. It's got to be a better place for sniffing glue than the bus stop.'

He frowned again. He didn't seem overburdened with a sense of irony. Perhaps that was an awful city trait of Emily's that she'd have been better off leaving behind, alongside her Oyster card and her ability to run up escalators. All that working with plants probably makes you understand life in a more profound way, she mused.

She looked towards the Nell and felt a frisson as she thought about Tamsin and Mickey and their unsophisticated but youthfully fleshed couplings. 'I guess I'd better be getting back,' she said. For what? To clean the stove yet again in order to kill the couple of hours before picking up Nate? 'Where's that blo— that dog of mine?'

Ben scanned the horizon, then bounded towards a hole in the ground where a fluffy black and white tail was whirling manically. He grabbed the tail, pulled, and out came the attached Rafa, who acquiesced to such treatment with surprising passivity. Gosh, thought Emily, he is masterful.

6

The Financial Controller

'I love your house, it's like a Pinterest page made flesh,' said Emily with feeling. Sasha thought she had a desperate but endearing enthusiasm about her. 'And you too, I wish I were wearing what you've got on.' Sasha wore a top she'd made herself from vintage Hermès silk scarves. 'Oh, look at your collection of blue bottles, they're beautiful. Where did you buy them?'

'I find them, all over. That big one you're touching was buried in the woods. It's amazing what you can unearth in the countryside.'

'You see, that's even better, that you forage for them and then upcycle them like that. It's just brilliant.'

'Does upcycle mean "use"?' asked Sasha, though she knew full well what Emily was on about, seeing as it was a word she herself employed frequently in the blog she used to promote her business. She updated it every day with bucolic images of her 'inspiration', which in turn sold more pieces of pottery – she'd post snaps of wild flowers, the sun dappling through the trees, Spike blurring past on a bicycle.

'Yes, I suppose it does.' Emily looked at Sasha and laughed. 'Oh, I see. Sorry.'

'I'm being mean,' Sasha said, giving Emily's arm a warm squeeze. 'Thanks for being so nice about my home. It means a lot to me. And I guess being good at finding things is my job now.'

'The ceramics that you sell? Oh that's lovely too.' Emily sighed. 'I need to get work of some sort.'

'You've got three small children, I wouldn't call that a holiday. Don't be hard on yourself.'

'Thank you,' said Emily, this time in a way that seemed to Sasha to be particularly heartfelt.

At that moment, Tamsin arrived for the second meeting the weekend wives had convened since the idea had first been mooted by Sasha and then leapt upon by Emily. She was, as usual, wearing sleek running clothes and a furtive expression. 'I can't be long' were her opening words.

'I was just saying,' Emily said when Tamsin sat down, still wearing her running jacket as if primed for a dash towards the nearest emergency exit, 'that I need to get a job. I never thought I'd miss being a patent attorney, but sometimes I dream about patents and wake up feeling really satisfied when I've got a submission off. I thought I'd really like not working. I was so sick of my office that it was part of the reason for moving up here, but it turns out that I'm not very good at feeling constructive without a professional construction around me, if you see what I mean.'

'I wouldn't know about that,' said Tamsin.

'What did you used to do?' asked Emily. Sasha gave her a look to try to warn her away from prying. Tamsin not working was a bit like Tamsin having no money – it was something not to be questioned.

'I've never had a job,' said Tamsin.

'What do you mean?' said Emily. 'You must have had one. Even if you gave it up when you got married. Which come to think of it is quite unusual in the twenty-first century. Probably even in the twentieth, for that matter. What did you used to do?'

'Coffee?' asked Sasha, keen to move the conversation on. To her surprise, though, Tamsin didn't seem particularly disconcerted.

'No, really,' she said. 'I've never worked. Not even when I was at school – there aren't many holiday jobs around here that you can get to without transport. Even now I still can't drive.'

'So I should have paid you for babysitting the other night,' said Sasha, still feeling guilty. 'Please let me pay now.' She grabbed her wallet and shoved a twenty-pound note into Tamsin's hand, trying to make the uncomfortable transaction as quick as possible.

Tamsin smiled sadly. 'This is the first money I've ever earned.'

Emily gasped in a way that Sasha felt was unhelpful. 'That's incredible! How on earth does that happen?'

'Quite easily really. I've never thought about it, or not too much. It's just the way it is. I met John when I was nineteen. He's much older and he's really successful and everything, so it made more sense for me to support him at home while he supports me financially. I messed up my GSCEs, you see, and I started doing some A levels but then eventually dropped out so I wouldn't have to do really badly in them too. So I was pretty much on the scrapheap anyway. He saved me.'

'You didn't need saving,' said Emily. 'Look at you, you're gorgeous and nice and kind. There must have been thousands of things you could have done.'

'No, there aren't, not really. I'm so stupid.'

'Says who?'

'Everybody. My brothers and sister are clever, but I think the smart genes had run out by the time it was my turn. Or my mother must have drunk during my pregnancy or something. The whole way through primary school, the teachers commented on how amazing it was that I was related to my siblings, what with them being so clever. My father always used to joke about how lucky it was that I was stupid, so he didn't have to fork out for a fourth set of school fees.'

'What do you mean?' exclaimed Emily. 'Your siblings went to private school but you didn't?'

'That's right. My father used to tell everyone, "no point throwing good money after bad", and they'd all laugh.'

'He really said that?' asked Sasha, feeling as though she could join in the conversation now it seemed that Tamsin didn't share everyone else's reluctance to talk about her lack of career.

'Yes, but it's true. I'm stupid. Just ask John.'

'But that's horrible,' said Emily. 'Nobody should think of themselves as stupid. I spend my life telling my children how marvellous they are at everything. Which is completely untrue, as it happens. Surely John doesn't think you're stupid, or else why would he have married you?'

'It's not a problem. He likes that I'm stupid. He calls me that all the time, but quite affectionately. Well, silly more than stupid, which is better, isn't it? He says I'm empty-headed, which I am. I don't think there's anything up here.' She pointed at her head. 'He says you could whistle through my ears.' She giggled as if to prove the point.

Sasha decided to broach the other unmentionable. 'Is that why you don't have any money of your own?'

'Yes, I'd only do something silly with it, or lose it. And I don't earn any money so it's only fair that I don't have any to spend.'

'What, not even – what's the old-fashioned word for it? – housekeeping money?' asked Emily. 'I'm not working either, but I still need money to buy food and pay bills.' She frowned. 'Though I don't seem to be getting much of that at the moment from Matt. At least I've got my savings. So how do you buy food or things for yourself?'

'John takes care of all the bills. I write a list of what food we need, he checks it and then orders for us online. I'm lucky like that. He takes care of all the boring stuff.'

Emily looked shocked. 'So he takes control of all the money, doesn't allow you to have any unaccounted for and is preventing you from getting a job? Please tell me I haven't got that right.'

'No, he's not stopping me from getting a job. I told you, I'm too stupid to get one and I can't drive. Who'd employ me?'

'This sounds remarkably like financial abuse to me.' Emily looked suddenly serious.

Both Sasha and Tamsin reeled at the word 'abuse'. 'Oh, you with your fancy pants city diagnoses!' said Sasha, trying to make a joke of it. 'That's just what one of my old neighbours in Los Angeles would have said. Everything was always a syndrome.'

'But it's true,' insisted Emily. 'It's a recognised thing. Make your wife look after the house, take away the money and any way of earning it, and you've turned her into a child or some sort of au pair. Except an au pair would be paid. And wouldn't have to have sex with you either. It's abuse.'

'It's not abuse. It's not like he hits me or anything,' said Tamsin. 'He looks after me. He buys me all these lovely clothes. You should see my wardrobe. It's walk-in and filled with expensive shoes. Even these,' she pulled at her running tights, 'are the best that money can buy. They've got two-way sweat wicking.'

'But why can't you buy your own clothes? I buy Clem's clothes because he's a seven-year-old boy. You're not a child.'

'I'd never buy myself clothes as nice as the ones John gets me. He's got amazing taste and knows me better than I know myself. He even gets me proper jewellery. I don't wear it out, he says that would be too dangerous, but it's lovely to own, honestly.'

Sasha pulled her cashmere cardigan tighter around herself. She loved clothes as much as she loved the things she filled her house with, and clung to them as reflections of herself whenever her sense of that was lost.

'Don't you think that's a bit controlling?' asked Emily, who wasn't going to let this conversation go.

'Or loving?' said Tamsin, hopefully. 'It's nice not to have to think about what to wear. Even on days when we're not going anywhere, he decides for me. Decisions do my head in.'

'Let's put aside the clothes thing,' Emily said. 'Why don't you think about getting a job, or maybe going back into education or doing some training? There must be something you're good at. What were your best subjects at school?'

Tamsin shook her head.

'You weren't good at anything?'

'Nothing.'

'Really?' said Sasha. 'You seemed like a happy teen-ager whenever I saw you. Much happier than you'd been as a child. Not someone who was failing miserably at school.'

Tamsin's face brightened at last. She looked towards the door, checked her phone was off and then leant forward conspiratorially. 'There was something.' She was positively glowing, and looked beautiful. 'It was the first and only thing I've ever felt really, really good at.' She paused.

'What was that?' asked Emily.

'Sex.' Tamsin smiled. 'Sex with Mickey.'

Sasha and Emily, for all the sophistication that their

careers and life experience had offered them, looked shocked.

'Gorgeous-but-rough Mickey?' said Sasha. 'God, you seemed so young. Please tell me you weren't having full sex with him? I know you were snogging, I saw that often enough, but you weren't having *sex* . . . I mean, proper sex, sex-sex?'

Tamsin nodded happily. 'It was so amazing. My brothers were brilliant at rugby, which Daddy made a big deal about, and Camilla was a county-level tennis player. And I remember thinking when I first had sex with Mickey, "At last! I've found a sport that I'm really good at." My brain never worked the way I wanted it to, and I always got out of any sport at school, but when I had sex with Mickey, everything just fell into place.' She giggled, looking like the teenager she had once been.

'Sex, brilliant,' said Emily, her shiny smiles for once replaced by a darker expression. 'So you can become a prostitute.'

'Emily,' admonished Sasha. 'That's really unhelpful.'

'It's just all so unfeminist. I'm sorry. It's my problem. I feel I'm letting the sisterhood down by giving up my job and leading my second-rate Stepford Wife life here, but really. Tamsin's gone from being her parents' under-valued child to John's.'

'Well I don't see how you're helping by trying to boss her into being something she's not. It's no good you trying to control her too,' said Sasha.

'Yes, you're absolutely right.' Emily put her hand to her forehead and seemed to deliberately force her face into an expression of positivity. 'But I can encourage you, Tamsin, can't I? Have you ever thought of seeing someone – a life coach or therapist?'

'And how's she going to pay for that?' said Sasha.

'OK. I'm sure there are special women's counselling services for people like you.' She leant forward and whispered, 'Victims of abuse.'

'But I told you, I'm not being abused,' said Tamsin, as forcefully as she ever said anything. 'Things like that are for women with black eyes from council estates, not happily married ones who live in houses like John's – like *our* house. It's perfect. I wish you could see it, then you'd realise how lucky I am. Next time we meet, you could come to our place, then you'll see. Please don't go on about this any more. I just want help finding Mickey.'

Emily looked pained. 'Of course I'll help you try to find Mickey. But also, the other thing, your lack of money, if I can help in any way, please let me.'

'I'm fine, really. I just need to see Mickey.'

'OK, of course. I'll let you know as soon as I hear anything.'

'Coffee, anyone?' said Sasha, letting out an exhalation, more disconcerted than she wanted to admit by Tamsin's revelations about John.

Tamsin and her marriage wouldn't leave Sasha's head. Like Emily, she wanted to help but did not know how in the face of Tamsin's protestations.

She had often thought that people's development could get arrested at the point at which they settled down into a long-term relationship. She had been twenty-six when she had met Ned, while he was thirty-one, and there was a part of them that was for ever calcified into that dynamic, of him that little bit more sophisticated and knowing, and her in a supporting role. How much more so must this be for Tamsin, who had been still a child in many ways when she met John. It was just a shame that the wild, red-cheeked Tamsin she remembered from the time of Mickey hadn't been the one to be preserved, rather than the skinny husk she had become soon afterwards.

If Emily was to be believed, Tamsin was married to an abusive husband, while she, Sasha, was possibly married to a rapist. It really was true, what she'd said to Emily about foraging: it was surprising what you could unearth in the country.

She couldn't stop thinking about Rosie and Ned, trying to shake away the picture of a girl only a few years older than Bailey wandering around London in the cold of the night with a pain in her heart and between her legs before, worse, being mocked and disbelieved.

'Then,' said Spike as she distractedly gave him his after-school snack, 'I did this awesome move and nutmegged the keeper!'

'What was that?'

'My goal.'

'Right. Well done you, was that at break time?'

'No, it was FIFA on the Xbox. I told you, Mum, my World Legends team beat Man U. It was sick.'

'I'm so pleased for you.' Even though Spike was now

nine, Sasha was relieved that she could still use the parental weapon of sarcasm disguised as sincerity. It wouldn't work on her daughter any more.

At that moment, Bailey arrived home from the bus stop. Her uniform was, as all the school's pupils put it, shit brown, with a regulation box-pleated skirt that was difficult for even the most brazen girl to hitch or take up. The whole outfit seemed to have been designed with the intention of making lissom teenage girls look as unattractive as possible, and would have made a good costume for a Miss Marple-themed party.

As if the uniform were not unflattering enough, Bailey accessorised it with hair that fell lankly over her face. While it seemed regulation among teenage girls to have great long straightened curtains of hair, Bailey's was badly cut into an approximation of a bob with a long fringe. By whom, Sasha wasn't sure. Bailey had long since forbidden her mother from dragging her along to her own hairdresser, Lucien.

Bailey looked a bit like a boy from an early nineties indie group, complete with hat pulled low with unwashed tendrils poking out from below it. At weekends, she furthered the impression with oversized hoodies and baggy jeans – 'boyfriend jeans', Sasha had read they were called in magazines, but Bailey wasn't following a trend and, she was fairly certain, didn't have a boyfriend.

'How was school?'

'Fine,' said Bailey, putting her thumbs through the holes she'd worn through the cuffs of her jumper and then sitting with her knees up and under it to make the whole thing even more shapeless. Sasha read the articles in online newspapers entitled things like 'My Daughter Dresses Like a Slut' and wondered why hers did not. Obviously she didn't want her dressing like a slut – though of course it was every woman's right to do so without fear of consequence – but on the other hand, dressing like a boy who hadn't updated his wardrobe since losing lots of weight at Slimming World didn't seem to be making Bailey happy either.

'Do any of your friends have boyfriends yet?'

Bailey did a teenage eye roll. It was irritating but almost a relief that she could manage something typical of her peers.

'Well do they?'

'Yeah, some. Most not. I don't, if that's what you're asking.'

It wasn't, in fact. It was a given that Bailey was not one of the precocious ones having sex in a disused farm building like Tamsin.

'You'd tell me if you ever did, wouldn't you? And you wouldn't do anything . . .' she glanced over at Spike, who was absorbed in kicking an indoor football perilously close to her collection of blue bottles, 'silly.'

'Sleep with someone without protection? No. I wouldn't. I'm going to be celibate anyway.'

Sasha laughed and then realised that Bailey wasn't joking. 'You don't know that, darling. One day you'll meet someone special enough for you to want to be, er, intimate with.'

Bailey shook her head. 'No I won't. I'll never want to

do with it someone, and more to the point, no one will want to do it with me.' She walked out of the room quickly, deaf to Sasha's cries and questions.

Sasha shuddered. She didn't want to think about teenage girls having sex, but the thoughts kept battering at the walls of her mind. Of Rosie, wandering the streets of London without her coat or her dignity. Of Tamsin, finally finding something she was really good at. Of Bailey . . . what of Bailey? The girl who even when out of her school uniform seemed to base all her sartorial choices on an effort to look repellent to men, and not in a kooky dungaree-wearing way either.

She'd been an incredibly cute child, with chubby cheeks waiting to be pinched and a rosebud mouth below watchful dark eyes peering from behind a shining block of thick hair. Always serious, even back then, but there had been something magnetic about such a thoughtful look combined with the dimpled knees and pudgy fingers of a pre-schooler. Now that watchfulness looked sullen, almost threatening. When had Bailey changed? It had been gradual, of course, starting with the loss of the little pearls of baby teeth to be replaced with the discoloured jags of adult ones, but this unrelenting misery was more recent, and getting worse since going back to school in September.

Bailey had left her phone in her coat pocket. Sasha had a quick look at it, despite remembering how angry she'd been when her own mother had read her diary. Again, her reading of scare stories in the newspapers made her think that she'd find Bailey had been sending out topless pictures or was being groomed by men in the takeaway shop by the bus stop near school.

She opened Bailey's text messages and found one from a withheld number. It was a photo of a bottle of Baileys, that deathly-sweet liquor that she and Ned hadn't really thought about when they'd come up with their coolly androgynous name for their daughter. With the photo was a message: *Why r bailey girl and bailey drink the same? Coz they both make u sick.*

Sick. That could be a compliment, but Sasha was savvy enough to know that it didn't mean sick in a good way here.

Bailey girl makes you sick.

Bailey, her lovely, inscrutable, well-behaved girl who was upstairs making a start on her homework. Her girl whom other mothers envied. She now thought of her as a girl who might be raped by a man or abused by a husband, like Rosie or Tamsin, but also as Ned's daughter, the teenager who was odd enough already without her father being exposed as anything other than Mr Perfect in LA.

What would she do with the Rosie revelation?

Nothing, she would do nothing. She would only do something if it became necessary to protect her family. The young girl wandering the streets of London without a coat all those years ago was nothing to her. The girl upstairs in the baggy clothes was everything.

Matt was irritable with her on the phone that evening, as per usual these days. Emily consoled herself with her standard single-mum supper – a bowl of Shreddies and a bottle of wine. That was one benefit of this weekend wife business: she only had to cook for the children and then not bother with a whole second sitting of dinner. She supposed there were women who made scallops for one or treated their bodies as gourmet temples, but she'd never met any that wouldn't always choose a version of breakfast for their supper if they were dining alone.

It wasn't strictly true that she was alone. There was another diner: Rafa. She poured out his dried chunks of brown and was struck by just how similar it looked to her own meal. 'You and me, boy, we're the couple of the house now.' To which he started licking himself a new patch of bald skin.

Then she began her other evening activity, which was to check her emails relentlessly for word from Jake V. Bond (hard to even think the name without heavily inverted commas) and to trawl the author's website for more clues.

While everything else was as normal that evening, this took her by surprise.

There in her inbox was a message from the author site she had looked at so many times. She stared for a moment, unsure what to do. Obviously it was as private as any letter and therefore should be delivered to Tamsin alone. On the other hand, if it were a letter, she knew she'd be tempted to steam it open. And to open an email and then mark it 'unread' would be the modern equivalent, and easier too.

Her hand hovered over the mouse just long enough for her to convince herself she was at least *considering* leaving it unopened.

And then she clicked.

7

Taking Steps

Tamsin walked to Emily's house as she did every morning, propelled by the hope that one day she'd have word of him, of Mickey. He had become so mythologised in her memory, sharp-limbed and illuminated in bleached-out sunshine, that there was a part of her that feared he didn't exist at all.

In the distance, she saw Emily returning from dropping off the children at school. As Emily saw her, she broke into a trot and then an undignified run.

'Tamsin,' she shouted. 'He's been in contact. It's him, it must be. Jake is Mickey. You've got a response to the message we sent on that author site.'

Tamsin looked around nervously, doing a shush gesture but unable to keep the excitement from her face. 'What did it say? What did *he* say?'

By this time Emily had reached her and was brandishing her phone. 'Here it is. Look, it's unread. I didn't open it, I promise.' She clicked on it and passed the screen of dreams to Tamsin.

Tamsin gulped and then read. *Hello you. It's me. I've been waiting. Can we ever go back to the Nell?*

'What does it say?' asked Emily. 'Is it good? Is it definitely him?'

Tamsin smiled, then frowned. Her legs felt shaky. 'It is him. Nobody else knows about the Nell or calls it that. I knew it as soon as I read that word in the book. Emily, look! He's been waiting for me, it's so romantic. He wants to know if we can go back to the Nell. We can, can't we?' She sought permission from Emily though it was not hers to give.

'I don't see why not. Nothing to do with me, but yes, of course you can.'

'I'm going to go there with him. I'm going to be with Mickey.' Tamsin sighed like the teenage girl she had reverted to.

'But be careful,' said Emily. 'You do know you can't really ever go back, step in the same river twice and all that?'

'What river?' asked Tamsin. 'There's no river there.'

'It's just an expression, you know, about how you can't recreate the past, because the place will be different or you'll be different.' Emily looked at Tamsin's hopeful face. 'You've changed since then, haven't you? He will have done too. He might be bald or fat. It's amazing how badly some men age.'

Tamsin shook her head. 'No, he'll be him. I know it. I know it from reading his book. He'll be the same. It doesn't matter what he looks like, because he'll be him on the inside.'

'How do you want me to respond?' asked Emily, as if all thoughts of caution were now forgotten.

Tamsin giggled. 'I don't know. What do you reckon?'

They stood next to each other, pondering the email

with girlish excitement, exactly as though they were the same age as Tamsin had been when she'd last seen Mickey.

'So you want to meet him?'

'Yes, yes, I do.' Tamsin was nodding vigorously to reinforce the point. 'I want to go back to the Nell.'

Emily returned home feeling the glow of a teenage love revived; a glow that was quickly cooled by the arctic wind blowing through her kitchen. Rafa was away from his usual place by the stove and instead was shivering under a fleece that one of the children had dumped on what she called the 'floor hook', since they seemed incapable of hanging anything on the rather attractive Shaker-style coat rack they'd put up on moving in. She touched her fake Aga and found its metal casket was giving off waves of cold rather than the moderate heat she'd been expecting. It was never an ideal heat source, behaving like one of those showers that had no temperature between scalding and freezing, but it at least generated some warmth if you sat almost on top of it.

'Bloody hell,' she exclaimed, 'not again.' This was another new country habit she'd developed: talking to herself. She checked the gas cylinder that was supposed to fire up what the estate agent had called 'the heart of the house' but which now seemed to be running on a very faulty pacemaker. It was spent. They got through them as quickly as she had got through expensive takeaway coffees in her last life.

Carefully closing off the top of the canister, she wheeled it through the door from the kitchen out to the garage, where it would be left for the delivery men to pick up and replace. A corner of the garage was dedicated to the one or two empty cylinders standing just to the side of the two new replacement ones. It was a system that ran with a pleasing regularity and efficiency.

Well, normally it did, but she could see from the coded labels that she had instead three empty canisters and no new ones, meaning that the gas company hadn't visited despite their promise to do so weekly to check and replace what was needed.

'How crap,' she said out loud once more, retreating to the kitchen out of habit but of course finding it no warmer than the garage. In fact, mysteriously it seemed even colder than outside, with her breath making clouds.

She put on her best intimidating patent attorney voice in order to rant at whichever worker was unlucky enough to pick up the phone at the cylinder supply company.

'I am very disappointed,' she said to the woman who answered, 'as well as extremely cold, to find that your men have not been to my garage to replace the empty gas canisters. This is particularly worrying for me,' she lied, 'as my elderly mother will be coming to visit us shortly.'

'Well,' said the woman at the other end of the phone, aping her pompous tone, 'we were extremely disappointed not to be paid for the last lot of canisters that we delivered.'

'I left the cheque tucked into the canister, as I normally do.' Emily knew this to be true because it never ceased to irritate her that she was still, in this day and age of online banking, having to find the chequebook and write a cheque, invariably getting the date or the figure wrong when she did so.

'That's as may be,' the receptionist said, masking her local accent in a faux posh voice, 'but we have been unable to bank the money from said cheque due to there being insufficient funds.'

'Oh. There's been some mistake, for sure,' said Emily, uncertain whether she was still allowed to be angry. 'I'll sort it out and get back to you. But I would be most grateful for a new canister once I've got to the bottom of this. It's still very cold and I'll have to microwave all our food.'

'We can't have that,' said the woman. Emily refused to rise to the sarcasm. She needed the power supply too much.

She rushed upstairs to the computer to check the joint account that she and Matt used for these sorts of bills. For her daily expenses, she was powering through the remains of her savings, all the money she had put aside over so many years of tedious office grind that was now being frittered on food and petrol rather than heels and cocktails.

The bank's homepage came up and she clicked on the button for Internet banking. She typed in the password, 'Caw5tone', the street where she and Matt had met in that house share all those years ago, with a sneaky numeral thrown in for extra security.

'Dammit,' she said out loud, when the computer bossily told her that she'd got the wrong password. She tried again, this time carefully watching her fingers. Still no good. She'd have to have another phone conversation. These had begun to scare her now that her formal voice was so rarely used, and she preferred to keep things online.

Of course when she got through to the bank's call centre, the young man she was speaking to asked her for the fourth and sixth letters of her password, and she failed.

'But that's what I'm ringing about. My password's been changed so I need to talk to someone about the fact that it doesn't work, but you're not letting me do that because I can't tell you the password because it's the very thing I'm calling about.' Kafka needed to come back to life and write a rant on dealing with call centres, she thought, then reminded herself that it wasn't the young man's fault; he was just some boy who was stuck working in a call centre despite the fact that he probably had a degree and thousands of pounds' worth of debts. Clem might be his in a dozen years' time.

'I quite understand, Mrs Dawlish.'

'It's Ms. If it were Mrs, it would be Hicks like my husband, the other person on the joint account . . .' She paused. Of course. She shouldn't be talking to the poor boy in the Newcastle call centre. She should be talking to Matt. *He* must have changed the password. 'I'm so sorry, it's not your fault. Don't worry about it. Have a good day.'

'Wow, thank you,' the boy said, unable to hide the surprise in his voice.

She rang Matt's mobile and left a message. Then she

texted him. Then, for good measure, she wrote him an email. The great thing about being married was that you no longer had to worry about being too keen or coming on too strong to the one you loved. Ha, the one I love, she thought to herself. They had reached that point in their relationship where they no longer said such things to each other. 'Is Daddy your one true love?' Zanna had asked her after watching *Enchanted* on DVD. 'Of course he is, aren't you, Matt?' she had said, and only afterwards thought, no he isn't, there are a million one true loves I could have had, all around the world. He is the one true love who I happened to meet and I am still glad of that.

She sat and waited. Why on earth would Matt have changed the password? And why wasn't there enough money in the account to pay for two piffling gas canisters? The whole of this ridiculous set-up and their separate lives was predicated around the fact that it was bringing them some sort of financial security. And if that wasn't the case, what on earth were they doing?

Years ago, Sasha and Ned had talked about what super-power they'd have if given the choice. Ned, ever the adolescent, had opted for X-ray vision so he could see women without their clothes on. Sasha had thought – hoped – he was joking. He probably felt the same about her choice, which was invisibility so that she could spy on Bailey, who'd just started nursery and was unhappy about being left there in the mornings. Sasha never believed the bovine girls who worked there when they assured her that Bailey was 'really happy when Mum's gone'.

And now here she was, thirteen years later, not yet invisible but still wanting to watch her children unobserved. There was something about the way Bailey refused to let her do pick-ups any more that worried her, especially since she'd been snooping around her phone and had seen that vile message. Of course, Sasha wasn't so deluded that she didn't think Bailey's problem with being picked up from school might possibly just be standard-issue teenage embarrassment about her parents, but she wanted to be sure. She read the newspapers; she knew that teenagers were getting into more baroquely awful things these days, things that made Tamsin's underage sex trysts in a disused grain store seem positively Enid Blyton-esque.

There was grooming for starters – not the waxing and preening type, clearly, in Bailey's case, but those poor girls she'd read about who'd been flattered and flirted with by minicab drivers and takeaway owners and before they knew it were sex slaves being plied with men and vodka in some horrible room above a chippy. She had felt a revolting frisson of relief, believing that this only happened to girls from dysfunctional families and children's homes, awful though she knew that made her in her smug middle-class world. But then she'd been listening to Radio 4 and heard a woman who sounded just like her, articulate and well spoken, telling of how her daughter had fallen in with these horrible men and been sold off cheap, despite their family holidays in French gîtes and shelves well stocked with children's classics.

Naked pictures on the Internet and sexting – that was another trap for Bailey to fall into. But though her maternal radar might be completely wonky, Sasha was sure that Bailey had no interest in boys or in taking pictures of herself and passing them to others. Her daughter was more about concealing than revealing. At the beach, she'd wear shorts over her swimsuit so as not to show her legs. Even from the age of seven, she'd always undressed and bathed in private – which might have been a sign of something, mightn't it? What, Sasha could not say.

Could she be sleeping with a teacher? That was the other idea that haunted Sasha. But Bailey's only male teacher had an old-fashioned non-hipster beard and halitosis. Then again, why couldn't she be sleeping with a female teacher? Sasha had read about that one too and couldn't decide whether it was better or worse. And, actually, Bailey's music teacher was improbably pretty, with her rosy cheeks and curly hair.

Why did all her anxiety around Bailey seem to involve sex? Why didn't she worry about drugs or guns? She'd tried to be the sort of right-on mother who avoided too many gender-specific toys (ironic really, since she and Ned were leading highly gender-specific lives). There were dolls for Spike and Lego for Bailey. But despite this, her worries about her daughter were all around her being female, centring on the fact that she had a vagina, on the simultaneous exaltation and degradation of women, especially those of the pubescent kind.

I never gave her dolls; now I worry that she will become one belonging to somebody else. She pushed aside thoughts of Ned and of John and of Mickey, of all the men who were there to remind her that there was no one both so valued and so unvalued as a teenage girl.

Something was wrong, that was all Sasha knew, and it had been for at least six months now. And she was going to find out what.

She parked the car a couple of streets away from the nice, not too pushy girls' private school that she herself had attended. She'd rather have sent Bailey to a state school, but sometimes, she'd thought, you had to put your family above your principles (as she had also told herself when she made the decision that Rosie's story would never be allowed to destroy her home).

Her coat collar pulled up and her beanie down, she was ready to go, ready to stalk. Just like Rosie. She shook her head. Why must that woman invade all her thoughts? She went into the charity shop opposite the stop where Bailey would catch the bus home and flicked through the racks permeated with the musty smells of others, while at the same time watching through the window.

She waited and she watched. She watched and she waited. A group of girls in the unfortunate brown uniform arrived like a river of chocolate, flicking their bags at each other with that girlish yearning for contact, speaking in their too loud, too upper-class voices, self-consciously aware that others were listening. Even through the glass, Sasha could hear their 'like, he's so annoying' and 'oh my God, I'm going to totally kill her, literally'. If any of them had ever spoken with a trace of the local accent, it had long been eroded, to be replaced with a generic posh-girl singsong. It was so different from the way she and her contemporaries had cultivated their mockney accents when they were students. Ned's now transatlantic tones were still tinged with some of that 'lumme lawks' cockney, as if he had been born within the sound of Bow Bells rather than Chichester Cathedral's.

No Bailey. Sasha presumed she'd follow on behind, maybe walking alone, a thought that pierced her heart since she herself had been – and still was – one of the popular ones. A fat girl appeared, tailing the others, then one with spots, and lastly the girl who'd been in primary school with Bailey and who had a mildly palsied leg.

Three buses arrived in quick succession to take the girls across town and to their various villages, and Sasha could imagine the other passengers sighing as these loud, entitled girls got on with their intimidating mass and mouths.

But no Bailey.

'Where are you going, my love?' John asked with a soft voice and a hard grip around her arm.

'For a walk. Got to get my steps up.' She spent so many lonely days with John travelling down to Kent or around the country to visit his various developments, but just when Tamsin wanted rid of him, he seemed firmly embedded at home. 'You'll be cross if Tammy doesn't do her steps for John-John, won't you?' she said in her best little-girl voice, the one he liked her to do in bed sometimes.

'Don't be long. I like to have you here by my side. I might as well be in Kent if you're not going to be next to me. I like you on that chair over there. So pretty against your hair, my beautiful girl.'

He did love her so much, she was very lucky. But not so lucky that she wasn't desperate to meet Mickey again. She could think of little else. When she was having sex with John on their 200-thread-count Egyptian cotton sheets, she was thinking of her and Mickey rolling off the foam mattress onto the dusty concrete of the Nell. When she drank her allotted glass of fine wine – just the one, John didn't like women who got drunk – she thought of the sickly-sweet alcopops and stolen vodka she'd knocked back with Mickey, and that time they'd both vomited into the bracken but then drunk some more and still had sex. When she sat beside John while he worked on the computer, she thought of sitting at a school desk next to Mickey and finding ways of touching him – dropping pencils, sharing textbooks, stretching her foot across the gap between them.

The fact that she was married and therefore had taken a vow to forsake all others didn't unduly concern her. Mickey didn't count. He had preceded John, he was the original. With anyone else it would be wrong, but Mickey was allowed.

Tamsin wasn't sure why she suggested that she meet Emily at the Nell to work on their plan to reunite her with Mickey, but it seemed appropriate. She glanced behind her as she left home. Well, not home exactly, the place where she was currently living. Given that she and John hadn't lived anywhere for more than a year, it would be madness to call it home. She saw the carefully raked gravel driveway where John had parked his black Range Rover (did they even make them in different colours?) and the perfectly symmetrical bay trees on either side of the door, which had been painted dark grey because that was what John said potential buyers would most like.

At first she'd been proud that she lived in places for which estate agents produced brochures when it was time to sell. She didn't need to imagine the one that would be printed for her current house – it was still so sharply decorated that it hardly seemed like a three-dimensional space already, but had the flat perfection of those shiny pages.

She glanced back behind her again but there was no John. He didn't suspect anything. Why would he? He knew there was nothing but space in that head of hers.

Emily had always been the one in charge of money in the family. But that was before they'd moved here, where she had been turned, or turned herself, into a 1950s wife. Matt had sounded as mystified as she was by the fact of the cheque bouncing, and promised to speak to the gas company. Which he duly did, and by that evening, the cylinders had been replaced and the family heart was once again beating, or at least faintly flickering.

So that was good. Less good was the fact that he had seemingly forgotten what the new password to the joint account was, and why it might have been changed in the first place. He said they could sort it out at the weekend. That was what they always said, but they never did. Everything slightly difficult or unpleasant got locked into an over-stuffed cupboard called 'the weekend' and was never seen again.

She kept Rafa tightly on his lead as she walked to the Nell, because she knew he'd otherwise disappear off down the many rabbit holes that pocked the fields. A little part of her fantasised about letting him go and leaving him there, not calling or looking for him.

He became frenzied when she approached the Nell. There was something about the place that he didn't like, but there were many things he didn't like and she was damned if she could indulge them all. She grabbed his collar and lifted him through the door as he snapped and writhed in her arms.

Tamsin was already there, standing at the broken, grimy window so that the light fell on her face in a becoming way. If Emily didn't know better, she'd have suspected this pose was contrived to show her to advantage, but Tamsin seemed strangely free from vanity for such an undisputedly beautiful woman. This, after all, was a person who didn't know how to access the Internet on her phone, so she was hardly likely to be practising her selfie face for hours in front of it.

Tamsin jumped and did the furtive look-around that Emily associated with her. Then she smiled in that way that took years off her face.

'I can't keep away,' she said. 'It's mad, isn't it? I just feel so close to him here.'

'It is cold, though, isn't it?' Emily shivered. 'I don't know how you did what you did in here back then.'

'It was spring when we started,' Tamsin said. 'April. And we kept each other warm. Please tell me, what did he say?'

Emily brandished the printout of the latest missive, this time not even bothering with the pretence that she hadn't taken a good look at it as soon as it arrived. It was longer this time.

Tamsin scanned it quickly, then gulped. 'Read it to me, I can't focus. I've never been good at reading anyway.'

Emily wondered if Tamsin's reliance on her as a conduit to Mickey would continue if the correspondence became, as she suspected it might, a little more steamy. She cleared her throat. She loved reading to the children, especially doing different accents for each character, but she realised that might be inappropriate here.

'OK then. "Tammy, my sweetheart. I can't believe it's you. I've so much to say to you. I've spoken to you every day in my head, wondering how you are, wondering if you and I can ever be together again."' Emily paused. Mickey or Jake or whoever this was did write in a rather adolescent style; no wonder they chose to become a young-adult author. It was as though both Mickey/Jake and Tamsin were trapped for ever at the age at which they'd been lovers, and perhaps meeting would be the only way to set themselves free.

Tamsin looked faint and leant on the wall for support. 'Go on,' she whispered.

'"I'm sorry for running away like I did. It wasn't what I wanted, I had no choice. They told me I couldn't let anyone know where Mum and I had gone as he'd find out."' Emily paused and looked up. 'What's he on about?' she asked. 'Who was he running away from?'

Tamsin frowned. 'I don't know. He never told me. He

just upped and left one day after we'd . . . after I'd told him . . . It was very strange, so sudden.'

'It seems like he's trying to tell you now,' said Emily. 'He was on the run from this man, whoever he was.'

'I hope so.'

'What do you mean, you hope so? It sounds like it must have been awful for him.'

'I know, I know,' said Tamsin. 'But it was awful for me wondering where he'd gone and thinking he'd chosen to just leave me like that.'

'Yeah,' said Emily. 'I know what you mean. Back in the day, when I was single and a boy didn't call or text me back, I'd fantasise that he'd been involved in an awful car accident. Which would be terrible, obviously, but at least he wasn't being silent because he didn't like me.'

'Is that it?' interrupted Tamsin. 'Does he say anything else?'

'No, there's more. I don't quite understand it, though. "I've thought about you both every day, wondering if you're together still or what your parents made you do. Please let me know and tell me how we can all meet again. I do and will always love you, M." What does it mean?' said Emily. 'You *both*? Were you involved in some sort of threesome?'

'God, no,' said Tamsin, blushing.

'But there were three of you in the Nell, that's what he seems to be saying. Just like in the book, I suppose. You don't have to tell me.' That was what Emily said, but inside she was thinking, yes you do, you owe me, I'm invested in this now.

'There was something. The day before he left, I'd told him about it. That's what he means.'

'I don't get it,' said Emily. 'Told him about what?'

'Poor Mickey, not knowing,' said Tamsin. 'All this time he's been wondering what happened. Poor, poor Mickey.'

'About what?'

Tamsin glanced towards the corner of the Nell, where the old cement sacks lay. Just then, her phone shrilled and they both jumped. 'John,' she said without looking at the screen. 'Hello. Yes, just walking. Yes, lots of steps I'd bet. Yes, of course. Very quickly.' She ended the call and fiddled with the rubber bracelet on her arm. 'What am I going to do? John will check my steps when I get back and I've been standing here talking to you. I'm an idiot.'

'He checks your steps?'

'Yes.' She waved the bracelet. 'This tells my phone and that tells his computer. He hates fat women.' She began running zigzags around the Nell like Rafa in one of his manic phases. 'I've got to go. I've got to run. Got to get my steps up.' All the while, she was darting around, and then she darted out and away.

'But . . .' said Emily, frustrated that the next chapter of the story was being denied to her.

8

The Blue Hatchback

This time Sasha left the car behind and waited nearer to the school. The other day, she had seen with her own eyes that Bailey had not taken the bus, yet her daughter had returned from school at the normal, expected time.

'How did you get home?' she'd asked her.

'By bus,' said Bailey.

'Are you sure?'

'Yes, of course I'm sure.'

'It's just that . . .' she had said to Bailey's retreating back, before deciding that it was better that she keep her espionage to herself.

So now she found herself at four o'clock on Friday afternoon standing in the side street opposite her daughter's school, wearing an old skiing hat and jacket of Ned's that she had unearthed and that she knew to be unfamiliar to Bailey. Her manic cloud of curls, that defining feature so admired over the years, was imprisoned within the moth-eaten wool, and her signature bright colours were dampened by the black polyester of the coat. In pursuing Bailey, she'd dressed like her, swamping herself in an andro-gynous gloom of clothes.

Just like the other day, she spied the brown sludge of

the girls as they were disgorged from the school, some immediately swallowed up by their illegally parked parents, others by the nearest newsagent's to get their sugar fix.

This time she saw Bailey and pulled the beanie further down her head as she did so. Her girl was alone, of course; she never invited friends over any more, nor was she invited to parties or sleepovers. While Sasha had always been able to take or leave friendship in favour of her own company, she wasn't sure that in Bailey's case it was a positive choice. 'We just want you to be happy,' she'd say to her, that mantra of parents that provoked anything but happiness in their children.

It was hard, as you tailed your child down the road, not to feel as though you were in a film, Sasha thought, especially when you'd worked in TV drama for years, as she had done. She had to treat it as an acting role to stop herself from questioning what she was doing. She'd snooped around her daughter's phone, the modern equivalent of reading a child's diary; now she'd taken it even further. As with all things to do with parenting, it was easy to dismiss the ethics of any choice with the all-powerful catch-all 'I need to do what's best for my child'.

As she walked, she distracted herself with thoughts of how this scene would be filmed. How would Ned frame it? Natural light, probably, with no music, just the sound of Sasha's breathing muffled beneath the turned-up collar of the ski jacket, and her quick footsteps.

Where was Bailey going? She was striding mannishly in the opposite direction to the bus stop, detached from all the other girls. She never looked round. Her head was down with her hair falling forward, while her arms were crossed as they pulled her coat tighter around herself. It was as if both hair and coat were curtains that she wanted to draw closed so that nobody could see in to her body and herself.

At last, about five minutes' walk from the school, Bailey slowed. Sasha darted behind a parked van as she saw her daughter glance around, but she quickly realised she wasn't looking for her. There was a car parked across the road, and the passenger door opened in readiness to swallow her up. Sasha broke into a run to get closer as she saw her walk over and get in.

She didn't care now if she was seen, she just needed to find out who was driving the navy-blue hatchback that was spiriting away her daughter. She didn't think it was a minicab, and the driver didn't look like one of those members of a grooming gang, but she needed to get closer to be sure. Cold shards of air stabbed her throat and she cursed her lack of fitness, as well as the impractical shoes that she hadn't quite been able to bear to leave off in her bid for anonymity.

It was no good. Bailey had gone.

Tamsin couldn't stay away from the Nell, but she knew now that she had to keep on moving whenever she went there to avoid John's suspicion.

She ran all the way there and then paced around – something that was hard to do since, like all places of childhood, the building was much smaller than she remembered.

When she felt sure that she'd done enough steps to allay John's doubts, she went straight to the corner, the place she thought of as theirs – hers and Mickey's – for it was where they had always lain, as well as stood up and knelt and all those other athletic things they had done in their joyful experimentation.

The corner was also where the terrible thing had happened, the memory of which she'd suppressed for all these years but which Mickey's message had dredged up again. She shuddered as she thought of it, tracing her fingers along the lines of the floor where it had happened, almost convincing herself that she could still see the stain.

Poor Mickey, she thought, he doesn't know what took place here after he left. Tamsin, never one for analysing subtexts in books, now realised the significance of Kez, the teenage boy sent back through time to reunite with Monkey/Mickey and Issi/Tamsin; the three of them together at last.

Poor, poor Mickey, she repeated, pacing the room once more. All these years he's been thinking about me, about us. Although Tamsin couldn't even work out how to use her smartphone, she was aware enough to know that most people traced their school friends and ex-lovers through the Internet. Mickey had probably tried to do that, but she was invisible to the world, a ghost of the girl she once had been.

All this time her love for Mickey had been mixed with resentment at his abandonment of her. He had run away from her, she had believed, the very day after she'd told him the awful yet wonderful news that she was pregnant.

Pretty pregnant too, judging by what had happened soon after and what she had seen. She'd never known for sure, but she remembered not even knowing when her last period had been. She wasn't the sort of girl to annotate her diary with little red Ps so that she'd always know. No, that recording of endless months divided into two had come later, now that she was supposedly trying to get pregnant. John's smartphone held within it a detailed record of both her periods and her cervical mucus, and yet she and Mickey hadn't needed such information, only action, to get pregnant.

He had vanished, leaving no trace, just as she now left no mark on the world. She hadn't even been sure of his surname because his mother was always changing it, sometimes to that of her latest partner, sometimes on some other whim. By the time he'd arrived in her life, he'd been to six different schools and had carried three surnames. It was remarkable how strongly he was himself when he was always being forced to adopt other names and ingratiate himself into new classes.

She had cried and cried, crazed with grief and hormones. It never once occurred to her to get rid of the baby – it was all she had of him – but she knew her parents would have 'encouraged' her to abort. So she wore baggy clothes and secretly enjoyed the curved hardness of her swelling belly. She had been much plumper back then, with famously big breasts, so it had been quite easy for her to disguise herself. She just had to keep going and she'd get a piece of him back. Then she'd have been able to find him. Even in her anger, she had known that

Mickey wouldn't really have left her, not if he had any sort of choice.

She sat down now and began to cry in a way that she hadn't for years. His leaving had cauterised her emotions and blocked her tear ducts; she'd become both emotionally and physically skinnier when he'd left. During the year after he'd gone, she'd slept with every half-decent boy at her school (admittedly there were only a few of them), then the man who worked at the pub, her parents' painter-decorator (that would have been the worst if she'd been discovered, because they really valued his good work), and finally, just before she failed her GSCEs, her physics teacher (young, good-looking, thought of as a bit of a catch. It seemed completely acceptable back in those days; she was sixteen by then after all).

Then nothing for three years. She'd got out of school and got on her parents' nerves. She'd wake up every morning with that feeling of excitement you had when you were really looking forward to something. Then the deflation upon realising that it wasn't going to happen, she wasn't going to see Mickey that day or any other.

Her parents told her she'd never amount to anything, unlike her high-flying siblings, and she knew they were right but wished they would stop going on about it.

And then into this half-world came John, her saviour. He saw something in her that nobody else had seen, least of all her parents. She was beautiful, he said, and just needed looking after, and she'd felt very nearly happy for the first time since Mickey had gone.

Her mum and dad had been overjoyed, falling on John

like the parents of a sick child upon a miracle-working doctor. They'd passed her over to him with relief, and then a decade later moved to be closer to those that Tamsin thought of as their real children.

She sat slumped in their corner of the Nell, knowing that she'd have to get up and start pacing again soon. The concrete floor beside her was cold beneath the inadequate protection of the cement sack. She shuffled along to look at it.

She squinted at the floor again. She could swear that there was still the faintest outline of the pool of blood that she'd spilled sixteen years before. Her fingers traced the stain before she got up to resume her steps and return to John.

Emily remembered that Sasha had observed that there were various phases to being a weekend wife. Phase one: the misery of missing your husband. Phase two: acceptance of his absence. Phase three: resentment of his presence.

She was still in phase two, she told herself, although this weekend might hover into the territory of phase three if Matt couldn't come up with an explanation as to why their online banking password had been changed and why the cheque to the gas canister company had bounced.

'Hello, darling,' she said brightly upon his return, trying to tap into the memories of phase one, when she'd been genuinely thrilled to see him each Friday. She was going old-school wife this time, all the better to get the truth out of him. He looked tired and she felt a pang of sympathy, quickly replaced with the refrain of the weekend wife: you think *you're* tired . . .

'Hi.' He looked taken aback at the effusive welcome.

'I've made roast chicken.' Ah, roast chicken, that piece of simple deliciousness which, alongside chips, sat at the centre of the Venn diagram of her family's food fads.

'Great,' he said, disappearing upstairs to wash away the city. Just a few months ago, he'd have hugged her, told her how lovely it was to be back and thanked her for providing a home-cooked meal with which to greet him.

'Kids,' she shouted, 'Daddy's here.' But he's not, she thought, his mind is somewhere else.

She followed him upstairs. He was sitting on the bed, wearing the gormless expression of someone staring at a phone screen, his fingers strumming it, his mouth slightly agape. Being lit from below made him look even more exhausted; he definitely had excess baggage around the eyes. She went round behind him and began to massage his shoulders as an act of wifely kindness but also as a way of getting a look at the screen. He quickly shut down the page he had been looking at.

'What was that?' she asked.

'Nothing. Just work.' He winced as she kneaded his back. 'That hurts.'

This hurts too, she thought, this feeling that I don't know you any more. If she were to bring this up at the next meeting of the weekend wives – the furtiveness, the checking of his phone, the distance – she knew what conclusion anyone sane would jump to. Well, not Tamsin, because she didn't seem to have a mind that jumped anywhere, but Sasha would raise those gorgeous eyebrows of hers and Emily would know what they were implying. A husband working away in the city – another woman seemed almost like an inevitability.

She needed to have sex with him, obviously. Sex to order was hateful. It was the opposite of sexy, but they'd need to do it. Marital sex – tiredly at night or furtively while the children were parked in front of CBeebies – was pretty unsexy anyway, but add in the fact that there was now only a weekend window in which to chalk it up, and the whole thing had become a chore that felt no more satisfying than descaling the shower head. Actually that wasn't true. It was a lot less satisfying than that – Emily *loved* descaling the shower head.

'Matt, why was the password changed on the joint bank account?'

'What?' He did a really fake distracted look, which was ironic, because most of the time at weekends he managed a very genuine one.

'You know what I'm talking about. The password. I couldn't access our account online. And why wasn't there enough money to pay the gas cylinder people?'

'I don't know.'

'If we don't have those cylinders then we freeze and can't eat. Is that what you want?' She sounded shrill, nagging.

'Of course not. I'll look into it.'

'But why?'

'I've said I don't know,' he snapped. 'For God's sake, Emily, stop bugging me.'

'I'm not bugging you. That's so unfair.' She stood up and moved away from him.

'You have no idea how stressful this is for me: commuting, being the breadwinner, everything resting on my shoulders . . .'

'Everything resting on your shoulders? Yeah, that's right, looking after your children, cooking all our meals, maintaining this decrepit house, walking that stupid dog . . .'

'Don't call him stupid!'

'He is. He's deranged.'

'Don't be mad, Emily.'

'I'm not the mad one. I tell you, he's got mental health issues.'

He laughed, and for a second she saw the old Matt, but while before they'd have been laughing at this together, now he was laughing as if he was mocking her. He wasn't there every day to see Rafa and his oddities; he just got the sane version of itself that the dog seemed to present at weekends.

'Can dogs even have mental health issues?' Matt asked.

'I don't know,' she said truthfully. 'Do you have to have language to have mental health issues? Do dogs have a proper consciousness?' They had, she realised, become like his parents, subverting their problems into conversations about canines.

'Come here,' he said, holding his arms out. 'I love you so much, I really do. Please let's not argue, not when I'm only here for such a short time.' She seeped into his embrace, and it was the warmest she'd felt with him in six months.

Or at least she thought it was, until she realised that one of the arms he had reached around her was holding up his phone, and that his eyes were focused past her shoulder on what it said.

Sasha was distracted by thoughts of Bailey as she went to the third meeting of the weekend wives, this time convening, as promised, at Tamsin's house. She'd have been tempted to duck out of it were it not for the fact that she was curious to see the inside of this palace for the first time. Tamsin and John were not given to entertaining.

She couldn't think of anything but four o'clock when she would resume her stalking, however. This time she'd be prepared and walk to the road where the blue hatchback had picked Bailey up.

When she'd asked her daughter how she'd got home, she had been given the usual flannel about the bus. There was no point expecting the truth from Bailey; she'd have to find it out for herself.

Tamsin's house was a new-build on the opposite side of the village, made of yellow brick and presented nakedly to the road by the lack of planting. It had all those things you read about in property magazines and which Sasha found hard to say without wrapping the phrases in the protective cling film of inverted commas: carriage driveway; double garage; open aspect. The girl who'd flunked her A levels and never had a job had come a long way, materially.

The gravel crunched beneath her feet as she approached

the door, which was flanked by two bay trees so perfect they seemed unreal. The faux-Georgian look of the place was undermined by a very modern buzzer with its own screen, presumably one of those video intercom things that seemed particularly inappropriate in a village where people prided themselves on saying that they could leave their doors unlocked (though they rarely actually did, as it turned out).

Tamsin came to the door dressed all in pale grey, as if to match the house's interior.

'Hello, Sasha. Do you mind . . . ?' She pointed at a row of slippers of the sort that you got in hotels. 'Don't worry, you'll be the first person to wear them.'

'You don't have many visitors, then?' asked Sasha as she slipped off her favourite boots, though she was pretty sure of the answer.

'None so far, apart from some work people of John's and their feet were too big for the slippers you're wearing. It's funny, but when we moved here, I was so proud of coming back to the village and living in such a big house. I thought my parents would be impressed. But they haven't been to visit yet.'

'Really? Why on earth not?' Her own parents, though they were getting frail, were a large part of the reason why Sasha had moved back to the village, and she couldn't imagine a world where she would not be close to Spike and Bailey. But then given that her daughter was lying to her, she had no reason to be smug.

Tamsin shrugged. 'They're so busy and they're so far away. It's odd to be back in your home village when it's not even your parents' home any more, if you see what I mean.'

'Yes, I heard they'd moved down south.'

'To be near Camilla's place. Mum does loads of child-care for her kids now.'

'That's funny,' said Sasha, 'I don't remember her doing much for her own children. Fortunately for me and my pocket money.'

'I think she did try, really I do. I just think she'd run out of that sort of love by the time they got to me. I feel like I was made up of all the bits that nobody else wanted and it must have been quite hard to love me.'

Sasha shook her head. That was possibly the saddest thing she'd ever heard.

'Let's go to the kitchen,' said Tamsin, who seemed quite reconciled to being so unloved.

It was the opposite of everyone's fantasy country kitchen. Like Tamsin's clothes, it was pale and cool, with everything built in and flat. There were no ornaments, no piles of letters and books, not even a tea towel or a mug left out on a work surface. 'Wow,' said Sasha, aware that some sort of reaction was necessary, especially since she was Tamsin's first visitor.

'Do you like it?' Tamsin said eagerly. 'John's got amazing taste. I'm so lucky.'

'Yes, it is incredibly . . . tasteful.' The kitchen opened out to what would be called a family room were Tamsin and John to have any relatives, where two sofas – pale, of course – sat still covered in plastic protection. Sasha gestured to them. 'Have they just arrived?'

'No, we've had them a while, but John thinks it more sensible if we keep the plastic on. I'd only do something silly like spill a drink all over them. We'll take it off when it comes to selling the house.'

'Are you moving soon?'

Tamsin sighed. 'I guess so. I haven't talked to John about it. But all the houses we live in are projects, if you see what I mean. We haven't lived anywhere for more than a year.'

'More of a show home than a home, then?' Sasha pushed, for she was beginning to realise that Tamsin was more robust than anyone gave her credit for.

'It is lovely, though, isn't it?'

'Yes, of course. But you moving on like this, it's like some sort of witness protection scheme.'

'What do you mean?'

'When someone has to remain in hiding for their own protection, or like those battered women who end up in safe houses hidden from their abusive partners.' Sasha saw Tamsin's face light up at the mention of this.

'Of course!' she exclaimed.

'Of course what?'

'I couldn't understand why Mickey moved away so suddenly and couldn't tell me where he'd gone. His mother had a violent ex.' Tamsin grinned. 'I knew he wouldn't abandon me unless he had to. They had to move to escape that man. Dave, he was called.' She did that misty-eyed thing that came over her every time she talked about Mickey.

Her reverie was interrupted by the electronic chimes of the doorbell. 'That'll be Emily.'

Sasha could hear the conversation about it being a shoeless house, and Emily's ever-exuberant exclamations of wonder.

'Isn't this place amazing?' she said on seeing Sasha. 'It's like a grown-up's house. Mind you, I love your house so much too, Sasha, and it couldn't be more different to this. They're both equally lovely.'

'Yes, very different.'

As Tamsin frowned over the built-in espresso machine, Sasha revived their conversation. 'You were saying, about Mickey having to move on . . . ?'

Tamsin turned to Emily. 'Do you remember me telling you about Mickey going away very suddenly like that, and I was a bit angry about it? Now I understand, at last. He had to leave the village overnight because his mother had this dodgy ex – they were always having to move on really quickly. That's why he arrived at my school right in the middle of term. His mum had pretty terrible taste in men and was always hooking up with these horrors. I should have realised it at the time, but it's only just dawned on me. Dave, it was all Dave's fault. That's why Mickey and his mum had to leave like that. He didn't abandon me because I was pregnant.'

'*Pregnant?*' said Sasha and Emily with one voice.

'Yes, with Mickey's baby,' Tamsin said cheerfully. 'I told you we were having sex.'

'Yes, you did,' said Sasha. 'But I suppose I hoped you were using contraception.' Dear God, she thought, Tamsin was only Bailey's age then. 'You were so young! You were underage, weren't you?'

'And what happened to the baby?' asked Emily. 'I'm sorry, do you mind us asking?'

'OK, but I've never told anyone this. Please, you mustn't tell John. He doesn't know any of it. Actually nobody does, only me, not even Mickey. There was no baby. I really, really wanted it, but it wasn't to be.'

'You had an abortion?' asked Sasha.

'Or there was no baby in the first place?' tried Emily, hopefully.

Sasha shivered as she thought of what might have happened to the baby. It was another worry in her mental Rolodex of anxieties for teenage girls – the unwanted baby flushed down a toilet. Oh yes, she'd read about those ones, too.

Tamsin shook her head. 'I was definitely pregnant. I took the test and everything. I remember thinking that it was one of the only tests I'd ever passed. I buried the stick with the little lines on it somewhere near the Nell. It may even still be there. I don't know how pregnant I was or anything. I got a bit fat – well, fatter; do you remember how much bigger I used to be, Sasha?' Her belly was now flat beneath the drapes of the yoga pants.

'Not fat,' said Sasha. 'But round-faced, I suppose.' And you looked a lot better for it, she added to herself.

'I definitely got a belly, but I didn't feel it move. I read a book in the library that told me I was going to feel that soon, but it didn't come.'

'Go on,' said Emily, gently.

'I used to go to the Nell every day after school, in case Mickey ever turned up. Which he never did. The last time

I went, I'd had these stomach pains all day, a bit like period pains, which I just thought were something to do with being pregnant.'

Sasha and Emily, with their five successful pregnancies and one early miscarriage between them, both touched their bellies protectively.

'But they weren't, as it turned out. They got worse and worse. I could hardly breathe, it hurt so much. I didn't know what to do. I hadn't told my parents and I couldn't go to Dr Stow because he'd definitely have told them – they were friends and stuff – so I just thought I'd sit it out at the Nell.'

'And what happened?' asked Emily, her face contorted with anxiety at the thought of the young girl going through this alone.

Tamsin sighed. 'I've never told anyone this. The pain was terrible. The worst period pains ever times a hundred. I sat in the corner waiting for them to go away. And my back was in agony. It was awful, and I didn't know what was going on. And then I felt down there and it was wet and I pulled up my hand and there were these chunks of blood, almost solid, like bits of jelly, and then it was so painful and something bigger came out into my hands and I think that was the baby.' Tamsin started crying.

'Did it look like, you know, a baby?' asked Emily.

Sasha went over to put a comforting hand lightly on Tamsin's back as she saw her wince at the memory.

'I don't know. I didn't really want to look. I felt a bit sick. The feel of it, of him – I always think it was a boy – was just so strange, that something like that should have come out of me. It was like a clot, but harder, more real. I was only young. I was a girl, a silly girl. I just dropped whatever it was, left it there, put some old newspaper into my pants and got myself home. Luckily Mum and Dad weren't there.'

Now there's a surprise, thought Sasha, angry at yet another example of their parental neglect.

'I put my clothes in the washing machine, had a bath, and that was that really. The water in the bath went very pink.'

'And what happened to the . . .' Emily paused, 'what was left behind at the Nell?'

Tamsin shrugged. 'I don't know. I never went back. I'd never gone back there until that day we bumped into each other when you were looking for your dog.'

Sasha tried to banish the image of a dog or a fox or some other creature coming across the dead foetus at the Nell, but that most likely had been its fate. 'I'm sorry, Tamsin,' she said. 'It must have been an awful experience. Did you go to the doctor?' Must not think of Bailey; it's Tamsin half a lifetime ago, not Bailey now.

'No, I just said, I couldn't go to see Dr Stow.'

'Well a hospital, then? It's really dangerous, you should have got checked out.'

'There was nothing to show. Mickey's baby was gone.'

Sometimes Sasha found it difficult to believe that Tamsin was now in her thirties. 'Well I know it's been a while, but you should go now.'

'Why would I do that?'

'There might have been a reason why you miscarried

the baby, or some of it could have been retained. I'm not a doctor, but I did have a miscarriage between Bailey and Spike – that's why there's a bigger gap between them than I wanted.' She paused. It still hurt when people asked her the ages of her children, because it reminded her of that unwished-for gap, which felt to her like a terrace of houses where one had been bombed out, or a perfect row of teeth with one extraction. 'Unless you get checked out, you won't ever know. It could affect your fertility.'

'I see.' Tamsin shrugged. 'John and I have been trying to have a baby, and because I'd been pregnant before, I just assumed it must be his fault.'

'Well get checked out now,' said Sasha. 'Please.'

'How can I? I can't get to the hospital without John knowing, and I can't tell him about this, can I?'

It was worse than Sasha had realised. Tamsin was a prisoner in her shiny new house. 'You can tell him it's because you're not getting pregnant. And then you have the appointment on your own; there's no reason why he'd ever find out what was discussed. I can take you if you want, or there are buses, just not very often.'

'Or I could take you,' Emily added. 'We want to help you. What you went through must have been terrifying and I'm sure you don't want to talk about it, but Sasha's right. It's important that you get checked out by a doctor.'

'OK.'

'And you've got to tell Mickey,' said Emily. 'He thinks there was a baby, a child. A teenager now, about the same age as your Bailey, Sasha. The age you were then, Tamsin, isn't that weird? It must have been awful for him wondering what had happened.'

'How can I tell him?'

'Write him an email.'

'I don't want to write it all down. I need to see him.'

'Yes,' said Emily with sudden eagerness. 'You must meet up with him. At the Nell! You both want to. You owe it to him to tell him what happened to your baby, and he owes it to you to explain in person why he had to leave you that way. It might make it all better again. And it's so romantic.'

'Hang on, Emily,' said Sasha. 'I think you've got to be a bit more careful about this.'

'Why? They need to be together. This is unfinished business.'

'Well, Tamsin is married, in case you'd forgotten. And married to someone that you yourself have suggested is financially and emotionally abusing her. Best-case scenario is that he's just a control freak.'

'I agree, but that shouldn't stop her doing what she wants,' said Emily. 'She and Mickey need to be with one another.'

'Not if that causes her ten tons of trouble.'

'She has to take that risk. A life without risk isn't worth living.' Emily's hands were waving dramatically now. Tamsin sat in the armchair, her eyes bouncing from one woman to the other as they discussed her as though she weren't there.

'Sorry, Tamsin,' said Sasha, realising that she and Emily were behaving like Tamsin's parents and John, treating her as though she were still a child without her own agency. 'What do *you* want to do?'

'I want to see Mickey. I need to speak to him. I can't believe that all this time he's been wondering what happened to our child.' Her eyes were shining with excitement.

Sasha felt beaten. 'OK, if that's what you want. But please be careful. Unearthing the past can be dangerous.' She thought about Rosie and that night of the poll tax riots, and shuddered.

As soon as Sasha left, Emily and Tamsin got to work on an email to Mickey – or the author of the book who claimed to be Mickey (though in Emily's mind there was no doubt they were one and the same). They felt like naughty schoolgirls lighting up a cigarette as soon as their parents had gone.

'You need to set up this meeting,' said Emily, tapping away at her screen. 'The time has come. Enough with the dithering.'

'You're right. I think. I hope,' said Tamsin.

'And there's only one place you can meet, isn't there? It has to be the Nell. What's John's schedule for the next few weeks?'

'I don't know. He just tells me on the day.'

'Have you got an online calendar or something? No, of course you don't, you're not online. Well, a paper one?' Tamsin shook her head. 'No, not one of them either.' Emily frowned. 'OK, what days does he usually go down south for work?'

'Mondays, and he stays for one or two days. Sometimes

he goes off again at the end of the week, but it's more often just after the weekend. He's got some new project in Scotland, too, so I think he might be away a bit more often now. It's part of the reason for moving here; we're kind of in the middle of the country.'

'All right. So we'll aim for a Monday, then.'

'But it's not every Monday. It varies. I never know from one week to the next. One day to the next, really.'

Emily suspected that this was another aspect of John's control issues, but didn't say anything. She didn't want to put Tamsin off arranging this meeting with Mickey, and she realised that Tamsin was easily derailed. She didn't ask herself why she was so desperate that they meet, for she knew she had become over-invested in the whole teenage romance just as her own relationship seemed to be slipping into middle-aged tedium.

Dear Mickey, she typed. *I have so much to tell you, so much to share.* Effective use of repetition, she thought. 'Do you want to tell him straight out about the baby?'

'I don't know.'

'I'm thinking not. It'll come out better face to face. Might be a bit brutal in an email, plus we don't actually know for definite that it's Mickey yet, do we? What next? "It has been so long and yet it feels like yesterday." Do you like that? It's true, isn't it? "But I cannot tell you all that has happened in an email. We can go back to the Nell." That's good because he asked you that question, didn't he? It's a proper exchange.'

Tamsin was looking dazed, which Emily took as acquiescence. 'Go on,' she whispered.

'I suppose now it's just coming up with some dates, isn't it?' said Emily. 'Are you happy to go for a Monday and hope that John's away or that you can slip out?'

'He did say something about being away the week before Easter,' Tamsin said. 'I don't know when that is, but maybe suggest the Monday of that week?'

'Good, yes, let's just check the dates. OK, that works. It will be a bit warmer by then, too.' Emily didn't know quite what she meant by that, but she had allowed her mind to flit through some disturbingly erotic thoughts of young, beautiful people engaging in wild sex at the Nell. 'Time? Eleven in the morning, I'd suggest. Shall I send?' She pressed 'send' before waiting for an answer.

'No,' said Tamsin.

'Sorry, too late.' Emily gave her an apologetic look.

'Too late . . .' repeated Tamsin.

'Or you could think of it as you finding Mickey about a decade and a half too late,' said Emily. 'Come on, he's written a book for you. The least you can do is meet him.'

9

Mad Dogs

Sasha waited, pacing by the front window at home, to see Bailey approach. Her parents had been unable to take Spike and free her up for an after-school session of daughter-stalking. Her mother was taking Dad into hospital about the ringing in his ears. There always seemed to be something these days, poor man, and she was relieved that at least she was nearby to help in whatever way she could.

She couldn't worry about her father today, since her thoughts were too occupied by her daughter. She knew that Bailey wouldn't rock up to the front door in the blue hatchback (and had there ever been a less threatening type of car for a would-be abductor? Surely it should be a black four-by-four with tinted windows, or a white van?), but maybe there would be some other clue as to what was going on.

'Mum, can I play on the Xbox?' shouted Spike as she fretted.

'Yes, all right.'

'Great.' He couldn't hide the surprise in his voice. 'Can I go to the shop and get some sweets, too?' he added.

'Yes. I'll go with you.'

He fist-pumped with excitement. 'Great. And can I buy as many sweets as I want with my pocket money?'

'Mmm, yes, fine.'

'Will you buy them with your money instead?'

'Mmm.'

'Get in!' he exclaimed.

She looked at her watch. Any minute now . . . The shop was right by the bus stop where she guessed Bailey might get out of the blue hatchback in order to maintain the pretence. 'Quick, Spike, just get your shoes on.' How many times had she uttered that phrase? She had always believed that the baby and then the toddler years would be the hardest she'd ever have to face as a parent. Nobody had warned her that although it became easier physically, it became harder emotionally as they got older.

She bustled Spike out on to the street and they strode towards one of the village's few remaining commercial enterprise. It was a newsagent's with a dwindling selection of magazines, some dusty birthday and anniversary cards and a small and random selection of food produce – tinned tomatoes, brown bananas and sugary cereals.

'So when I was on FIFA, right, I took on the Legends . . .' Spike began, apropos of nothing, as they walked.

'Spike, I'm not interested in playing Xbox and even less in listening to stories about it.'

'And the Legends had every Ballon d'Or winner like ever and I had this youth team of nobodies . . .'

Sasha decided to let him drone on. It was almost comforting, and there were only so many times you could tell your child that they were being boring without feeling like a right bitch.

It was almost dusk and she hated this walk, along a very narrow path beside a busy A road. On the whole, in this part of the country, when you went for a walk, you went for a drive first.

As they rounded the corner, there it was: the blue hatchback. Though she had expected it, she couldn't quite believe she'd been right. 'Come on, Spike.' She began to run, leaving her nine-year-old exposed to any swerving driver instead of putting her body between him and the road as she usually did.

She got to the bus stop just as the blue hatchback pulled over to let Bailey out. She saw her daughter's look of panic as she realised that she'd been rumbled, before looking towards the driver's seat.

Sasha's mouth gaped open in recognition of the person driving the hatchback. 'Rosie?' She couldn't quite absorb what she was seeing. There were too many separate worlds melding together, as though somebody had shaken a giant bottle of vinaigrette. The oil and the vinegar should not mix, but Bailey had become emulsified into that confused night from over twenty years ago.

'Hi, Sasha,' Rosie said, as calmly as though she were a fellow mother helpfully giving her daughter a lift home. 'I'm glad I caught you. I've got something for you.' She leant over to the glove compartment of the car and pulled out an envelope which was addressed to her in loopy, posh-girl handwriting. 'Bye, Bailey.'

Bailey, still looking shocked at being caught, managed to wave before dipping her head so that her hair fell over her face and contorting her arms so far around herself that it was as though she wanted to stop herself from breathing.

'What the hell?' asked Sasha.

'What?' stropped Bailey. 'So I got a lift home? What's the problem?'

'Who is that woman?'

'Rosie, obvs,' said Bailey, striding forwards in the direction of home.

'Well I know that, but how do you know her?'

'She rescued me.'

'Rescued you from what? From whom?'

Bailey shook her head. 'You wouldn't understand.'

Sasha took a deep breath, realising that anger would get her nowhere. 'Please try me. I promise to be very understanding.'

Bailey's stride had quickened into a trot and then a run. Spike was still intoning something about the Xbox as if they'd never been interrupted. She grabbed his hand and dragged him along behind his sister. 'Bailey, Bailey,' she shouted. 'Please, you've got to tell me.'

When the children were small, she'd learnt numerous strategies on how to deal with intransigent toddlers and temper tantrums – time-outs, the naughty step, positive reinforcement. But there didn't seem to be any equivalents for teenagers, and Sasha felt that she flailed between cajoling and admonishing with no logic and no partner on hand to back her up.

'Bailey!' she shouted again as Spike whined behind her about having a stitch.

Thinking about Tamsin and Mickey's reunion gave Emily a warm romantic glow that just about managed to quell her anger at Matt. She'd got nowhere at the weekend. She'd tried to have sex with him in a tragically old-fashioned attempt to get the truth out of him about what was going on with their bank account, but he'd very deliberately put his pants on and slept on the far side of the bed. Every time she'd broached the subject, he'd managed to avoid it by tickling the nearby tummy of either a child or the dog.

If he wasn't rough-housing some small being, he was on his phone. It seemed to have become an extension of his hand, and his face was constantly lit up with a ghoulish blue. She'd tried to check it, obviously, but as with the bank account, he'd changed the password away from 2002, the year when they'd first got together.

We don't have shared jokes any more, she thought sadly. They had been the glue that had both got them together and kept them together. When they'd first met at that scruffy flat in Finsbury Park, they had fallen in love over their mutual mocking of Jay, the boy who'd signed the contract on it in the first place and so thought that meant he was the landlord's conduit. Jay had been obsessively clean (oh how tragic, they had thought at the time, though looking back, some of his complaints now seemed to Emily to be utterly reasonable). He would sink into a pool of passive-aggressive sighing if the shower wasn't dried after use, if items of shopping were not cleaned with a paper towel before being put in the fridge and if the hand towels were not washed every day. 'It would be nice,' he'd say as if to himself, 'if someone other than Jay-Jay could do something around here.'

One evening, when just the two of them had been at the flat, Matt had found a Post-it note on the sugar jar reading *Please put don't stick wet teaspoons in me!*

He'd sighed and put on a reedy voice that was an excellent imitation of Jay. 'I do wish Jay-Jay didn't have to keep writing these polite notices to teach his flatmates basic manners.' He then wrote out his own note, which he stuck on the fridge door: *Please stop writing annoying passive-aggressive Post-its!!* followed by three smiley faces.

Emily and Matt had been drinking that night (Jay's stash of wine, natch) and thought this was the funniest thing ever, so funny that they celebrated it with some fervent snogging, followed by some surprisingly successful, for a first attempt (and second and third attempt thereafter), sex. That the sex was so good was particularly astonishing given that both of them had been giving in to the temptation to do impersonations of Jay-Jay throughout the proceedings. So amused were they that they decided to add more Post-it notes to his bedroom door and the bathroom. One of them read,

Jay-Jay wishes that his flatmates wouldn't have such noisy sex because it's turning him oooooooon! while Matt stuck one on Emily's door that proclaimed it to be *Home of the sexiest woman alive.* It was possibly at that moment that she fell in love. In one night, he'd been transformed from polite flatmate to lover and, finally, future husband. It felt so inevitable in its rightness that Emily would have married him the next day if he'd asked her.

Jay, of course, was less amused when he found the trail of Post-its. So unamused was he that he insisted they both move out by the end of the month, forfeiting their deposits as they did so.

They felt like outlaws, and Jay's overreaction just brought them closer together. They found a one-bedroom flat for a reasonable rent and moved in, going from the platonic to the living-together relationship without even a few dinners out in between. Jay was even toasted at their wedding – the man who had helped them fall in love. In fact, until Matt had started working away during the week, the mention of Jay-Jay had always been enough to bring them both out in a fit of giggles.

But not any more. Nowadays Emily's shared jokes were with Nate rather than Matt. They'd got all out of sync on their box sets, and so at weekends she'd watch TV alone while he stared at his phone or computer some more. She'd even written him a note this weekend in the style of Jay, but he put it aside without the merest trace of recognition or a smile.

'Rafa, don't do that,' she admonished as the dog snapped at her fingers while she tried to put his lead on. The more she worried about her marriage, the more Rafa seemed to sense her vulnerability. The weird behaviour had definitely increased lately. His underbite seemed more pronounced, or perhaps it was just on display more as he growled and glared at her from his corner in the kitchen, the warm spot by the stove.

While Matt had dismissed the idea that Rafa might have mental health issues, Emily was becoming convinced that he had some sort of canine form of obsessive-compulsive disorder. He kept licking patches of his skin so that they were now bald, and other times he'd chew his own tail. He'd become so territorial that Emily was afraid to walk past him to get to the garage, but at other times he was almost aggressively affectionate towards her, reluctant to leave her side and constantly humping her leg. Matt thought it was she who was mad, and perhaps she was. The combination of the move, his absence, Rafa and unemployment was making her doubt herself.

She dragged Rafa along the pathway to the fields. He was resistant, but walking him was her central task of the day and she wasn't going to let go of her only structure. When friends from her old life asked what she did all day (that 'all' always being stressed sceptically), the 'you know, walk the dog' was most important.

'Rafa, you little—'

'Hello, Emily.'

She stopped what she was about to say ('fucker', as it

happened) to find herself standing far too close to hand-some Ben, Tania's husband, and his model Labradors.

'Oh, hi, Ben, I was just trying to chivvy Rafa along. Come along, my darling boy. I mean Rafa, not . . . obviously.' Idiot.

Ben gave Rafa that quizzical look once again and then turned to his far more appealing pair of dogs. 'Shall we walk together?' he asked.

'That would be lovely.' If Rafa obliged. 'Which way do you recommend?' He gestured in the direction of the Nell, and off they went at a pace set by his mannish strides. And he was very manly, well over six foot, with appealingly weather-beaten skin. She banished the knowledge that he used to work in financial PR from her brain and went with the whole Lady Chatterley and Mellors thing that occasionally flitted across her thoughts unbidden.

'How are things?' he asked.

Emily wondered whether he really wanted to know and whether she should actually tell him. 'Fine, fine. Well, it's been quite hard to adjust. Part of the reason we made the move here was so that I could give up work, but I've missed it more than I thought I would.' Was this more information than he had asked for?

'But it's so good to get off the hamster wheel, isn't it?'

'Yes . . . though at the same time, there's something quite comforting about the hamster wheel. At least you don't have to worry about where you're going, you just go round and round.'

'Where are you going?' he asked.

'Gosh, how profound you are. That's the question I ask myself almost daily.'

'No, I mean, where are you going now?' he said. 'Do you have a specific walk you usually do with Rafa?'

'Oh, right, I see what you mean. No, wherever. Towards the . . . that old farm building.' She stopped herself from calling it the Nell, but she couldn't stop herself from thinking about the two lovers who used to meet there. She blushed. It's because he's a man, she told herself, and I have no exposure to men any more. Exposure, she thought, expose oneself, exposed to the elements at the Nell. Stop it, stop it. At that moment, Rafa barked sharply while baring his teeth at her. Oh my God, he knows, he can see inside my soul. 'Good boy, calm down.'

'Where did you get Rafa from?' asked Ben. He was the sort of man who remembered the name of your dog. I couldn't tell you the Labradors' names, Emily thought. Probably something traditional and no-nonsense like Rex and Goldie.

'Wiltshire,' she said. 'Well, he was actually delivered to us. Like an Amazon parcel. Luckily we were in or they'd have had to leave him with a neighbour.' She laughed, but he looked serious.

'No, I mean what sort of breeder?'

'A breeder breeder, I guess. This probably sounds a bit daft, but I looked up Jack-a-poos on the Internet and this one had a litter and they were for sale and it was just before the move and we wanted to get a dog in time for that so, we went for it. It wasn't Christmas, but he was a bit of an impulse buy. It was to celebrate moving up here. My eldest was a bit sad about leaving his school, so it was a sort of bribe too.'

'Did you check out his parents?'

'Rafa's parents, you mean? One was a poodle and one was a Jack Russell.' Obviously, she thought. 'I don't know which way round it was, though, whether it was the mother or father who was the poodle.'

'But you didn't meet them?'

'Meet the parents? What is this, Jane Austen?' She laughed, and as ever, Ben maintained his earnest, thoughtful expression.

'You should always meet a dog's parents and see where they're kept, what their welfare is like, see if there are children around. Preferably you'd find a Kennel Club-approved breeder.'

'Well he's hardly going to enter Crufts, is he?' Emily was feeling defensive. It had been a long time since anybody had told her off like this, and it was bringing out the recalcitrant teenager in her.

'That's the trouble with hybrids. Much harder to verify, but it should still be possible to check out their lineage and the place where they were born.'

Emily realised what an utterly ignorant townie she must appear. Getting Rafa had all been about the cutest breeds with the silliest names. 'Why are you interested?'

Ben shrugged. 'He seems quite unusual. And he doesn't look anything like a mix of Jack Russell and poodle, either. What did the vet say about him?'

'We've not been since coming up here, but we saw a

vet recommended by the breeder in London and got all his jabs done. They said he'd had most of them done before we bought him. It was part of the price.' The more she spoke, the more naïve she sounded.

'I think you ought to take him to the vet here. I really recommend Jenny Naldrett, she's amazing.'

'I will do.' Emily looked at the glossy coats of Ben's Labradors and felt the kind of inadequacy she used to feel on standing next to a beautiful woman at a party, both of them being what one might call groomed.

'I've seen a man hanging around that farm building,' said Ben.

'Really?' said Emily. 'What do you think he was doing there?'

'I don't know, he was too far away. It's odd, because I've been coming here for years and there's never been anyone, and now I've seen that man as well as seeing Tamsin a couple of times.'

'Oh. I think she likes walking. Did you talk to him?' Could it be Mickey? She shivered at the thought of that mythical boy being all grown up and so close.

'No, why would I do that?'

'Curiosity?'

Ben frowned in a way that suggested this was not an impulse he was given to indulging.

'How far do you want to go?' Emily asked, and then realised what that had sounded like. 'I mean, on the walk.' Oh God, that made it worse. She'd never found a man without a sense of humour so attractive before, which she blamed on moving to the country. At that moment,

Rafa started doing his sex-preventative snarling once more and then turned back towards home.

Tamsin hid behind the trees as she watched Emily walk away with Ben. For a minute she had thought they were going to go into the Nell, which had made her feel an uncharacteristic fury. It was her place, hers and Mickey's, and nobody else was to go there.

She slipped in through the brambles and went towards her favourite spot. But it was different. There in the corner, in *their* corner, was a bundle of wool. As she got closer, her heart began to beat faster.

This was not just any wool; this was a dark green army surplus store jumper. She lifted it up to look at it. Yes, it was exactly like the one from back then, the one he'd worn every day. She pulled it towards her face and breathed in deeply. It even smelt the same, a delicious soapy, worn smell that could only belong to one person.

It was exactly like the one from back then.

It *was* the one from back then.

Mickey had been there.

Sasha waited until the children had gone to bed before even looking at the envelope that Rosie had given her. She would have imagined that she'd have ripped it open immediately, but she had a sense it would contain bad news, and by not looking at it she wouldn't let the bad news in.

Besides, she'd been busy trying to get some sort of

truth out of Bailey, who had responded to her barrage of questions with silence.

'How do you know that woman?' Sasha couldn't even say her name out loud in front of her children.

'That's none of your business,' Bailey had said.

'It's every bit of my business. You're my daughter.'

Bailey snorted. She had always been a strangely compliant child, missing out on the toddler-tantrum phase, instead plodding through childhood with a patient sense of acceptance. But ever since the summer, and especially since the beginning of term, she'd changed. Sasha's friends had warned her that she wouldn't be blessed with an easy child for ever, but she hadn't been expecting this sort of teenage rebellion, so unlike the one in the textbooks.

By the time she'd gone to bed, she couldn't face opening the letter. It would be silly, more rubbish from that woman, more truths as Rosie saw it but lies according to her husband. And if she had to choose between them, she'd choose the word of the father of her children, wouldn't she? Protecting Bailey and Spike was all that mattered, and she seemed to be failing in that at the moment. No, she would leave the letter until tomorrow, a decision that gave her a small sense of power, a belief that she, not Rosie, was in charge here.

She also knew that if she read it late at night, she'd have no choice but to discuss it with Ned. If she put it off until tomorrow morning, then she'd have to wait a few hours until the LA dawn.

The next day, she dropped Bailey off at the bus stop

(waiting to check that she got on the bus) and then Spike at the primary school, before coming home. She loved 9.15 on a weekday. She'd make herself a cup of coffee and breathe out in relief that the shouting about shoes and bags was over for another day. Then she'd begin work, knowing that by 2.30 she'd be gearing up for the second leg of her mothering.

But today she wouldn't be working. She made her coffee, comforting herself in the ritual, then fetched the envelope. It took her five minutes of staring at it to remove its contents.

It wasn't a letter, but a printout of an email. And it wasn't from Rosie, but from Ned, or so it seemed. Was it possible to fake emails? Presumably it would be quite easy, but this one had Ned's current email address emblazoned across the top as if by way of truth. More than that, it read like something Ned would write. There were too many details that could not have been faked. The mixture of public-schoolboy repression with Los Angeles therapy-speak was so characteristic of her husband.

Rosie, it began, and even that degree of familiarity was chilling. *Thank you for your email. I'm actually glad you got in touch with me. I know it's been a long time, but I've been thinking about what happened, or what you thought happened, a lot. Maybe it's because I have a daughter who's now a teenager, or perhaps because I've been doing a lot of thinking about the past and how it can affect the way that we feel in the present.*

Yes, or you've been having a lot of expensive therapy

– a luxury for which Sasha felt she had neither the time nor the money. Nor in fact the option, given that it wasn't as prevalent in the village as it would be on the West Coast. Any therapist around here would be a middle-aged mother who'd retrained after having children. Sasha knew this because it was something she herself had considered. Ned had probably been told by his therapist to write letters to anyone he might have wronged. Where's my letter? she thought. She went back to the printed-out email.

Or maybe it's some sort of mid-life crisis!

She blanched at the jaunty exclamation mark, which seemed as out of place as a red dress at a funeral. She could picture his handsome face as he made mention of middle age, pausing to wait for someone to tell him how remarkably young he still looked.

I don't remember much about that night. It was a long time ago and we were both very drunk. I know you feel that I did wrong to you.

He was keeping it neutral, maintaining what was known as the NHS apology – we're sorry that you feel that you did not have an acceptable level of service – never admitting to being wrong.

And I think you may be right.

Sasha froze. *May*, it was only *may* be right, but this was so much further towards some sort of acknowledgement of guilt than he had given her or told her that he had admitted at the time. She took a breath and a gulp of coffee before reading on. She had an urge for her first cigarette in thirteen years. Either that or a shot of morphine.

I've never said this to anyone before, but I don't think I told the whole truth when I was asked about it at the time. I never lied, I don't think, but I was never asked all the questions that perhaps I might have been.

It was so weaselly; he was being evasive after all these years. Just give her the truth, Sasha thought. Just give me the truth too.

It's funny, but what you accused me of is perhaps the only crime where everyone can be telling the truth. What I never said or told anyone before is that I knew at the time that you weren't keen on doing what we did. You told me. But I never would have gone on if I hadn't genuinely believed that it was what you wanted, even though you said something different.

What? She said no, Rosie said no and you chose to disbelieve her?

And even though you maybe made out that you didn't want to, I think you enjoyed it, didn't you?

Sasha cringed. He sounded like one of those footballers who was accused of date rape, rather than a mature, educated man who might be able to understand the idiocy of his words.

Despite what happened afterwards, the email continued, *I have some good memories of that night and I like to think you do too.*

Was he trying to flatter Rosie into agreeing that it was a night of love? That he was such a great lover she gave him post-coital consent? Sasha couldn't understand what he was trying to achieve with this half-arsed confession of possibly, maybe, perhaps a little bit of guilt. It all seemed to go back to the assumption that he and everyone else had made at the time – that Rosie wasn't pretty enough to rape and that Ned was too good-looking to ever have to.

But if you don't, then I'm really sorry.

Oh God, thought Sasha with fury. Is he apologising for forcing himself on her or for not being a satisfying lover?

Please tell me I'm forgiven.

And in that last line, Sasha felt that the only truth in the email was contained. It was the nearest Ned came to an admission of guilt and the nearest he came to explaining why on earth he was writing the stupid email. He wanted absolution. Popular, handsome Ned couldn't bear to live life knowing that someone hated him. It wasn't about making Rosie feel better, it was about making himself feel better. He wasn't sorry that he'd hurt her, that he'd possibly raped her and then stood by while others ridiculed her; he was sorry that someone in the world didn't want to ruffle his hair and tell him how wonderful he was.

Sasha felt angry on Rosie's behalf. But then, not that she could admit it, she felt angry for herself too. Not because she'd married a liar, but because this email was evidence that could be possibly used against Ned and might destroy the pretty perfection of their separate lives. She would never have been able to articulate this fear to herself, for it was shameful. She wasn't angry so much that he was bad enough to rape a woman (there, she'd said it, if only in her mind), but that he was stupid enough to put himself in a position, by writing an email over two decades later, where he might get punished. And not just him; them, their family: her gorgeous, innocent, clueless Spike and her poor, anxious, closed-off Bailey. They were the ones who'd be punished most.

10

Fish Fingers with the Kids

Tamsin cradled the jumper as if it were a precious artefact, the central piece from the final haute couture collection of a recently deceased fashion genius. She would let her own wardrobe of expensive clothes burn before she allowed anything to happen to this ageing piece of wool.

As soon as she entered Emily's house, she presented it to her.

'It's a jumper,' said Emily, sounding unsure of how she was expected to respond.

'Yes.' Tamsin sighed and clutched it closer.

'You remind me of Clem and the polyester fleece blanket he can't sleep without.'

Tamsin nodded dreamily.

'It's a special jumper, isn't it?' Emily asked.

Tamsin nodded.

'Belonging to Mickey?'

'Yes,' Tamsin sighed.

'That you've kept all this time?'

Tamsin shook her head. 'I found it,' she whispered. 'At the Nell.' She could hardly believe it even as she said the words out loud.

'Really? I didn't see it when I bumped into you there.'

'It wasn't there then. It only appeared last week,' said Tamsin. 'He's been there, don't you see?'

'Oh my God, I wonder when? He might be the man that Ben saw hanging around. Right, well this definitely speeds things up between you, doesn't it? He must definitely want to see you.'

Tamsin nodded eagerly.

Emily glanced out of the window. 'And at least the weather's better now too. God, it's exciting. I can't believe you're going to be reunited after all these years.'

'You'll organise it for me, won't you, by emailing again to sort out the details, and . . .' Tamsin paused, unsure of what she was trying to say, 'can you keep Mickey's jumper somewhere safe for me?' She was putting it carefully into one of those specialist plastic bags that John had bought for her in order to keep her summer and winter wardrobes entirely separate and protected.

'Yes, of course, but I'd feel happier if you kept it. I'd feel awful if anything were to happen to it. Look, Rafa's eyeing it up already – he's got an unerring instinct for chewing anything of sentimental or monetary value.'

'Oh God, please don't let him eat it.' Tamsin clutched it closer. 'But you've got to take it for me. I just don't know where to hide it.'

'Tamsin, your house is the size of the homestead of a Southern plantation owner. Surely you can find a little corner in which to put it?'

Tamsin continued to plead with her eyes.

'I see. It's John, isn't it? You're afraid he'll find it and work out what's going on. That's paranoia.'

'He knows everything. It's amazing. I can't do anything without him finding out about it. He knows I come here to talk to you almost every morning. It's like he's God.'

'No, there will just be some sort of app on your phone that tracks where you are. If you left it at home, he'd be none the wiser. Or give it to me and I'll try to disable it.'

'No.' Tamsin recoiled. 'Don't touch the phone. Then he'll definitely know that something's going on and he'll stop me. He knows I wouldn't be able to change it without somebody else's help. He knows I'm too stupid for that. He'll stop me from seeing you. He'll stop me from leaving the house.'

'Has he done that before?'

Tamsin looked embarrassed.

'How? Did he physically restrain you? Lock you in the house? Did he hurt you?'

Tamsin's shoulders drooped. 'No, he's never hurt me. He's never hit me or anything like that. It was in the last place we lived, near Stratford. We lived next door to a teacher. A woman – so *that* wasn't the issue; it wasn't like anything could happen between us.'

'So what was the problem?'

'We became friends. She was lovely. She was the first friend I'd made since Mickey really. Before you and Sasha. I told her how sad I was about having messed up my GSCEs, and she suggested I go back to college to retake maths and English and then I'd be able to do A levels and maybe get a job one day. She helped me with my applications and it was all organised that I'd start going to evening classes at the local further education college.

I was lucky, we lived in a town then so it didn't matter that I couldn't drive.'

'And?'

'For some reason, I didn't tell John about it. I don't know why. Lucy, my neighbour, kept saying, "Oh, John must be so proud of you," so I didn't tell her that he didn't know. It just built up and built up and then it was the day I was supposed to be going to my first maths class in the evening. And I told John and he went mad, he was so angry.'

'Why? Because you were trying to educate yourself or because you'd done all this behind his back?'

'He said it was because I'd kept it secret from him while Lucy knew, and that made him feel small. He's very sensitive about that. He says that a man and a wife should always be each other's everything. He said it wasn't the GSCEs, that wouldn't have been a problem, but that he should have been the one to organise it all. He said he was proud of me wanting to get some sort of education and that he'd do everything he could to help me succeed.'

'Hmm,' said Emily. 'And did he?'

'No,' conceded Tamsin. 'Not really.'

'And he actually stopped you from leaving the house to go to the college? He physically stopped you?'

'Not at all. He just said I shouldn't go and I obviously didn't go against his wishes.'

'And what about Lucy? She must have encouraged you.'

'I never spoke to her again. John thought she was interfering. Said she was a lesbian. I don't think she was, though. She was married with two children.'

'Blimey, he probably thinks I've got designs on you too,' said Emily. 'If he even knows that we're actually friends rather than someone you randomly visit first thing each morning.'

Tamsin blushed.

'Anyway, if this Lucy was your neighbour, how did you avoid her?'

'I just didn't go out for a while.' Tamsin shrugged. 'It was all right, as the supermarket delivery was very reliable, so I didn't really need to. And then we moved. First into a rented place down the road while we finished the house, and then here.'

'Where there are precious few buses, no trains, and you still can't drive. Poor you, it must be hard.' Emily paused. 'Tamsin, have you thought about where all this is leading?'

'What do you mean?'

'If you meet with Mickey . . . *when* you meet him, what are you hoping for?'

Tamsin blushed again.

'OK, that,' said Emily. 'But what about after that? Have you given any thought to where all this could lead?'

'Oh no, I hadn't.'

'Well perhaps you ought to. What's John going to say when he finds out?'

'He's never going to find out.'

'But if you see Mickey and if you . . . you know . . . and then you fall in love . . .'

'We never fell out of love,' said Tamsin.

'Exactly. So you meet up again and you fall back in love, and then what? Do you have any money?'

Tamsin shook her head. 'I don't.'

'Literally nothing?'

'I don't even own a wallet. I don't need money. John takes care of me. At least I didn't need any money. Do I need money if I have love?'

'Well yes, you do, I'm sorry to say. I never realised until I didn't have any of my own just how important it is. Something would be a start, just some petty cash.'

'Can you lend me some?'

'Not really,' said Emily. 'Sorry, that sounds harsh. I really wish I could help, and I would do if I could. If I had an income of my own . . . but I don't.' She looked at Tamsin's trousers, which were definitely leather rather than 'leather look'. 'If it comes to it, I reckon I could put some of those lovely clothes John buys you on eBay for you. I bet Sasha could help with that too. But this is mad talk anyway, since a) we don't know what's going to happen, and b) you live in a vast mansion with a built-in Italian coffee maker. I'm sure you can do better than a few hundred quid if it comes to it.'

Tamsin shook her head. 'I don't own anything. The houses are all part of John's business. I sign things sometimes but I don't know what they are.'

Emily was distracted by checking her emails on her phone and started flapping her arm with excitement. 'Seems like Mickey has got the same idea as you – I didn't need to chivvy him, he's responded to our message. He wants to meet tomorrow at the Nell. Eleven o'clock! What shall I say?'

'Yes, of course. I'll be there.'

Tamsin stroked the bag that held the jumper. In only a day, she'd be able to stroke the man who wore it.

Talking to Tamsin allowed Emily to forget about her own money issues, but as soon as Tamsin left, they came flooding back. Somehow just looking at Rafa made all the bad stuff fill her head, just as the way he barked made her put aside those vaguely lustful thoughts about Ben that she enjoyed.

The joint account debit card had been rejected at the supermarket the day before. It was fine, no problem, she just got out her own one, but the money in that account was dwindling and not being replaced by any income. What would happen when she couldn't rely on her personal account any more? Matt, of course, could offer no explanation as to why their joint account had been so eroded. It was as if the balance statement she printed out at the cashpoint machine told her not only how much money she had in the bank, but how much trust remained in her marriage. Both were heading for overdraft.

Rafa was being worse than usual this morning, as if his behaviour, too, reflected the turmoil in her head. He alternated between sniffing manically in every corner of the kitchen and conking out with his back legs splayed behind him as if trying to make sure he got an even suntan. When he woke up, he'd either start worrying his bald patch or make growling noises at Emily. He was a furry embodiment of all her life's ills since moving up here. If it weren't for her friendships with Sasha and

Tamsin, she'd have gone even madder than she had already.

Her head hurt too. All week she'd been feeling sick and headachy, which at least gave her something other than celebrity gossip to search for on the Internet. Not pregnant. Obviously. Her symptoms fitted the description of a migraine, although she'd never suffered from one before. Perhaps it was something to do with the country air. Either that or a brain tumour, but she decided not to google that one just yet.

And she felt sleepy, too. Funny how doing so little could make her feel so tired.

Time to wake Ned up on the other side of the world. Sasha's hands shook as she logged on to the computer and waited for his face to flicker into view, a disembodied piece of him that she could see and hear but not touch. Or punch.

'All right, darling?' he said, rubbing sleep out of his eyes, obviously having decided to take mockney out of his well-stocked wardrobe of accents that day.

'Not really.' She held up the printout of the email that Rosie had given her.

He squinted. 'What's that then?'

She pushed it towards the screen, a strangely lo-fi via hi-fi way of sharing an email, but then she wasn't the one who'd printed it out in the first place. 'It's an email.'

'From whom?'

'You. To Rosie.' She examined the screen for his reaction. It was almost a relief to see him visibly crumble, so at least she didn't have to question its authenticity any longer.

'What does it say?'

'I think you know what it says; you were the one who wrote it. Or have you written lots of emails like this one?'

He sighed. 'I have written her an email. But just the one. It was part of my therapy.'

'I thought as much.' Somehow this confirmation made Sasha feel more angry than anything else. 'Well you'll know what this means, then. That she's got proof.'

'Proof of what? That I'm sorry? It doesn't prove anything else; it just means that I'm sorry she feels so upset about it all these years later.'

'No it doesn't. I've read it. I've read it over and over again. It proves that something regrettable happened that night.' Sasha flinched. Regrettable – what an inadequate word. She was falling into the trap of wanting to minimise what had happened through euphemism. 'It suggests that you raped her.'

'No it doesn't. Because I didn't. Look, I've told you, I don't remember what happened, but I know she's messed up and going on about it all these years later, and I just didn't want that aggro and guilt.'

'The guilt of knowing that she felt messed up or the guilt of having done it?'

'Jesus, Sasha, stop acting like a DA.'

'We say barrister in this country.'

'For God's sake. What I'm saying is, don't act like I'm on trial. I'm not, I've done nothing wrong.'

'You think you did nothing wrong, but then you say you can't really remember.'

'I'm pretty certain I did nothing wrong.'

'Well she's got enough evidence now to take this to the police if she wants.' Sasha started to cry.

Ned put his hand out to the screen, just like in those prison films where the prisoner was behind a window and could only talk to his wife via a telephone. 'Sasha, love, please don't cry. There's nothing to cry about. This all happened so long ago and nothing is going to come of it now. I'm sorry I wrote that email. It was supposed to make things better.'

'I hate myself,' she managed through her tears. 'I hate that I don't know whether I'm more upset about the fact that you might have raped a girl and ruined her life or that you're stupid enough to write a letter that might get you, *us*, into trouble.'

'But it won't.'

'It could do. If she wanted to take this to the police, it could do. Oh God, there I go again, worrying more about others finding you guilty than you actually being guilty. I just want to protect my family. I almost don't care about some other woman, and that makes me feel terrible. I went on feminist marches and bloody look at me now. I have a stupid nothing mum-business rather than a job; I live for and through my children, which I'm not even managing very well any more since our daughter is miserable but won't tell me why; and I don't care whether my husband raped someone or not, I'm just a bit pissed off that he might get caught and ruin our weird but pretty life. Why, Ned, why did you write to her?'

'I told you, my therapist said it might unblock me.'

She put her face in her hands. She didn't want to look at him any more, nor for him to see her.

'What do you want to do?' he asked finally.

'I don't know, I really don't.' She opened her mouth to say something about how Rosie was now stalking their daughter, and then closed it again. One thing at a time. She was used to dealing with Bailey and Spike's problems on her own, and she'd manage this one too.

Emily cooked fish fingers for the kids, with enough spare for her to pick at. She didn't much like fish fingers, she hadn't even as a child, but she didn't dislike them enough to make something separate for herself later.

'Come on, guys, eat up,' she admonished. 'I'm not going to force the vegetables on you, but please eat some of the fish fingers. Imagine how big the fish must be to have fingers that size.'

Clem shook his head. It was unlike him not to have corrected her deliberate misunderstanding of the process of battering cod. 'I've got a headache,' he said.

'Me too,' added Zanna.

'Me three,' Emily finished. She really did; it was horrible. 'I wonder if we've all got the same thing. I really don't want us getting ill. All the more reason to eat something: it will make you strong enough to fight the bugs.'

Zanna started crying.

'What is it, darling?' Emily asked through gritted teeth. The sound of the crying was ricocheting around the rawness of her mind. Make it stop.

'I don't want bugs crawling inside me,' Zanna sobbed.

Emily waited for Clem to tell his sister how stupid she was, but he was clutching his head now and harmonised Zanna's tears with some wailing of his own.

This single-parent-in-the-week thing was too delicate to withstand illness. It barely worked when they were all well. She needed to go to bed with a wet flannel over her forehead herself, not deal with three sick children. She felt a resentment towards Matt that even in her migrainous state she knew was unfair.

'My tummy hurts,' added Nate, and she realised hers did too. She felt tired, so very tired, of everything. She didn't care about the bloody fish fingers and what the children ate or what they did; she just wanted them to all go to bed, followed shortly by her.

Usually she found it hard to believe that anybody else's children might bicker as much as hers. Sometimes she wondered whether they'd moved to the country in order to be able to shout without the neighbours hearing. But not today. Today they were model children, seen and not heard. She felt a vague disquiet that they were being so harmonious, but mostly she felt grateful. Maybe this was what other people's mealtimes were always like.

Even Rafa was being peaceful today, seeming happy to gnaw away at the bald patch from his bed in the corner of the room.

The children all flopped into bed clutching their stomachs by seven, and Emily went to bed not long after. She felt a mixture of exhaustion and excitement, mingled with the thumping headache. Tomorrow Mickey and Tamsin were finally going to meet again. She was reading the copy of *Text Back Time* that she'd bought for herself, swept up in the mix of fiction and reality that was the love story of these two teenagers. Only a few pages in and she felt her eyes closing, until she fell asleep with the light on.

She woke in the mire of half-sleep to hear Rafa barking. He sounded nearby; he was in her room. Damn dog, he'd got out of the kitchen. They had rules about him being allowed upstairs, where he would invariably pee and poo despite the extensive training they'd done.

'Rafa, you little bugger,' she said out loud. 'Am I not even allowed to sleep in peace?' Her head was throbbing, although she didn't think she'd had much to drink the evening before. Well, no more than usual.

Her bedside light illuminated the room enough for her to see that he was running around the room in a haphazard way, as if he'd drunk one of those vodka and energy drink cocktails. This wasn't abnormal behaviour for him, but it seemed even more manic than was characteristic.

'Please calm down, Rafa, you're scaring me.'

Instead he leapt on top of the bed and went for her face. She shielded herself with her hands, terrified that he was about to savage her, but instead he began licking her. It would have been affectionate, but he did it with too much ferocity, like he was trying to take a cast of her features with his tongue.

'What is it?' she asked. Stop talking to the dog, Emily, he can't understand you. He barked in reply, as if she could speak mad dog. This is the bit in the film where I'm supposed to translate, for him to tell me that there are burglars in the house or a child has fallen down a well. 'Please leave me alone,' she said, burying her head beneath the pillow. 'I need my sleep and you'll wake the children.'

Too late, as Clem wandered in, looking ashen even in the dim light. 'Mummy, I don't feel well.'

'It's Rafa, he's woken you. I'm sure you're fine, darling. Come and sleep in my bed.'

He tottered towards it and then heaved, vomiting over not just the carpet but the duvet too. As ever when her children were sick, she felt that mixture of sympathy, fear and irritation. Why did they never make it to the toilet? But more, what's wrong with them and was there a way for her to take on their pain on top of all that she was already feeling? Clem began to wail, and Rafa joined him in an awful symphony of frenzied grief.

'Please be quiet, you'll wake the others.' Every cry bored through her.

Clem began to sob. 'Not Nate. He won't wake up. I kept pushing him. I thought he was being annoying, but I really think he won't wake up.'

Emily felt a shudder of fear welling inside her, and for a second she thought she too would throw up. 'What do you mean?'

'I was scared when I felt ill and I wanted him, but he wouldn't move.'

She leapt out of bed and almost fell over, so dizzy did she feel. This was more than fear – she felt in some way incapacitated, as if she'd been drinking the same noxious cocktail as Rafa. She skirted round the pool of sick and went into the corridor to go to the boys' room. The light was on, as it was every night, but for a second she felt so disorientated that she couldn't work out which room they slept in.

'Nate, Nate,' she shouted when she'd finally worked out where she was going. She pushed at his immobile body, but Clem was right, he wasn't waking. They were all ill at the same time, but with what? Some sort of winter vomiting bug, though it wasn't winter? What else could make them all ill at the same time? She tried to think but her brain was cloudy as if she'd been poisoned.

Poisoned! That was it, but by what? Then despite the mugginess of her mind, it came to her: gas. Yes of course, it's gas! She'd always felt uneasy about the gas canisters for the not-Aga Aga, imagining that one day they'd explode into a fireball of action movie proportions. And if it was gas, then it must be leaking from either the stove or the canister. The last time she'd changed it, she'd been disconcerted by a hissing sound as she'd done so.

The fear made her feel faint, but she needed to act. She ran over to the bedroom windows and threw them open, then went to Zanna's room to do the same. She shoved her daughter as hard as she could, but she was in the same state as her little brother.

Think, think, think. Vague memories of public safety advertisements came to her. If you think there's a gas leak, what do you do? You don't turn on the lights, that was it, don't flick the light switch or the whole place could go up. She needed to get the children outside to the fresh air, but she didn't dare go downstairs where it would be worse. The roof; there was a flat roof over the garage. But the garage was where the spare gas canisters were. And the front door was next to the kitchen. Oh God, oh God. The roof, I'll take them to the roof.

She grabbed Zanna and staggered with her dead weight towards the window in the corridor that led out to the roof, then did the same for Nate, leaving them in a pile like discarded coats at a party.

'Clem, darling,' she shouted as she ran back into her own bedroom, 'you've got to be strong for me, do you understand? I need you to help me.' She flung open her windows to try to revive him as he lay on the point of passing out on her bed. 'Please, darling.' He nodded, and she dragged him up, surprised by the weight of him. He's growing up. Please let him grow up.

He managed to stagger to join the others by the window on the landing.

'Listen to me, Clem. I am going to open the window and you are going to climb through it and sit very still on the roof.'

His eyes were half closing, but even in his stupor he

registered surprise. 'But Mummy, you said we were never ever to go out there.'

'I know, but I think there's some poison in the air inside the house and I need you to get away from it.'

'And you.'

'Yes, and me. I've just got to get you three out first and then find my phone so we can get some help. Do you understand?'

He nodded, and she helped him out. 'Don't move, do you understand me? Stay away from the edge and make sure that Zanna and Nate do too.'

She nearly buckled under the weight of her littlest child, but managed to shove him through the open window. 'Get him, please, Clem, help me.' Clem grasped Nate's legs while she held on to his head, with his body balanced over the ledge. She leant over and managed to deposit him on the pebble-dashed roof. God, it was ugly. It rather ruined the rural idyll she had once imagined.

'Good boy, you're such a clever boy. Now we need to do the same for Zanna. Can you do that?' She manoeuvred her daughter in the same way, noticing that she seemed to be stirring. This was good, of course, but bad too, since she might stumble towards the edge of the roof. 'Clem, I'm going to get a duvet, but you have to make sure you all stay safe, do you hear me?' She grabbed the duvet from her bed and shoved it through the window to join the most precious things in her life. When she'd given up her job and they'd moved here, she'd fantasised about the sort of madcap picnics they'd have and the memories their marvellous mother would make for them. This seemed to be a sick version of those dreams. 'Please, Clem, stay together under the duvet. Imagine it's a ship and the roof is the sea. You're not safe if you're not under the duvet.' The March night air was crisp, and each gulp of it made her feel more awake and alive.

Right, what now? Phone, where had she left it? Charging in the kitchen. She grabbed a flannel from the bathroom to put over her mouth, took a deep breath, and ran down the stairs, away from the light of the upstairs corridor.

She made it to the kitchen, where either the fear or the reality of the gas seemed to seep through the flannel. It was pitch black. Damn it, she hated the suffocating dark. Back in London, she could have relied on the permanent orange glow outside the windows, but not here. Something wonderful, she'd thought, we'll see the stars every night.

Grappling her way through the darkness, she found the phone and wondered for a second whether disconnecting it from the charger was as dangerous as switching on the light. She felt as though she were a bomb disposal expert choosing between the red and the blue wires as she pulled it off. Pause. No, it was fine. The house didn't blow up.

Through the window, out on to the roof, where her three children were huddled like well-fed refugees. She smiled gratefully at Clem as she heard Zanna crying, feeling a relief that she hadn't experienced since those first cries they'd unleashed on being born.

'Which service do you require?' said the emotionless voice on the other end of the phone.

'Ambulance, no, maybe a fire engine, I don't know. There's a gas leak and we're out on the roof.'

Nate too had woken up and was crying along with the others. Never had Emily been so pleased to hear their whines. She joined in, but with tears of thankfulness.

Another enticement of the countryside was the fact that the nocturnal noises would be owls rather than sirens, but Emily smiled as she heard their wailing, preceding the flashing lights of the ambulance and fire engine.

The firefighters weren't the hose-carrying hunks of a cheesy calendar, but Emily still swooned as she saw a pair of them sweep up her children and carry them down from the roof. By now, the three of them were chattering excitedly about the firefighters' uniforms and all the attention. Embarrassed about her weight, Emily made it quite clear that she could climb down the ladder on her own, something she instantly regretted as she began to sway with vertigo, gas poisoning and adrenalin.

Then into the ambulance with the children, where they were told that they'd have to go to hospital for observations. Bliss, thought Emily, a place filled with experts where she wouldn't be responsible for her children's safety any more. But then her relief was curtailed by her eldest child.

'Where's Rafa?' asked Clem. The others immediately began to clamour for him too.

'I don't know. Shit . . .'

'Don't swear, Mummy,' said Clem. He began to cry again. 'I want Rafa.'

She stood up, still shaky, vaguely aware of the skimpiness of the T-shirt she slept in. 'Don't worry, I'll find him.'

'You're not going anywhere,' said the paramedic. As a mother, there was usually something so comforting about being talked to as though she were a child. But not this time.

'I've got to. He saved our lives.' Her voice shook as she said it. Rafa saved us and he might die. A vision of a scruffy black and grey ball of fur curled up by the dodgy oven flashed into her brain.

'The firefighters will get anyone out still left in the house. Who is it? Is it another child?'

'Our dog. He was the one that woke me up. If it hadn't been for him, we all could have . . . I don't know.'

'We'll let the firefighters know.'

'Please, let me go. Or let me at least talk to the firemen. He's not just a dog, he's part of the family.'

'I want Rafa,' wailed Clem.

'Me too, my love, me too. Please,' she said to the paramedic. 'We need Rafa. We love him.'

'I promise you,' said the paramedic. 'We will inform the fire service and make every effort to ensure that your dog is rescued.' Without physically barring her path, he stood, arms folded, in such a way as to make it very clear to her that she was not to approach any of the firefighters, gabbling of lost canines. She looked at her phone and texted the most reliable person she could think of: Sasha. It was only then that she realised she hadn't spoken to Matt, and she belatedly rang him next. Like the hardened country-dwellers she'd so long mocked, she'd become the sort of person who thought of the dog first and her husband second.

As they drove away towards the hospital, she looked back at the house, half expecting to see it consumed in a gas explosion, but it stood there – without flames – just as it always had. The house could go – she'd almost be pleased to see it destroyed – but either the remains of the gas poisoning or the thought of a little charred Rafa made her feel nauseous once more.

Sasha didn't know whether the sound of sirens had woken her or whether she hadn't yet been to sleep. If she had slept, it had been fitful, pocked with dreams of Ned and a random girl she'd been at primary school with and hadn't thought of since.

Sirens were the sound of the city. She couldn't remember the last time she'd heard them racing through the village, and their rarity made them threatening. Her children were fine, in their beds; her parents had just gone away, Dad's tinnitus and all, on holiday, again; Ned was in LA, of course.

Could it be Tamsin? The more she heard about her relationship with John, the more Sasha was haunted by images of a murder-suicide. He had all the hallmarks of that sort of man: the control, the lack of friends, the ambition. Or maybe Tamsin would finally crack. That book, for which Sasha felt responsible, could tip her over into some sort of madness.

She'd never get back to sleep now. There might be some online bids for her pottery from America, so she could usefully go and check on that. Or phone Ned, she supposed, but she was done talking to him for the moment. He had said all he had to say and she felt no nearer the truth, or indeed what that truth would mean to her family.

Her phone pinged with a text from Emily. She shuddered. People didn't text at two in the morning with good news.

We've gone to hospital. Firemen should have Rafa at ours. Can you get him? Careful, gas in house.

Then a second text arrived. *We're fine.*

Rafa? Who was that? Sasha found that once she had her first child, she developed a perfect memory for children's names, rather compromised for their mothers, and just called their fathers Mark or Dave and hoped for the best. But Matt was Emily's husband, she knew that, so where did that leave this Rafa?

She got dressed pondering the question, and wrote a note to Bailey in case she woke up before she got back. Rafa, gas, hospital; all odd but apparently all fine.

'Rafa,' she said out loud. It made it more familiar and she could hear it in an exasperated shout. It was that scruffy dog of Emily's, the mongrel. Sasha, despite her country upbringing, was not a dog person, especially when it was as unattractive as that one, which had what her friends in LA would describe as 'English teeth'. So she was getting up and out in the middle of the night to rescue a dog from some gas? It was the sort of malodorous creature that was probably the source of it.

So the sirens had been for Emily then, not for Tamsin, and all was fine. She breathed out in relief, but was unable to shake the feeling that Tamsin still needed protection from John and from Emily's encouragement of her romantic fantasies. Sasha hadn't seen much of Tamsin back then – she'd been off at university and then working in London – but she had seen enough to know that she'd been destroyed once by her relationship with Mickey and it could happen again.

Tamsin lay in bed, listening to the sirens swirl past. She didn't wonder who they sounded for because she could think of nothing but tomorrow.

She wanted to sleep, she really did. She would look so haggard otherwise. But she couldn't. Just a few hours more and she'd be with Mickey once again. It had been sixteen years since she'd last seen him. She thought back to that awful time at the Nell when she'd told him about the pregnancy and he had promised he'd be with her for ever, that they'd keep the baby, that the three of them would make it work out somehow. If she had known then how long it would be until they met again, she'd have drunk a bottle of weedkiller there and then.

Never wondering how Mickey might look after all this time, she worried only about what his impressions of her might be. She was thinner, of course, and she considered this a good thing. At least, it was something that mattered a lot to John and, it seemed, to the rest of the world. The rare instances when she saw her family, they all commented on it – her mother approvingly, her sister reproachfully ('You don't want to go getting any thinner' was the standard refrain from the milky plumpness of her maternity).

Mickey, she thought in her limited imagination, would look exactly the same, a scrawny red-headed boy with scruffy clothes and the charisma of a rock star. Oh God, that body of his, the six-pack produced by lack of food rather than tedious abdominal exercises, the way he moved like a dancer in and out of her. She had wanted her flesh to eat him up and be eaten by him.

John snored beside her. He'd told her that he was off early tomorrow morning, and she clung to this promise. She wanted to turn on the light to reread *Text Back Time*, to stare at the bad line drawing of the author, but John was a light sleeper and hated being disturbed. It would only turn into a row about how important his work was and how her shoes didn't pay for themselves. No, row was the wrong word; more like lecture.

Shoes, what shoes should she wear tomorrow? And clothes? She couldn't help but wonder if she should be choosing something easy to remove.

If John hated her turning the light on, he'd be even more disturbed if she put her hand between her thighs – she was throbbing so hard she knew that sleep would remain elusive. Just a few more hours.

*

Emily's house was flanked by a fire engine, but there was no sign of an ambulance. Sasha didn't know whether she was supposed to knock for entry or how on earth she was going to explain her mission.

Fortunately one of the firemen walked past just as she had parked up.

'Hello,' she said, and then felt idiotic.

'Hello,' he replied, evidently perplexed by the presence of a random middle-aged woman in the early hours of the morning. 'Can I help you?'

'I hope so.' She got out her phone and brandished it at him. 'I got this text, you see, from Emily. She lives here.'

'She was very fortunate.'

'Really? I don't know what happened exactly.'

'I don't know how many times we have to ram home the message of gas safety for people to take it on board. I don't understand why on earth anyone still uses those gas canisters for heating purposes.'

Sasha felt defensive on Emily's behalf, sensing a note of 'tsk, these silly women' in his tone. 'Well it would help if the gas mains extended this far. Have you any idea of the cost of heating oil in comparison?'

'I know the human cost of gas leakage,' he said rather pompously.

She knew she couldn't afford to irritate him. 'I'm sure you do. Terrible business. We're lucky to have a good fire service in this area.' She had no idea if this was true, having fortunately never needed their services. 'You're so very knowledgeable that I wonder if you could help me.

Emily is very concerned about the whereabouts of her dog.' That sounded so silly, she couldn't believe she was saying it out loud. She was most certainly not a dog person, and she'd rather thought that Emily wasn't either.

'A dog, you say? I wouldn't know about any dog,' he said, and Sasha felt her throat unexpectedly constrict in fear.

11

Too Ugly

Emily didn't know if it was the effect of the gas poisoning or just the general weirdness of the situation, but since that first blast of cold air when she'd opened the windows in the middle of the night, she'd felt as if she were in a dream.

The hospital was wonderful. Seeing all the drunk, injured people staggering into A&E gave her a kiss of nostalgia for all those visits to a crowded London hospital when Zanna had stuck a bead from a flip-flop up her nose or Clem had fallen head first off the kitchen table. There was something so pleasing about the competency within chaos that hospitals represented.

The doctors and nurses had seemed to know exactly what to do. Since leaving the structure of her job, Emily now realised that she'd been floundering in uncertainty, and for the first time, here she was and she didn't have to make any decisions. Nobody was relying on her; she wasn't in sole charge of her children and their safety. She had failed in that, but this felt like a sort of relief, as if the thing that she most feared – them being in danger – had finally happened and they had survived.

Of course the children hated having blood tests, but it

had been good to know that although they had been poisoned, it was not at such a dangerous level as to cause any long-term damage. Poor little Nate had the highest levels of toxin in his blood of the three children, being the smallest, but Emily was surprised to find that hers were even higher.

She explained to the doctor that she'd gone downstairs, near where the gas canisters and the not-Aga Aga were, to retrieve her phone. In the country, doctors and waitresses were as likely to be white British as anything else. That never happened back in London. His name was Dr Smith-Goode, of all monikers. She'd never met one of those in the city in all her trips to A&E.

'Could that be the reason why my levels are higher than the children's?' she asked him.

'Well yes, obviously, because gas is heavier than air,' he said, as if everyone knew that. Which actually Emily hadn't known, but now she'd never forget.

'Oh right, yes, of course. I didn't know what to do, whether to take them out through the front door or on to the roof.'

'You did the right thing not going downstairs with them,' he told her. 'The smaller the person, the more dangerous carbon monoxide poisoning is.'

'What about dogs? Very small dogs?'

'I'm a doctor, not a vet. But canaries were sent down mines as an early-warning system for miners, as they'd keel over and die if there was gas in the air. So I suppose it would be the same for dogs.'

'Oh,' she said, and began to cry.

Dr Smith-Goode tried to look sympathetic, but she thought she caught an eye roll through her tears. He was used to dealing with human misery, and the fate of a tiny, mad and very ugly dog probably felt trivial to him.

'But,' he said, 'I think you're all going to be fine.' Yes, he definitely wanted her to buck up and think herself lucky.

'Are you absolutely sure there aren't any long-term effects of the poisoning?'

'Fairly sure. Of course, it's possible, though unlikely. We'll ask you to report back to us if you spot anything. How long had you noticed the fluey symptoms before last night?'

'I'm not sure. Maybe a week.'

'Well, you need to look out for any neurological abnormalities.'

Oh God, brain damage. 'Such as?'

'Inability to concentrate, dramatic mood swings.'

'Gosh, that's me all the time. How would I tell?'

'Really?' Dr Smith-Goode looked interested.

'I'm joking.' His expression told her she really wasn't funny. 'Lots of us have mood swings, don't we? Well, women.' Oh no, now she was making sexist jokes. She was a feminist-turned-self-hating-woman.

'I see. Well if you could keep a diary, and one for the children, to note down moods and any other changes, that might be a good idea.'

Clem and Zanna certainly seemed in a cheerful mood, especially as Emily and Nate had oxygen masks put over their faces to bring down the levels of carbon monoxide in their blood. This of course caused much mirth for the older two.

'Nate, you look like such an idiot in that mask,' said Clem.

'Like a robot,' added Zanna.

Nate's protests were muffled by the mask, and Emily had to remove hers to intervene, almost relieved that the gas hadn't impaired her children's fundamental ability to fight over anything. She'd once seen them have full-on fisticuffs over a discarded herbal tea bag.

Nate removed his too. 'I'm a superhero.'

The others scoffed at this, at which Nate thumped his sister.

'Stop it, all of you!' Emily heard herself shouting, and as so often at these moments, she found she didn't care that it made her sound like a terrible mother. Well at least she didn't until she realised that Dr Smith-Goode had entered the room, whereupon she shut up and pulled the clear plastic bubble back over her mouth, hiding behind it.

Another blood test for her and Nate, and then at last sleep in the knowledge that they were fine, they were all really fine. Emily thought she'd never be able to drop off, that her mind would be whirring with all the horrifying what-ifs and the regretful if-onlys of the night's events, but she found herself drifting off into a dreamless world.

She didn't know how many hours had passed, but when she awoke with a start, Matt was sitting by her bed.

'Rafa,' she said by way of greeting.

'No, it's Matt,' he said, with his propensity to make glib jokes in a crisis. She thought he'd lost that ability when they'd moved up here.

'Do you know what's happened to him?'

He shook his head. 'I thought you didn't like him.'

'I never said that.'

'I think you did. Anyway, you didn't need to. You looked at him as if he were pure evil.'

She started crying. 'He saved our lives.' Matt stood up and hugged her. He hugged her without even checking his phone behind her back. All the confusion and terror of the night came back to her. 'Oh God, it's been awful. We could have been killed, all of us.' She felt him shudder with fear. She herself was alternating between giddy relief and fearfully going over what might have happened had Rafa not alerted them.

'I know, I know. It's all my fault,' said Matt, looking a bit tearful himself. She'd always loved the fact that he found it easy to cry.

'Why's it your fault? I wanted to move out here. I drove us here. And I presume I'm the one who connected the gas cylinder in such a crap way as to gas us all.'

'But I should have been here for you. I should have checked those stupid canisters. I'll never leave you again, I promise.'

Even in the haze of tiredness and emotion, she was thinking more rationally than him, which gave her hope that perhaps she wasn't going to be intellectually impaired by the gas for ever. 'Don't be daft. We can't afford that.'

He sighed and opened his mouth as if to say something, and then closed it again.

She looked at him with narrowed eyes. 'What is it, Matt? There's something you're not telling me.' So it was another woman. That would explain all the secrecy around his phone, the sense that when he was at home, he wanted to be somewhere else.

'I've . . . There's something . . . I've been keeping something from you.'

Oh God, it was true. He was having an affair. That was what everyone told her might happen when she became a weekend wife. How could she have been so stupid? She tried to ask the question, but no words came out.

He looked at her with horror. 'Oh fuck, not *that*. There's no one else. Don't be daft. I've always known I'm punching above my weight to be with you. I so don't deserve you. I love you so much, you're so much better than me.'

She waved away his protestations. She realised that although she'd felt distant from him, she'd never not loved him on some instinctive level. 'So what is it?' she whispered.

'This is so hard to say. I don't know where to begin.' He sighed and looked away. 'I'm so ashamed.'

'What? Just tell me, what is it?'

Dr Smith-Goode decided at that moment to make his pompous appearance. Just piss off, she thought, longing for those more humble London doctors.

'You'll be very pleased to know that your children all

seem quite well now. As do you. I expect you want to be with them in the children's ward.'

This was not a question, but a potential judgement on their parenting, so off she and Matt trotted, with her hissing questions all the way along the corridors.

Sasha sat staring out of the window with Rafa curled up on her lap. I'm not a dog person, she kept on telling herself, I'm not a dog person. But the combination of his tiny neediness and her sleep deprivation stirred memories of Bailey and Spike's babyhood, sparking in her a painful nostalgia. She'd honestly believed that the milky messiness of those first few months with a new baby were as hard as it was ever going to be. She shook her head at such naïvety. Being a mother as they grew older became physically easier, that was true, but so very much harder emotionally. If she had fully under-stood how much more complicated it was going to become, she wondered whether she'd have given them up for adoption there and then. It was one thing to be woken from sleep by a crying baby, but another to lie awake in the early hours with worries circling your head endlessly, like a plane trying to land at a busy airport but never quite making it.

Rafa alternated between sleeping, shaking and growl-ing. None of which was, admittedly, like the gorgeous snuffling of a newborn, but he appealed to that instinct in her. I could look after you, she thought, and you'd never tell me I was stupid, or didn't understand. The worst thing was when Bailey said nothing at all, but that kind of went with the territory with dogs, so the lack of words was less bothersome.

When the fireman had said he knew nothing of any dog, she'd been terrified.

'Dog?' he'd said. 'We all thought it was a furry rat.'

She'd been confused for a second, and then realised that he was making what might pass for a joke in emergency services circles.

'So you've found him?' she'd asked. 'Is he . . . is he all right?' Her voice a whisper. 'Is he alive?'

'Bloody is,' said the fireman, 'but my mate will have to have a tetanus injection because of that horrible mutt.'

Sasha's body had sagged with relief. 'Thank God.'

'You say that, but you're not the one who's been bitten. It's really more than we should have to put up with. He could sue.'

'So where is Rafa . . . the dog now?'

'In a cage, where he belongs. One of the fire investigation dogs' cages. Now they *are* useful animals.'

She was taken to the back of the fire engine, where in the corner a grey rat-like thing was whimpering. Sasha was no dog whisperer, in fact she'd probably be more a dog-shouter, but she made the sort of shushing and calming noises that had once worked on her children. At that point, Rafa gave her what seemed to be a smile – either that, or he was baring his teeth, revealing an unfortunate underbite. She felt an unexpected rush of sympathy for him. With his fur falling over his face and his cowed body, he reminded her of Bailey. 'Can I take him home with me?' she'd asked, and the fire service had been only too glad to get rid of him.

Her memories of the middle-of-the-night rescue were rudely interrupted.

'Oh my God, Mum, what is it?'

She looked up to see Bailey, fully dressed and ready for her sensible breakfast of porridge and herbal tea, staring at Rafa with wonder.

'It's a dog. Though I do admit it's difficult to tell.'

Bailey peered at Rafa with curiosity. 'Is it ours?'

'No, absolutely not.' Sasha laughed, but there was a part of her that felt sad at that fact. 'It's Emily's, the family who moved into the house at the end of Meadows Row. Kids at St Peter's with Spike, a bit younger. They got gassed last night.'

'Like the Jews?'

'No, not like the Jews. It was an accident, unlike the Holocaust. They're fine, but I got called up to rescue Rafa, who'd been left behind.' See, thought Sasha, other people think I'm a heroine, even if you don't. 'Do you want to hold him?'

Bailey took him gently on to her lap and immediately seemed to relax, her shoulders opening out instead of being hunched as they usually were. She smiled as she ran her fingers through Rafa's fur, and Sasha felt joy at seeing this rare event.

'Mum, there's something I've not been telling you.'

Sasha wanted to say *I know, I'm your mother, I've known that you've been keeping secrets*, but resisted, instead nodding encouragingly.

Rafa too looked more relaxed with Bailey, as if he recognised another damaged soul. Emily had always called him the nutter dog, but he seemed rather wise.

'It all started at the end of Year 9.' Bailey sighed, and again Sasha bit her tongue. She looked imploringly at her daughter, who didn't look back, choosing to concentrate her gaze on the salt-and-pepper fur ball on her lap. 'There are some girls who don't like me much.'

Sasha couldn't resist that awful maternal urge to make everything better and ram solutions into her daughter's face. 'There are always some girls who won't like you, sweetheart. They're probably jealous because you're so clever and funny and lovely.'

Bailey snorted. Sasha worried that she had blown it. Must be quiet, must not try to fix it. 'Sorry, love. I'm going to make us both a cup of tea and not interrupt any more.'

'They started writing stuff online about me. They did this poll where everyone had to vote on who was the ugliest girl in the school, and I got the most votes.'

Sasha concentrated on watching the kettle. She didn't want to turn around and look at Bailey, to make her hesitate or, worse, to appraise her appearance. The kettle was close to boiling, as was she. There was a visceral, violent fury welling up inside that she'd never felt towards anyone. She wanted to find the girls who had dared do these things, and to hunt them down and kill them – no, torture them first and then kill them. If one of them had been stupid enough to wander into her kitchen at that moment, she was sure she'd have grabbed the kettle and scalded her smug, complacent face so that no one would ever vote her the prettiest on Facebook ever again.

Calm down, Sasha, she told herself, scared by the powerful rage she felt.

'They called me hipster boy,' Bailey continued.

'What? Isn't that a good thing?'

'Because they said I had a beard like someone who lives in East London. And I like checked shirts.'

'Quite the wits, aren't they?'

'They think so. They also called me fur-face and wolf girl.'

Boiling water is too good for them, thought Sasha, I will hunt them down and pour bubbling hot wax over them and see how they feel about depilation now. That'll be a Brazilian they'll never forget. 'I'm sorry,' she croaked.

Bailey shrugged. 'S'not your fault. And it wasn't so bad. I mean, like you always say, sticks and stones . . .'

'. . . may break my bones.'

'Yeah. I kind of knew they were stupid and annoying and it didn't really matter.'

That's my girl, Sasha thought, but she knew there was worse to come.

Bailey continued. 'So like it was fine and stuff, but then it wasn't.'

'What happened?' Sasha was desperate to find out but at the same time was desperate not to know. She wanted to remain in a state of ignorance, for she knew that whatever it was would make her so angry that she'd never want to sleep again. That every night when she went to bed, she'd be plagued with imaginary conversations with whoever had hurt her daughter.

'They kept saying I was too ugly to rape.' Bailey looked embarrassed. Sasha had tried to be the sort of parent who could talk about sex with her child, but Bailey had never let her.

'That is not OK,' said Sasha, quietly, fearfully.

'No, it's all right. Words will never hurt me.'

Sasha's heart actually seemed to cleave at her daughter's stoic bravery, but then she thought, if words can't hurt her, what did? There was silence.

'Please, Bailey.' She stirred the tea bag in the boiled water so vigorously that it burst, vomiting its leaves into the cup.

'There were these boys from Drapers.' This was the nice boys' school that Bailey's nice girls' school did debates and drama with. Sasha remembered those boys, who despite their parents' money were, on the whole, not particularly nice after all. One day, soon really, Spike, her darling skinny-ribbed boy, would probably be one of them.

'And?'

'So Annabel, Christy and Ella would get these boys to follow me to the bus stop every day. Well maybe not every day, but it didn't matter if they did or not because I was afraid every day, which was the worst bit. I spent all afternoon wondering if they were going to be there or not. In a weird way, it might have been easier if it had been every day.'

'What did they say?' What did they do? thought Sasha, but she couldn't even voice the question. She turned round to look at Bailey, who was deep red and stroking Rafa manically. He didn't seem to mind too much, perhaps still suffering the effects of the gas poisoning.

'They'd follow behind me, really close, so that I could feel their breath on my neck, and they'd be saying, "too ugly to rape, too ugly to rape", over and over again. Like a chant.'

'Oh sweetheart, I'm sorry. That's a horrible thing to have to hear.'

'That's how it started, but that's not all.' Bailey's head drooped.

Sasha said nothing, but allowed Bailey to continue to tickle Rafa's tummy.

'They followed me . . . Oh God, this is so embarrassing. I can't talk about it.'

'Do you want to write it down?' This was a parenting technique she'd read about in a book a long time ago.

'That would be even worse. I don't want to see it in writing. I really don't.' Bailey sighed and took a deep breath, as if preparing to dive to the bottom of a swimming pool. 'They'd follow me and then two of them would hold me and one of the others would . . . he'd . . .'

Sasha held her breath, waiting for her daughter to speak. No, no, no, a voice in her head kept saying. If it was what she feared, it would be a punishment for what Ned had done, might have done, all those years ago.

'He'd like go as if he was going to force himself on me, kissing and stuff, I suppose, and then he'd pull back and make gagging sounds and they'd all say "too ugly to rape" again. And laugh. A lot.'

'So they didn't do anything to you, actually *do* anything? You know what I'm talking about, don't you?'

She nodded. 'Rape.' There, she'd said it; it was just a word, please God, let it be just a word. 'No. That's the thing, I'm too ugly to rape. One time, they had a competition where they dragged me into an alleyway and opened my shirt and like, sort of, pulled me out of my bra, and then they all pulled down their trousers and pants and stuff to show that none of them . . . like, they were all soft. These are teenage boys, Mum. Annabel says she can't walk past a boy without him . . . they say stuff like it's the Eiffel Tower down his pants. Ella says she only has to look at a boy and he – sorry, Mum, I'm only saying what she says – and he shoots his load. When those boys did that competition to check that none of them found me in the slightest, littlest bit attractive, one boy did get hard, like a tiny bit, and the others were all like "urgh, you've got a semi, you fancy her, you want some of her Bailey's Irish Cream", and then they pushed him towards me. With his pants down.'

'And did he do anything?'

'No, he drooped when he got near me. Because, obviously, I'm too ugly to rape.'

'Don't be silly, Bailey, he didn't do anything because

he was surrounded by his friends and that's hardly condu-
cive to being . . .' Sasha paused, looking for an appropriate
word, 'aroused.'

'No, I'm hideous. I'm wolf girl.' She shrugged, heart-
breakingly stoical.

Sasha felt pulled in all directions. Relieved that her
daughter had not been abused – well, at least not pene-
trated. Aggrieved that these horrible snotty, spotty boys
would reject her lovely, clever, unique Bailey. And furious
with those vile girls and boys from their nice comfortable homes who could be so cruel to someone so beloved
and special. And kind, smart, quirky Bailey *was* special.
All that time Sasha had worried about her being
different from other teenage girls, when she should have
celebrated it. Why be like all the other girls when those
girls were so shallow and heartless? She put out a hand
towards her daughter, wanting to pull her into a hug,
to sit her on her lap as if she were still a small child.
To at the very least remove the flatulent canine that was
between them.

'I feel so ashamed,' Bailey said.

'Darling, you've nothing to be ashamed of. It's those
girls, that horrible Annabel who I've never liked, and
those boys. They should be mortified. Their parents
will be.'

'Don't tell anybody!' said Bailey.

'But I have to. We have to find some way of putting a
stop to this. It's assault and it has to end. We need to do
something for you and for anybody else who might be a
victim of bullying.'

'But then everyone will know.'

'I'm sure it will all be handled discreetly. You have nothing to be ashamed of. You're the victim here, not them.' Her damn mobile began to ring, but Sasha ignored it. Nothing should interrupt Bailey now she had finally begun to tell her what had been corroding her delicate teenage soul.

Bailey hung her head. 'You don't understand. It's the fact that I'm so disgusting and everyone knows it. I'm ashamed of that. Everyone will know that it's true, that I really am too ugly to rape.'

Sasha looked at her, and so much of the last six months began to make sense. She now understood why her daughter had, almost overnight, begun to wear those shapeless, baggy clothes and hide behind an unwashed curtain of hair. She was trying to own her rejection. It's not that I'm too ugly to rape, she was saying, I have chosen to make myself so. The poor girl was mortified at being considered 'unfit' by a revolting group of teenage boys, but also, probably, ashamed that this should cause her such anguish. She was as much shamed by not being abused as by the threat of it. There had probably been a terrible part of her that had wanted the boy with the flaccid dick to be able to attack her, just to prove them wrong. Her darling girl had been suffering for all these months and she, her own mother, hadn't been able to find a way for her to talk about it.

But somebody else had.

'Bailey, I'm so sorry this has happened to you, and we will work out a way, together, to try to make things better.

But there's one thing I need to know. How did Rosie become involved? Why was she giving you lifts?'

'I don't know really. Luck, I guess. About a month ago, she happened to be in the side street and saw what happened with the boys. The usual, the pulling open my coat and stuff, and then the chanting.'

Rosie 'happened' to be there, thought Sasha. In a conversation filled with unwelcome revelations, the fact that her daughter was being stalked by a woman who felt wronged by her father was of little comfort. And yet, as with all her feelings about what she had heard that morning, there was ambivalence. A small part of her felt grateful that Rosie had been there to protect Bailey when she herself had failed.

'Rosie intervened, told them to fuck off. Those were her words. And the boys just ran away.' Bailey gave a rueful laugh. 'Honestly, they were pathetic, so scared of this little woman.'

'And she started giving you lifts?'

'Not every day. Just on some days, as she works part time. She'd text me to let me know when. But it was enough to mean that the boys didn't know where I would be. They used to ambush me on the way to the bus stop, but I went a different way to meet Rosie, and so when I did catch the bus, they stopped being there.'

'Rosie helped you break the pattern?'

'Yes. But it was more than that. She talked about stuff with me. Like a mum but not my mum.'

Sasha flinched.

'Not like you're a bad mum, honestly,' said Bailey. 'It's

just that I knew you'd be upset and go to the head and all that.'

'Exactly as I've just said I will.'

'Yeah. Rosie didn't try to fix it or anything, she just listened. And then she talked about female empowerment and how rape isn't an act of desire but of power and that what they said, the too ugly bit, was crap and that I should be proud there was something inside me that stopped them. That I was too powerful.'

'She made you feel better.' Sasha felt ashamed that Rosie should have recognised the glory of Bailey's uniqueness before she had done.

'Yes. I sort of know now that it's not my fault that they didn't have sex with me. And it's not my fault that they followed me in the first place. The thing is,' said Bailey, 'Rosie has got experience of this kind of stuff, and she's really sorted about it now.'

Really? thought Sasha. So sorted that she's ingratiated herself into the life of my darling fifteen-year-old daughter.

'In what way?'

'She told me that years ago she actually did get, like, raped I suppose, by this man, and nobody believed her because they said she wasn't good-looking enough for it to have happened. But it did and it showed me that what you look like has nothing to do with this sort of thing. Like, there are old ladies who get attacked by men years younger than them. It's about power. Rosie said those boys didn't need to, because they were getting power just by not doing so.'

'She's right.' Sasha said the words and then a second later, she felt them. Rosie is right.

But if Rosie was right, what did that make Ned?

And following those thoughts to their logical conclusion, what did it make her for wanting to ignore whatever had happened with Rosie all those years ago?

Tamsin tried to keep cool. She couldn't let John suspect anything. Today, an ordinary day in March, she was finally going to be reunited with the only man who'd ever really mattered.

'Are you all right?' asked John.

'Yes, fine. What do you mean?'

'You look a bit flushed.'

This made Tamsin blush some more. 'Yes, maybe I feel a bit hot, now you mention it. Perhaps I'm getting this flu thing. There's a lot of it going round.'

'Going round where?' asked John.

'Nowhere. I'm sure I'm fine.'

'You ought to stay in bed just in case,' he said.

'Maybe I will.' She smiled and rubbed his arm. 'But please don't worry about me, honey. I'll call you if I feel worse. Aren't you supposed to have left by now?'

'Why don't you get back into bed. Wear this.' He pulled out a coral-coloured negligee. His taste was usually so impeccable, but Tamsin thought the colour would do her flushed cheeks no favours.

'Of course. Whatever you say, John.'

'And text me a photo of yourself in it later. I don't want to be worrying about you. You know you're very delicate, my little one.'

'You really take care of me.' She'd said that a thousand

times and had really meant it, but today she was just going through the motions.

'I'm the only one who cares about you. Not your parents, not these friends you've started seeing, not your brothers or your sister. Remember how you were when we met? You were a mess. I've been taking care of you ever since.'

She turned around to get into the negligee and then into bed, figuring that the quicker she acquiesced, the quicker he might leave. She had waited sixteen years to see Mickey again. She did not want to wait another sixteen. She had two and a half hours to go – time for John to leave and for her to get herself ready. After all this time, so little time.

'Where's Rafa?' was the first thing Clem asked her when they'd been reunited in a family room. They were all considered well but were hanging around in an awful abeyance that reminded Emily of the last time she'd stayed in hospital, in fact the only occasions she'd stayed the night: the three times she'd had her children. You were all dressed and desperate to go home, but then they kept you hanging about with inexplicable bureaucracy and form-filling.

'I don't know, sweetheart. I'll try Sasha again. She was supposed to be going to find him but she's not answering her phone.' She shook her head. 'Still no answer. I'll text her.'

Matt held her hand, looking equally anxious. That damn dog had been a symbol of their move out to the country and now it seemed to have become a vessel for all their hopes for the future. If Rafa was OK, they would be too.

She looked at Matt. 'What we were talking about earlier . . .'

He glanced at the children, sitting playing with his phone on the bed. 'Sorry. Please don't worry. It was a problem. It's not any more. I promise you.'

'But you will tell me?'

He nodded. 'It's been awful. But it's OK now. I hope you'll be able to forgive me.'

Emily felt doom claw at her body in a way that she knew had nothing to do with the after-effects of the gas poisoning.

Sasha dropped Spike off at a friend's house for breakfast with profuse apologies and a box of Shreddies. Bailey sat next to her in the car, still with Rafa on her lap.

They drove in silence. Her daughter would not be going to school today. She would go back there, possibly, but not that day or that week. Sasha tried to suppress the hatred she felt towards Annabel and the others. They were pretty girls, much as she herself had been at that age, and she remembered that even the skinny-legged hair-flickers were beset by all the uncertainties of adolescence. Well that was what she tried to think, but instead she entertained thoughts of hanging them off the bridge across the motorway by those glossy locks.

There had probably been girls to whom she had been casually cruel at school. When you were rich in the currency of femininity, it was all too easy to laugh at those who were poor or bankrupt. For all those girls, the plain ones, the fat ones, the spotty ones, the greasy-haired ones, the shy ones, she felt a belated pain.

She waited at the junction that signalled the end of the village. Their tiny main road, blocked on both sides by parked cars, was perpendicular to one of those country A roads that claimed the lives of at least one motorcyclist and an eighteen-year-old boy with a new driving licence every year. The parish council argued to no avail for traffic lights to stop the big beasts of the main road. In the Darwinian logic of traffic, they were the lions, and they weren't inclined to take pity on those antelopes trying to make it out of the village.

Taking a glance at Bailey, who was staring out of the window, she vowed to concentrate on this manoeuvre. She never knew why she worried about cancer when this junction, which she attempted almost daily in a bid to escape the village towards the sunlit uplands of the local supermarket, would be far more likely to put her in hospital.

Someone let me in, she mentally commanded the speeding cars that passed her making the sorts of noises more normally associated with Formula 1. She saw a large black Range Rover slow down and indicate left into the village. The protocol was, in these cases, that the driver coming from the village would be allowed to pull out first on to the main road, because everyone knew that otherwise you'd be forced into playing chicken ever to have any hope of escape.

She readied herself to pull out, but the black hulk of the car just swung in, denying her a precious opportunity and almost forcing her into a ditch as it did so.

'Bastard,' she shouted, catching sight of Tamsin's husband John at the wheel. Wasn't that just typical of him? Not content with controlling his child bride (admittedly a child bride now over the age of thirty), he was also the sort of dick who never let in other cars.

'Mum, don't swear,' said Bailey, the first words she'd uttered since they'd got into the car.

'Men, they just think they own everything: the roads, our bodies, our minds. The bloody leg room on the bus.'

'When was the last time you caught a bus, Mum? Anyway, I didn't know you were such a rad fem.'

'I was. Then I wasn't. Now I think I am again.' She glanced over at Bailey and smiled. 'There's nothing like having a teenage daughter to make one wary of men.'

'Thanks,' Bailey said. 'I think.'

Thank goodness John had finally left to drive to Kent. Tamsin only had an hour to go. Not that she even required that time; there was no need to wax or pluck, since living with John meant she was always kept in a date-ready state of perfect hairlessness. Although when she thought about it, she'd been all natural the last time Mickey had been anywhere near her, apart from some rudimentary leg-shaving. Maybe he didn't like smooth women. An hour, however, would not be long enough to grow all her pubic hair back.

An hour to go. The timer in her head that she now realised had been running for sixteen years was finally approaching the alarm.

Sasha left Bailey with Rafa while she ran into the hospital to find Emily. It was mean of her, she realised, not to have called with reassurance about the dog, but she'd been distracted by Bailey and now she needed to see the sweet relief at her good news to cleanse her palate of the bitterness of all she'd heard.

She only just caught them as they stood, a confused family of refugees wearing coats over their pyjamas, in the hospital atrium.

'Sasha,' said Emily with anxiety. 'Where's Rafa?'

'Look outside.'

Bailey stood with Rafa's head poking out of her black coat. He seemed to have twisted his underbite into a canine smile.

The whole family burst into various levels of excitement. The children shrieked while their parents let out loud exhalations of relief. They all ran outside to greet him.

'Rafa,' said Emily, her eyes welling up again. 'You saved our lives, you damn dog.'

He made weird noises that were neither animal nor human, a growling hum that was hard to interpret. Bailey carefully put him on the pavement, where he celebrated his survival with a sort of break dance, rolling over and then spinning.

Emily crouched down. 'I'm so sorry, Rafa, that I ever said those rude things to you.'

'Why were you rude to him?' asked Bailey indignantly.

'I don't know. He just seemed so weird. And he was the only person I had to talk to until I became friends with your mother. He became a sort of talisman for all my problems. I thought he was mad. Well, either him or me, I couldn't decide. You must admit that he is a bit strange.'

Rafa bared his teeth by way of acknowledgement or denial.

'He's not weird,' said Bailey. 'He's just got problems with his teeth.'

'What do you mean?' asked Sasha in surprise, not having thought of her daughter as having any veterinary knowledge.

'It's obvious. He grinds his teeth like I used to until I got my brace. Do you remember those headaches I used to have every morning? His teeth don't fit his mouth for some reason. What sort of dog is he anyway?'

'A Jack-a-poo, allegedly,' said Emily, reminded of the conversation that she'd had with Ben where he'd questioned Rafa's provenance. 'Oh God, I think he might have come from a puppy farm.'

'A what?' said Sasha.

'It's a puppy breeding factory,' said Bailey, filled with teenage righteousness. 'You must never, ever get a pet from one as it only encourages them. They're all about making money rather than animal well-being. It's really important to see your family pet at home, where it's been born, and to meet its parents.'

'How do you know so much about it?' Sasha felt that she was getting to know Bailey as if they'd only recently become acquainted.

'Because I want a dog. I've wanted one for ever. I've got lots of pictures on my phone of my favourites. You can imagine what Annabel says about me liking dogs.'

'Why didn't you say?'

'Because I knew you'd say no. You hate dogs.'

'I promise you now, in front of these witnesses, that we will get you a dog.'

Bailey rushed over to hug her, and Sasha felt as if it had been years since she'd had her daughter's arms around her. It made her feel both saviour and saved.

'I'm such an idiot,' said Emily. 'I think you're right. I think Rafa is like one of those Romanian orphans that needs to be taught how to love. That's what Ben was trying to say to me.'

'Ben?' said Matt with suspicion.

Sasha could have sworn Emily blushed. 'Tania's husband. We sometimes walk the dogs together and I think he was too polite to spell it out to me. I think he might have post-traumatic stress disorder.'

'Who, Ben?' asked Matt.

'No, Rafa. Seriously,' said Emily. 'Maybe he was kept in a small cage like a battery chicken. Maybe he's inbred and he's got a Habsburg chin. He gets really panicked in small places.'

'He bit the fireman when he tried to put him in a cage,' added Sasha.

'That's it. It's because he remembers his childhood. He's definitely got PTSD.'

Matt laughed. 'You're always ascribing weird psychological syndromes to people; now you've started on dogs.'

'You're so right,' said Sasha. 'She does like labelling human quirks. Like you said John was financially abusing Tamsin. Mind you, if he treats her like he treats other drivers, he's certainly got aggression issues. He almost ran me off the road on the way here.'

'He what?' said Emily with alarm.

'Aw, that's nice of you to be so concerned about me. I thought he was going to let me out as he turned into the village, but oh no, not a bit of it. He was in quite the hurry.'

'Shit,' said Emily, and her children turned to her in fascination.

'We're fine, don't worry,' said Sasha.

'I'm not worried about you. It's Tamsin. She's meeting Mickey today.'

'What?' Sasha looked at Emily's stricken face. 'Where?'

'The Nell. Where else?' Emily was pacing frantically in her best imitation of Rafa's manic tail-chasing. 'John's not supposed to be here. He's supposed to be away, down in Kent for work as usual. That's what Tamsin thought. I wonder if he knows somehow?'

Sasha looked worried, and then shrugged. 'Even if he

does know that Tamsin's meeting her ex-boyfriend, he's not going to know where she is, is he?'

'I think he will. I think he's put one of those "Find My Friends" apps on her phone so he can keep tabs on her. She said he always seems to know what she's been doing. He might go there – and I don't know what could happen.'

'God, Emily, did you not perhaps think of the consequences when you started encouraging Tamsin's ridiculous teen romance?'

'I know, I know. It's just . . .'

'Just what?'

'It gave me something to do,' she said pathetically. 'We need to go there to warn her.'

'Having seen the way he was driving, he's certainly dangerous. Anyway, how do we know that this person you've been contacting is the real Mickey? Even if it is, he's got to be some sort of weirdo to have written this book. He might harm her.' Sasha knew she was wrong to think that all men were abusers, but nothing that had happened recently was dissuading her of the notion.

'I don't have the least idea what you're talking about,' said Matt. 'But we don't have a car here, since Emily and the kids came by ambulance and I came by minicab.'

'Come on,' said Sasha. 'I'll take you back in mine.'

'Can you fit us all in?' asked Matt.

Sasha did a quick headcount and nodded. 'No worries, it's a seven-seater.' She'd bought it so that her parents could come away on weekends with them. And though they had, she'd never needed to fold down the extra seats, since Ned had never been there with them. 'Emily, you and I can.go to the Nell and see if there's anything going on.'

'We need to hurry,' said Emily, checking the time on her phone. 'They're supposed to be meeting at eleven.'

12

Return to the Nell

Tamsin stopped for a second as she approached the Nell. The brambles had grown wilder in the spring sunshine, making it look even more enchanting to her. It had been so cold last night as she lay awake, but now it felt like summer would one day come. But even with the sun on her face, she'd known to leave some blankets there the previous day, just in case.

She pushed her way through and the door opened easily, now that it had been forced so many times. Checking her phone for the time, yet again, she realised she had ten minutes to go. How should she position herself? If she sat on one of the blankets, she'd have to scramble up, which would ruin the moment. Maybe she should stand by the window so that the light would fall through its metal-veined panes to light her becomingly. Or would it make her look old? She would look old, wouldn't she, while in her mind Mickey was still a skinny boy.

He had filled her thoughts for so many years, but she had long since stopped daring to hope that they'd ever see each other again. The first year, that hope had been the only thing that had stopped her raiding the paracetamol cupboard, but after that it had faded as she had become thin and wan.

She had imagined their reunion so many times, but had never fully realised the vision. It was more 'Mickey!' then 'Tammy!' and a blurry embrace, then a happy-ever-after without any clue as to what that might entail. Other times, when she needed to get herself wet for John, she'd allowed her mind to fashion from her memories what the TV called 'scenes of a sexual nature'. But even those were a bit hazy, like an old-fashioned soft-porn film, where what was shown was more about the loving embrace than the rude mechanics.

Five minutes to go.

Four.

What if he were late?

She checked her phone again.

Two minutes to go.

Then, suddenly and yet so expectedly, she heard a man's exclamation as he grappled with the brambles, and the door opened.

'It's all my fault,' said Emily from the passenger seat of Sasha's car, Matt having been banished to sit with the children behind them.

'Hmm.'

'You're supposed to make me feel better. Oh God, what have I done? What do you think John will do?'

Sasha shrugged. 'Listen, we don't know if John even knows something is going on. We don't know if Mickey is actually going to turn up. For all we know, someone else might have masterminded the whole thing and is pretending to be Mickey. Maybe Tamsin herself, because she so longs for it to be true.'

Emily was wide-eyed. 'Do you really think that?'

'No, I don't. It's too far-fetched. Tamsin isn't as silly as she believes herself to be, but I don't think she's got it in her to cook up such a complicated plot. Though even if the book was written by the real Mickey, it's still a bit weird.'

'You're right. But what if they, you know, reignite what went on before?' She glanced back to see if the children were eavesdropping, which inevitably they were. 'And John finds them. In flagrante delicto.' She knew the children didn't understand the phrase.

'I think I know what that means, but I suspect it's too cold for that sort of thing. But like I say, I don't think we should speculate. You like drama, don't you, Emily? That's what got you sucked into this in the first place.'

Emily felt chastened. She wanted Sasha to like her so much, but she'd seen through her altruism into the hollow life that she had been living. 'You're right, of course. Are you always right?'

Sasha gave a rueful laugh. 'No, absolutely not. I feel I've been wrong about so many things. But I'm going to try to put them right.'

'It's almost eleven. He could be there.'

'John or Mickey?'

'Both. I know you can't drive any faster . . .'

'So please don't ask me to. When are you allowed back into your house?'

Emily hadn't thought about that, though she wasn't sure whether this avoidance had been deliberate. In between worrying about Rafa, Matt's unrevealed revelations and now Tamsin, there hadn't been a lot of space in her gas-addled brain. 'Good question. I guess I need to speak to the fire people to check if it's safe. I'm not sure I ever want to go back. Last night was awful. I keep thinking about what might have happened.' She shivered.

'You're probably still in shock.'

'No, just cold. Can I borrow something to wear when we get to yours?'

'Of course. Then we'll head off to the Nell. I'm sure it will all be fine.'

If it's not, thought Emily, it will be my fault.

Tamsin turned around to face the door, hardly able to believe that the moment she'd waited for all these years had finally arrived.

'Oh,' was all she could say as she saw . . . not red-haired, skinny Mickey; so very definitely not Mickey.

She stood still, waiting for him to speak, but he did not; he just stared at her as if appraising a painting that he might buy.

At last she spoke. 'John. What are you doing here?'

'I was about to ask you the same question.'

'I was just, er, hanging out.'

He glanced around the asphalt grey of the room, his gaze alighting on the blankets, blankets from his home, in the corner. 'Waiting for someone?'

'No.' Oh no, Mickey, please don't come now.

'You come to this place,' he glanced around it again, with even more disgust, 'rather a lot, don't you?'

'No,' she repeated.

'But you do. Don't lie to me. Why are you lying to me, Tamsin?'

'I'm not,' she stuttered.

'You can do nothing without me knowing. That's because you're my wife.' He emphasised the 'my'. 'Your phone tells me exactly where you are, and it told me that you kept coming to this horrible place.'

'It's not horrible,' she whispered.

'What did you say?'

'I said, it's not horrible.'

He shook his head. 'Then you're even more stupid than I thought. I can't believe you'd do this, behind my back, after all I've done for you.'

She was afraid of how calm he was being, but then she realised that she didn't care. What could he do to her? If she didn't see Mickey, she'd die again anyway, like she had died inside all those years ago. No one could hurt you when you were already dead. It was Mickey she worried about. If he turned up here and there was some sort of confrontation between him and John . . . well, Mickey had never come out of it very well when his mum's boyfriend Dave had turned on him.

'I'm not stupid,' she said. 'Well, I have been very stupid, but I think it's possible that one day I won't be.'

John's body went from rigid and forbidding to softer, his arms unfolding and opening towards her. 'Love,' he said, 'it's fine, I don't mind that you are.' He walked towards her, his arms now above his head as if in surrender, but she knew that was not how he intended it to be.

Sasha and Emily dumped the car in the lay-by at the side of the road, stealing the space from an Audi that was indicating that it wanted the same spot, and started to hurry over the fields towards the Nell.

Being distracted by Tamsin's predicament had allowed Sasha's mind some clarity over the whole issue of Rosie and her own marriage, like the way solutions to problems came just as you were about to fall asleep. The less she thought about it directly, the more her path emerged until she was almost at the point where it felt as though there was no longer any decision to make. Just people to be told. Or not. Would it really make any difference to the way her life was lived?

It was strange, but she felt a sort of kinship with Rosie now, and gratitude that her actions had delivered Bailey back to her. She, Bailey and Rosie were a circle of women who needed to protect one another as no one had protected Rosie back then. 'Everyone,' Ned had said to her by way of defence, 'knew it was impossible that I'd have had to force myself on her.' He was handsome Ned, she was plain Rosie, obviously. That was what they had said, that Rosie was too ugly to rape, just as they were saying to Bailey now.

There were so many ways in which her marriage had died, but it had taken Rosie to show her that there really was no pulse.

Emily suddenly stopped, sending Sasha crashing into her.

'Shh,' she said, ducking behind a tree and beckoning for Sasha to do the same.

'What?'

'I saw a man go in there. Right ahead of us.'

'Mickey?'

'I don't know. I've never met him. It was too far away for me to see anything really. I suppose I don't even know if it was a man.'

'What should we do?' asked Sasha.

'I don't know.'

'Well it was your idea that she meet Mickey.'

'I know, I know. I don't think we should interrupt. If we go round the back, we can look through the window in case something goes wrong.'

'Like what?'

Emily shrugged helplessly. 'We're just keeping her safe.'

They manoeuvred themselves round the Nell, through the brambles, as quietly as they could until they reached the window. It was hard to see through the patina of dirt that coated it. Sasha longed to clean it like the smeared lenses on the glasses she now had to wear for reading. But gradually her eyes became accustomed to looking through the gloom of the dirty panes, and she could make out two figures, a man and a woman. They were embracing.

'Shit,' whispered Emily. 'It's John, isn't it?'

Sasha squinted and could see that it was not so much an embrace as Tamsin collapsed in supplication in John's arms. 'Where's Mickey?'

'I don't know,' said Emily, her voice shaky. 'If he turns up . . . I feel so guilty. I should never have got so involved.'

They crouched with their backs against the wall beneath the window, getting their breath back while trying to work out what, if anything, they should do.

'What do you think is going on?' asked Sasha.

'I don't know. I don't understand any of it really.' Emily gave a quiet giggle of barely suppressed hysteria. 'I'm so relieved that Mickey's not here. I was worried something terrible would happen and it would all be my fault.'

Their calm was jolted by the sound of a twig snapping.

'What's that?' said Sasha.

'An animal?' said Emily, hopefully. 'There are lots of rabbits round here.' She shimmied up to look through the window again. 'Oh God.'

Sasha leapt up to join her. 'Oh God,' she echoed.

Tamsin had moved herself so that she could keep an eye on the door, while remaining locked in John's embrace. And then, there he was, just as he had promised.

As soon as she saw him, she wondered how she'd ever thought she wouldn't recognise him. He looked so different and yet so much the same. Less hair, more body, but still so utterly him, with the swagger that never seemed arrogant and the look of amused curiosity that he'd worn when he'd come into the classroom all those years ago.

She tried to gesture behind John's back with her arms and eyes that he should retreat. It was hard, because every cell of her wanted to shout his name and run to him, but she had to protect him as she'd never been able to do back then, when his little white body had been bruised by Dave. Some muscle memory made her own body twitch in longing for him.

'Tammy,' he said out loud. His voice was posher than before, and deeper.

John immediately disentangled himself and turned around.

What to do? She had to let Mickey know that she had been waiting for him and that John wasn't supposed to be here, but how to do so without enraging John? She felt as if Mickey had caught her being unfaithful with another man, when of course her intention had been to commit adultery with *him*. She should never have slept with anyone else when Mickey had left. It had been an act of betrayal. Marrying John had been the worst of all. She shrugged off her husband and ran forward to Mickey, standing in front of him, not touching. She felt as though she was looking into a mirror that showed her how she had once been, what she might have become.

'Mickey, I'm sorry. I don't know what he's doing here. I've been waiting for you for so long.'

John looked at her in confusion. 'Mickey? The one your parents told me about? The skanky little twat who broke your heart?'

'That's the one,' said Mickey, smiling at Tamsin. 'I'm so sorry, Tammy, believe me. It was Dave. I had to leave, I wasn't allowed to tell anyone where I was.'

'I know,' said Tamsin. John had evaporated; now there

was only her and Mickey, just as there had been all those years ago. 'I didn't for ages, I thought you'd abandoned me, but now I understand what happened.'

'I would never leave you,' he said. 'I won't. I've been trying to find you for so long. I've been searching and searching, trying to find clues, your electronic trail, but you're a ghost. Your parents sold their house, didn't they?'

'How did you know?'

'I had an alert set up with one of those property search websites that let me know when anything in the village came up for sale. That's when I started to write the book. I thought that if they'd moved, I'd lose you for ever, and even if I never saw you again, I wanted to remember it all. I felt sad that we'd never go back to your old house. Do you remember that time they were on holiday and we had the whole place to ourselves?'

Tamsin shivered with delighted recollection. They had closed all the curtains and shagged in every room, including her parents' bedroom, on top of her mother's favourite quilt, the one that was dry-clean only.

'I wrote to you at that address, lots of times, but you never replied.'

'I never got the letters.' The teenage rebellion that had led her to frenzied underage sex with Mickey in the Nell revived in her. 'Fuckers that my parents are. They say they want the best for me, but I don't think they ever did. I wonder if they read them.'

'Probably burned them. Pikey Mikey was what I was called in the village, wasn't I?'

'Oh Mickey, I'm sorry. If I'd known . . .'

John gave out a sound, a groan or a moan, something almost inhuman. Mickey and Tamsin turned regretfully away from each other to look at him.

'He's nobody, Mickey. There's only been you.'

This dismissal rallied John. 'Nobody?' he shouted. 'I'm your husband.'

'You're married?' asked Mickey, his voice honeyed with hurt. 'I never married.' He took a step backwards, as if retreating from her.

She nodded, filled with despair. 'But I'm not married in my heart. I never was. I feel like life stopped when you left.' She didn't care about John and what he heard, only that she should explain how she'd never stopped loving Mickey. 'When you left, I was broken. It felt like he rescued me, but I know now that he didn't. Nothing has really touched me since you left. Reading your book was the first time I've been alive in all these years.'

'I wrote it for you. I was desperate. All the searching . . . and nothing. I was worried you were dead.'

'She will be,' shouted John, finally shaking off the paralysis that Mickey's arrival had caused.

Both Sasha and Emily leapt away from the window and ran around to the door of the Nell. Emily had only met John a couple of times, when his voice had always been loud, confident, brooking no argument. This was higher-pitched and full of misery, despite its threat.

'Shit,' she muttered. Everything she had heard about John made him sound like a monster. And people in the country often had guns, didn't they, even rather urbane property developers like him? It had been her fault that Mickey and Tamsin had met like this, and it would be her fault if anything happened to them.

Her brisk walks with Rafa meant that she was fitter than Sasha and arrived at the door first, covered in scratches and out of breath. The door had been left wedged ajar by the spikes of the brambles, and she didn't have time to stop and wonder what she might see.

Sasha cursed the nettles, Emily, Tamsin and then the brambles, before cursing her own lack of fitness. She almost hurtled into Emily, who was marooned at the entrance to the Nell, transfixed.

The door was only ajar by about thirty centimetres, meaning that in order to see what was going on, she had to put her head down below Emily's, making them resemble some two-headed beast.

Despite the kerfuffle she and Emily were causing, the protagonists within were able to ignore them, so engrossed were they in each other. As she crouched below Emily, Sasha felt as though she were acting in a farce, while Tamsin, John and the man she supposed to be Mickey were in a drama that she was hoping would not turn into a tragedy.

Far from carrying a weapon or threatening Tamsin and Mickey in any way, John was on his hands and knees before them, keening with grief. Sasha rebuked herself for being repulsed by the sight of a grown man crying great snotty tears, but she had known John for too long to feel much sympathy.

She viewed the scene taking place in the corner of the Nell. Tamsin and Mickey were clutching at each other like the lost teenage lovers they were. Sasha recognised him from all those years ago as much by his stance as by his looks, which had inevitably changed over the decade and a half. When she'd lived at her parents' for that brief few months in her twenties, wherever she went she'd see Tamsin and Mickey, their hands in each other's jeans pockets, extravagantly snogging, or, as Sasha and her friends had so accurately described it when they were that age themselves, 'swapping saliva'. It fairly seemed to dribble off their faces as they'd sat at the bus stop glued to one another.

And now here they were, wrapped around each other as if they were still adolescents with the world against them, but with John taking the role that Tamsin's parents had once played. Back then, they had been the barrier to this great love affair, which might never have flourished with such lasting effects without this impediment.

'Please, Tamsin,' John sobbed, seemingly undone with grief. 'I love you. Don't say that you never loved me.'

Sasha felt a pang of pity, but then reminded herself that what John had shown Tamsin was not love, but control. Maybe he thought they were interchangeable.

Emily muttered, 'Bollocks' at this. Sasha pinched her leg to quieten her, which only resulted in a loud 'Ouch!' Fortunately, the trio at the centre of the drama were too self-absorbed to notice.

But it was as though Tamsin had somehow heard the 'go girl!' thoughts of her friends. 'I don't know, John. I'm not sure you do. I always thought you must love me an awful lot to put up with how weak and useless I was when we met, and how I stayed that way: no job, no friends, no nothing.'

'I did, I do, I love you. I looked after you. I will look after you,' he shouted.

'You say that. But now I see that you didn't love me in spite of my weakness, but because of it. You did nothing to help me become the person I could be. The person I was when I was with Mickey.'

Mickey and Tamsin looked at each other and clung together even harder. 'I love you, Tammy,' Mickey muttered.

Love, present tense.

John groaned some more, then stood up, his face now angry rather than distraught. 'You were nothing when we met.' His finger was jabbing at Tamsin, who stood still, made resolute by the clutch and crutch of Mickey. 'You were a mess who couldn't get out of bed and didn't have a thought in her head. I made you.'

Sasha felt Emily bristle. She felt the same antagonism towards John.

'You can't make people,' said Tamsin. 'I don't think.' Her voice wavered a little.

'Look at you,' he said. 'You're so beautiful now. You live a life that most women can only dream of. You wear those clothes and you sit on my sofas, the ones I choose, the ones that I pay for. You've contributed nothing to our lives and now you say you never loved me.' He paused. 'You ungrateful little whore.'

'Come on, mate,' said Mickey.

'Don't you "mate" me,' spat John, turning on him. 'Who do you think you are? That's my wife you're holding. *My* wife. Her parents told me about you and how you just fucked off one day, leaving her with a broken heart and no GSCEs.'

'I didn't. I had no choice.' He turned to Tamsin. 'I had to go and I couldn't get in touch with anyone because of my mum's ex. Dave threatened to kill her.'

She nodded, now tearful.

'She's my wife,' repeated John. He emphasised the 'my' again.

'Well, she's the mother of my child,' said Mickey.

Sasha couldn't see John's face, but he reeled backwards in shock before saying, 'She's infertile, you fucker.'

She could have sworn that Mickey swaggered slightly as he said, 'She had my baby, didn't you, Tammy?'

Tamsin shook her head.

'See?' said John. 'You're nothing to her, you lying piece of scum.'

Tamsin had been mute as the menfolk fought over her, but now she spoke. 'He's everything to me, John. I was pregnant with his baby. I'm sorry, Mickey.' She began to cry. 'I lost it. Over there.' She gestured towards the corner of the room, underneath the window.

'You lost it?' asked Mickey.

'I don't know why. But it was awful. It just came out, far too early, and I was left with nothing of you.'

'You were pregnant before?' asked John. 'And you never thought to tell me? Or your parents? You don't think this information might have been relevant to us when we were trying for our baby? Our much wanted, *legitimate*' – he shouted the word – 'baby?'

'Yes I was,' said Tamsin, so quietly that Sasha could barely hear her. 'But it died inside me. I couldn't keep it alive because I'd died inside too, when Mickey left me. You always called me your living doll, but I wasn't. I was a dead one. That's why it was so easy to dress me up and tell me what to do, because there was no real me left when Mickey had to leave.'

A roar of pain sounded from John as he came to the belated realisation that his life was a sham. He pulled something out of his pocket that glinted in the light that came in diluted by the dust of the window. Mickey and Tamsin jumped back in fright.

'Jesus,' cried Emily, and she and Sasha pulled at the jammed door as one and burst into the Nell. Sasha could see now that he was brandishing an old-fashioned Swiss Army Knife, the sort of gadget that came in special catalogues for men and boasted twenty different blades including a tin-opener and an implement for removing stones from horseshoes.

John looked round at the interruption. 'What the hell?'

Mickey stayed frozen, staring at John, but Tamsin lurched forward and deliberately pushed her left hand into the knife. As blood spurted out, Sasha felt her mouth fill with bile.

Tamsin stood holding her hand up like an emblem as blood continued to drip on to the concrete floor, just as it had done all those years ago. She almost seemed to be smiling, proudly displaying the stigmata of her wound.

'Stop,' was all she said.

Sasha went to her. 'You need to get this seen to. It could have cut an artery or something.' She turned round to look at John, who was now lying sobbing on the floor. He had seemed so big and powerful, his cars increasing in size as his wife diminished, but now it was as if the curtain had been pulled back to reveal a feeble man pulling the levers. He hadn't been attracted to Tamsin because he was strong, but because he was weak and she was even more fragile than him.

They all stood frozen for what seemed like an age, with the bleeding woman at the centre of their pageant.

'Stop,' Tamsin said again. She looked with wonder at the gaping wound in her hand, feeling somehow as if the blood draining out of it was giving her power rather than taking it away. He can't hurt me any more, nothing can. She had chosen to let the blade enter her to protect Mickey. She had not been there to stop his mum's boyfriend, but she could stand between him and her husband.

'Please, Tamsin, you've got to do something about that hand,' said Sasha again, while Emily looked as though she were about to be sick. Through the blood on her hand, Tamsin thought she could see something white – fat or bone, who knew?

Mickey took off his jumper and began to wrap it around her hand in an attempt to staunch the flow. She smiled at him. If only he'd been there with her all those years ago, when she had been bleeding before.

'Get her out of here, Mickey,' said Sasha. 'Both of you, go to hospital and get it sorted.'

'But what about him?' Mickey asked.

'Take the knife too,' ordered Sasha. 'Look after it in case we need to give it to someone later.'

Tamsin watched Mickey pick the knife up. She hadn't been frightened when John got it out. She'd spent so long being scared of him and his reaction to her – if she put on weight, wore the wrong clothes, spoke to anybody he hadn't pre-approved – that she felt as though she'd used up all the fear she might have had and there was nothing left but pity.

John started howling again, and she now felt only revulsion. This is for all the years you didn't even let me have pocket money, she thought. This is for our neighbour Lucy, this is for stopping me from getting an education, this is for making me eat budget cereal while you got the expensive muesli for yourself. What had she been so afraid of? That he might hurt her? He'd done the worst she could have imagined by bringing that knife out, but it wasn't enough. All it had needed was a few minutes with Mickey for her strength to come back to her and defeat John.

She stood over him for a second, enjoying the moment, then turned and walked out of the Nell with Mickey, perhaps for the last time. He held her hand with his jumper wrapped around it and she felt a memory so powerful it was as if she, like Kez in the book, had finally travelled back in time.

*

Emily felt a delayed shock at the sight of the blood, for which she felt responsible. When she had helped arrange this meeting, she had never foreseen violence, but then again she'd never thought any of it through. If something had happened . . . It hadn't, she told herself, but the frightening 'what if' only added to the same feelings of hypothetical doom that she'd been carrying from the gas leak the night before.

The children, Rafa, Matt, now this. It was all too much and she felt her legs wobble.

'Think,' said Sasha, breaking through her confusion.

They looked at John, who was still lying on the floor, his face splattered with some of the blood that Tamsin had dripped over him. Even prone, he was quite a big man, with a body that looked gym-honed. He was rolled into a foetal ball, sobbing.

'Yes, right. Think, I must think.' Even in her haze, she hadn't lost her desire for Sasha to like her. She stepped back and beckoned Sasha to confer with her. 'I think we leave him here. Enough time has passed, hasn't it, for Mickey and Tamsin to have got away?'

'We can't just leave him,' said Sasha, glancing over to the man felled by misery.

'Why not?'

Sasha looked thoughtful and then shrugged. 'Maybe you're right. He hasn't got anything he can hurt himself with, unless I suppose he smashes a window. But they've got those metal vein things, haven't they, so he can't do that.'

'And if he does hurt himself some other way?' said

Emily. Sasha tried and failed to look shocked at the suggestion that they might leave John to self-harm.

They began to shuffle quietly towards the door. Emily turned to survey the Nell for the last time. It was undeniably ugly, with its grey concrete floor, windows threaded with dirt and air of creepy abandonment. John's sobbing body in the centre of the room made it all worse. She knew it had once been a place of beauty and love for Mickey and Tamsin, and she had, shamefully but only briefly, imagined herself doing something similar with Ben there, but now she knew she never would; nor would she ever, in the words of the book, return to the Nell.

'Do you think he's going to be OK?' she asked Sasha, after they had wriggled through the gap in the door.

'I don't know. I don't really care. He's vile.'

'And what about Mickey and Tamsin?'

'I don't know about them either. I'm afraid I don't share your optimism about the wisdom of reviving teenage romances, but I do see that Tamsin looked happier with her hand dripping blood in a horrible agricultural shed than I've seen her look in years. Since she was a teenager in fact. Perhaps they are each other's soulmates after all. They've both got sort of stuck, haven't they?'

'What do you mean?'

'Tamsin needs to go back to that time in order to finally grow up, and . . . well I don't think you write novels for children unless there's a part of you that hasn't moved on either. It was really quite good, that book.' Sasha looked miserable for a second. 'To be honest, I can't really worry about Tamsin. I've got problems of my own. Well, not exactly problems, decisions, things to do. I've got to move on as well.'

Emily was suddenly reminded of Matt and his unrevealed revelation. 'Oh my God, me too. Matt's going to tell me he's having an affair or something.'

'Really? That doesn't seem very characteristic. He's always been a good man.'

'Yes, he is a good man, but he's got something to tell me. Something pretty serious. Oh dear.'

'What?'

'You know how you said at Tania's party that the divorce rate for weekend wives must be at least two out of every three? I reckon Tamsin's one down, don't you, but I hope the other spot isn't taken by Matt and me.'

'No,' said Sasha with a faint smile. 'I reckon you're OK.'

13

Out of His Misery

As they approached an Audi badly parked on the verge just beyond the lay-by, Mickey got out a key fob from his pocket, pressed it and the car's lights winked in response.

'Oh,' said Tamsin, surprised that he owned a car, let alone this one. In her head, he couldn't drive, just like her, but if he did own anything, surely it should be a camper van or a beaten-up Mini?

'What's wrong?' Mickey asked, looking anxious. She realised that he was just as concerned as she had been with everything about their reunion being perfect, a hope that had been rather squashed by the appearance of a knife-wielding husband.

'Nothing,' she said, climbing into a shiny seat, carefully sticking her bloody hand out of the window so as not to drip on to it. The car had an almost artificially clean smell of pine- and smoke-tinged grooming products. A bit like Mickey himself, who she had imagined would smell of grass, both the sort you lay on and the sort you smoked. 'I'm a bit surprised by your car, that's all. I think I sort of imagined you arriving here on a wild horse or a painted caravan.'

He laughed. 'I think you're confusing me with Jake V.

Bond. That's not me – well, I wrote the book, but I'm not the same as the person described on the back cover. I'm sorry. He's the me that I suppose I wished I could have become.' His voice was different now too, having lost all traces of the Northumbrian accent he'd arrived at school with.

'I'm not who I wanted to be either. So if you don't live in a caravan, where do you live?'

'In a very normal but quite nice flat in London, and I work as a systems analyst for banks.' Tamsin nodded as if she knew exactly what this meant. 'I'm really good at it so I can choose my contracts now, hence being able to write a book in my spare time.'

So he was well paid, though to someone like Tamsin who'd never earned anything apart from the note belatedly pressed into her hand by Sasha for babysitting Spike, all jobs were strange species of golden remuneration.

'I really loved it.'

'Thank you.' He shifted gear, and she couldn't help watching those hands, smooth and hairless, that had once stroked every part of her body.

'What made you write it?'

He looked intently at the road ahead. 'I had a girlfriend.'

Tamsin winced. She knew it wasn't fair to expect him to have remained celibate all these years, especially since she'd got married. 'And?'

'It wasn't working between us so she made me go to couples therapy with her to try to sort things out. I talked about you and the Nell and I realised how stuck I was.'

Just like me, thought Tamsin. 'Go on.'

'So I began to write it down and it all came pouring out as though it were yesterday. And while I was writing it, I realised that with a few changes, I could turn it into a work of fiction, a book about our boy going back in time to meet us.'

'I always thought of our baby as a boy too,' she said. 'Go on.'

'I wasn't intending to publish it or anything, but when I finished it, I showed it to a friend who's an editor, who passed it on to a colleague of hers who works in children's fiction. She suggested I add more of a plot, so I did the bit about the cat murderer.'

'And did you think that somehow I'd get to read it? It sounds mad, but as soon as I opened it, I felt like the book was a message to me, that you were talking to me.'

'Yes, though that came later, once it looked as though it would get published. It was irrational, but I thought, why not? There seemed no other way of finding you, what with you not existing on the web.'

'I changed my name when I got married. John insisted.' How could she have done that? It was as though she had vaporised the girl who'd loved Mickey by burying her along with her name.

'I donated all my author's copies to the primary school in the village more in hope than expectation. As far as I was aware, you no longer lived here anyway.'

'It worked! I did read it because of one of those copies. Sasha, the woman at the Nell, had it at her house because of her son.' From the moment she had met Mickey, it had felt like fate – that he had ended up at her school just when she needed him, that years later his book should have come to her. 'And when I read it, I knew, I just knew. The Nell was our word.'

'Yes, and one that only you and I knew. It had to be our secret.' He sighed. 'You're not the only one with a different name now.'

'What do you mean?' she asked.

'Mum and I, we had to change our name again when we left here. It would have been pretty easy for Dave to find Bonnie Scora, not the commonest surname. I'm Michael Campbell now. We had to keep running away, and in the end, it seemed easier to get whole new names.'

In their different worlds, Tamsin realised, both she and Mickey had been pretending all this time to be different people while at the same time remaining exactly the children from the Nell.

'So why Jake V. Bond?' she asked. 'Why not Michael Campbell?'

'Writing young adult fiction doesn't really fit in with the job of a systems analyst. It wouldn't have made any difference to you finding me anyway, since if you did read it, you'd know who wrote it whatever the author's name was. I just hoped you'd find the website and contact me that way. If you wanted to. You and our boy . . .'

'Oh Mickey, I would have kept the baby, I really wanted it. I'd have done anything to have something of you.'

He nodded, his eyes filling with tears.

'It was awful,' she continued.

'I'm so sorry.'

'No, I am. It was so unfair. I hate my parents for stopping me from getting your letters, and Dave for causing you to go away. I hate John too. I know it's not his fault, but he's helped keep me in this sort of nothingness that I've been in. I've been asleep and I've only just woken up.'

'Aren't I supposed to kiss you for that to happen?' Mickey said, showing that mix of shyness and cockiness that she had first fallen in love with.

She couldn't stop herself from grinning, and then the grin became a giggle, just as it had all those times when he'd passed her notes in class telling her about the deliciously filthy things he'd wanted to do with her. And she wanted him to do them now, too, just as much as she had done then.

Since the next-door village wasn't on any tourist trail, the local pub that Matt and Emily sat in that afternoon was untouched by notions of gastronomy or charm. The menu was on laminated plastic with at least fifty dishes, none of which could have been prepared fresh but would come out of the aptly named coffin freezers flanking the back door that led in from the car park.

The children had been left with Matt's parents, with Sue looking ecstatic about the prospect of having them to herself, a fact that surprised Emily, since she'd always presumed that her mother-in-law preferred dogs. The kids were fine, Emily told herself, but she knew she'd be haunted by the fear that the exposure to gas could have some long-term effects despite the doctor's reassurances, like getting a low grade on their maths GSCE or failing to get into a good university. She had to put aside those worries for now, though, to concentrate on a more pressing anxiety.

'So,' she said to Matt. 'You were saying you had something to tell me, back at the hospital.'

'I did?'

'Don't give me that, Matt. What do you think we're sitting in this pub for? I need to know.'

He sighed and looked into his pint morosely. 'First of all, I'm sorry. Let me say that.'

'You're scaring me. Please tell me what it is.'

'I've been really, really stupid. I've messed it all up and I don't know if you can forgive me.'

'Try me.' She almost didn't care what the revelation was, she just needed him to tell her.

'When I was down in London, I developed, well, a habit.'

'A habit as in a custom, like walking in the park, or a habit as in smoking crack every day?' she asked.

'Not crack or smack, no, as it happens. But it was – is – I suppose, an addiction.' He looked up to the ceiling as if seeking divine inspiration, and was then distracted by the television on the wall that someone had switched on to show that day's sporting events, his face taking on the gaping expression it always seemed to when absorbed by a screen. She snapped her fingers in his face and he looked back at her with reluctance. 'I've always liked sport,' he continued.

She'd read about those middle-aged men who became obsessed with triathlons and Iron Man competitions. That didn't sound so bad, though it did involve the wearing of Lycra. 'Right.'

'I hated being away from you. I could see that it was driving us apart. Every time I came home on a Friday, I felt like an interloper, a third wheel, that I wasn't a real member of the family any more, but a stranger.'

'What's this got to do with sport?'

'I wasn't making enough to provide us with a cushion. We needed that extra money just to cover the cost of living in two places.'

'I know. The financial cost of the weekend wives' life-style,' said Emily. Not to mention the emotional cost.

'Exactly. Without you bringing in money, I felt that me being able to live up here all the time, all of us together as a proper family, was just slipping further and further away. Everything was just so much more expensive than we'd calculated. How did we get it so wrong?'

'That's my fault too.' It felt like this was the first time they'd admitted to each other how utterly ridiculous their sums about moving to the country had been. For some reason they'd naïvely believed that everything would be half the price outside London, which was true of property but not of anything else, especially not petrol, which they needed twice as much of.

'I felt this awful kind of breadwinner thing that we'd never had before, and it made me feel rubbish. I wasn't being a proper man and providing for you all. That's what moving here did – it made us into the sort of family that I never thought we'd be. You're the clever one with the great job, not me; it's one of the things I loved about you when we got together.'

She nodded, feeling ashamed that her temporary

boredom in her job and greed for a nice kitchen that opened out on to a garden had led to them all being so miserable. 'I completely understand, I do, but you've got to tell me the thing that's bothering you. This habit you developed.'

'I felt trapped. Like we'd be in this silly situation of me mega-commuting every week for ever unless I did something about it.'

Emily and Matt had always leavened seriousness with humour, and she was determined that this time should be no different. It was all too weird as it was. 'You became a male escort, didn't you?'

He smiled, but wanly. 'No, this is where the sport comes in. I always enjoyed watching sport and I know a lot about it. So I thought I'd try to make some money out of that knowledge. Not initially, but that's how it developed. I didn't have much else to do in the evenings, when I was either at the horrible Travelodge or making a nuisance of myself on other people's sofa beds.'

'I don't get what you're talking about.'

He gulped. 'I placed a free bet on a website, one of those sites that are always advertised on TV in the middle of matches. And I won!' He looked childishly delighted. 'It was quite a long shot, who was going to score and when, and I got it right, right down to the nearest minute and that it was a header.' He looked misty-eyed. 'They gave me fifty pounds. Well, fifty pounds in credits to make more bets.'

Emily stared at her smart, lovable, wonderful husband in disbelief. What an idiot. 'Go on,' she said, careful to try to remove judgement from her tone. They give you a freebie to suck you in, you fool; even heroin addicts know about that one.

'I wasn't so successful with the second lot of bets.' You don't say, thought Emily. 'Actually that's not true. I made enough on one of them, the cricket if you want to know.'

I don't want to, no, I just want to know how much of our money you've blown.

'So I placed some more bets with the money I'd won. It wasn't like it was even real money at this point, it was still off the back of the first free bet. It was harmless. I wasn't making any money but I wasn't losing any either, and it gave me something to do in the evenings. I was so lonely.'

Emily felt a pang. She'd never considered that he might be lonely; she'd just resented the freedom of his life, which she imagined as a metropolitan idyll of child-free care-lessness, filled with pubs and pints, booze and banter, in contrast to her own existence of unrelenting domesticity. 'I see. When did things change?'

'Quite quickly. I realised that if I actually started making money with the bets then I'd be able to give up working in London and move up here properly to start freelancing from home, like we'd planned when we did this. I didn't want to make a living out of it or anything, just enough to get me out of this mad situation we were in. And I couldn't do that fiddling about with the credits I'd got from the free bet.'

'So you started using our money? From the joint

account?' The joint account that she knew now to be depleted. She could see where this conversation was heading.

He nodded. 'And things were going all right to begin with. I won some, I lost some, but after six months or so I was about three grand up.'

'That's good. But I'm sensing you're not three grand up now.' The words were coming out of his mouth, but she couldn't believe them. She had thought many things of Matt, but she'd always loved the fact that he was so sensible. Yes, sensible; it sounded so boring and unsexy, but the alternative was far worse. Sensible was the one thing that in the end she valued above all else in her husband and the father of her children.

'I had a bad run.' He hung his head in shame.

'I see.' And she did, it was all making sense now. 'I remember you being very distracted. Since before Christmas. Always checking your phone, watching sport all the time. Even when you were here you weren't here, if you see what I mean. You used to jump every time your phone buzzed.'

'I'd set up some alerts on the events I'd bet on. It felt like work to me, so that even when I was here, I was working.'

'So where are we on the bad run?'

'Pretty bad.'

'How bad?' She had no idea what the figures might be in all this; it might as well have been Monopoly money, a feeling that Matt had evidently shared when he was making these ridiculous bets. Was bad a four-, five- or

– oh God – six-figure sum? He was looking at the TV screen intently once more.

'Matt!' she shouted, clicking her fingers in his face again. 'For God's sake, stop it! We're supposed to be talking and you're looking at the bloody sport. Can't you see how much that's going to annoy me? I feel like I'm talking to one of the children and I'm having to tell them "no toys at the table". Now, *now* of all times, concentrate on what I'm saying. We need to swap places so you can't even be tempted to look at the TV.' They did. 'So you were about to tell me how much of our money you've blown.'

'It's complicated.'

'I used to have a big job, remember. I think my tiny brain can probably understand it if you just tell me the sum involved.'

'It was twelve thousand pounds.'

She slumped in what she thought might be relief. Yes, it was bad; it was all their savings, savings that they didn't really have given the size of their mortgage and their lack of adequate pension provision and the fact that it was money she had to live off, but it wasn't so much that they'd be made homeless or have to stop eating or putting on the heating. 'Hang on a minute, you say *was* twelve thousand. What is it now?'

He gulped again and she saw him glance into the mirror behind her head.

'Matt, you're watching the TV through the mirror! For God's sake, what do I need to do to make you stop?' She threw a coat over his head so that he couldn't see anything and continued to talk to him through his make-shift burka. 'Tell me what you mean by *was* twelve thousand pounds.'

'I don't know.' His voice was muffled by the coat. People were looking at them and she was, of course, aware that they must look ridiculous, a grown woman sitting in front of a talking coat pile. 'Can I take this off my head now?'

'No. Not until I get to the bottom of this or the landlord turns the TV off. What do you mean, you don't know?'

'I've got this accumulator.'

'I don't know what that is.'

'It's a bet made on a series of bets. They're all connected and you have to win all of them to win the overall bet, but obviously the odds increase the longer the bet is.'

'I understand. And how much more money are we going to lose because of this accumulator? How big is our debt going to be by the time you've messed up that one?'

He shook his head. 'Not much bigger. It was only a ten-pound initial bet.'

'So what does it have to do with anything?'

'The final bit of it rests on two NFL games.'

'Two what?'

'American football,' he explained. 'The Chicago Bears – it's tonight, in the afternoon US time but we won't know until the small hours. And then one more after that.'

'But Matt, what on earth do you know about American football?'

'I had a lot of empty evenings. Actually I've done quite well so far on NFL.'

She shook her head. 'So you've bet on them winning or losing or whatever, I don't care. And if it goes as you want it to, then what?'

He looked pathetically hopeful. 'Then the debt is down to a few thousand. Just over three.'

She understood immediately. Without intending to, he had sucked her into the world of gambling, as she now found herself instinctively hoping that the Chicago Bears, whoever they were, did whatever it was he wanted them to do.

But she also understood that if he won the bet, they might lose the war against this addiction of his. She wanted him to win the money, yes, of course. But if he won, he'd be vindicated: a complicated accumulator bet would have paid off (well, *almost* paid off) the £12,000. And she knew enough about gambling to know that if he won, he'd be far more inclined to carry on wasting their money on this high-stakes game.

Somehow Matt had contrived to turn her into a gambler herself – what did she value more: the dent in their debt that winning the accumulator would make, or a husband who would be more likely to never want to bet again?

She now understood the meaning of the phrase 'heads you lose, tails I win'. She couldn't be sure which outcome would be best for her, for him or for them.

Bailey was waiting for Sasha when she got home. They sat on the deep velvet-covered armchairs by the stove in the kitchen, clasping their mugs of tea and then their knees as Sasha told her daughter of the events at the Nell.

'So you just left John crying on the floor?' Bailey asked, enraptured by the whole tale, with its winning combination of teenage love and adult idiocy. 'Bloody hell, Mum.'

'Do you think we shouldn't have? What would you have done?'

Bailey visibly blossomed as Sasha asked for her advice. Why hadn't she ever realised that it was not her job as a mother to fix things, but to enable her children to do so? This feeling of warmth and communion was like falling in love. She felt giddy, joyous, despite what she knew to be true of her marriage. 'I don't know. He does sound like a twat.'

'Yes, he is. I thought he might be evil, but seeing him lying there, I realised that he's just pathetic. And it's partly Tamsin's fault. For years she let him get away with it.'

'Mum, that's victim-blaming.'

Bailey was doing that teenage thing of making it all about her. 'No it's not,' said Sasha. 'It's about making choices. And the way that things that happen now can shape the rest of your life. You're going to be OK, sweetheart. You can move schools now, or wait until sixth form, but you're going to be OK. Better than that, you're going to be brilliant. Not because I can fix things for you, but because you managed to tell me what was going on and because you're wonderful. You're already on the way to fixing it yourself just by having told me all about it.'

The curtain of hair that had been closed for the last

six months was opened and Sasha could see her daughter's face once again. And it was beautiful, smiling and open.

'Bailey, do you have a number for Rosie?'

'Yes,' she said with suspicion. 'You're not angry with her, are you? She was only trying to help.'

Sasha shook her head. 'Not angry, no. But you don't need her any more. You can sort this out for yourself.'

'With a little bit of help from you?'

'Maybe a little. But mostly you.'

She put the number into her phone and went to lock herself in the loo to write her message uninterrupted.

Rosie, your work here is done. I promise I will punish Ned, but please don't let Bailey have to share that punishment. I will lose a husband but get back my daughter. For this I am grateful and I hope it is enough for you to find some peace.

She paused and then added three words.

I believe you.

Waiting in the hospital was torture. Not because her hand hurt; it might well have done, but Tamsin was anaesthetised by the shock of it all. No, she just wanted to be alone with Mickey.

When her faith wavered, she just looked at her hand. All those years spent cowed by John, and just meeting Mickey again had given her the strength to stand up to him, wielding a knife and everything.

They used the waiting time to stare at one another and smile, then to find out more about the years in between, which somehow seemed to be a shorter time than the eight months they'd actually spent together. He understood about the wreckage of those years and how it had led her to marry John and exist in her half-life since then. She learnt that he hadn't been married but had had two long-term living-together relationships that had been blighted by his inability to move on from the past.

His job, she discovered, had something to do with computers. Ironic, really, since she was the only person in the country who wasn't computer-literate. Despite moving from school to school with his flaky mother, he'd made a success of his life thanks to intelligence and determination. She was ashamed that with her greater material advantages she'd been unable to do so.

'I don't have any money,' she told him.

He shrugged. 'I've got plenty.'

Did this mean what it seemed to mean, that he was suggesting they would be together? She hardly dared ask, but then she looked down at her hand and said, 'What do you mean?'

'I mean, I've got somewhere to live.'

'That's not a caravan,' she said.

'No, but I could get one if you wanted.'

She laughed. 'Or a house boat.'

'Or a tent. Tammy, I'd live anywhere with you.'

'We don't know each other.'

'But we do, don't we?'

'Yes.' She struggled to reconcile the feeling that if she stayed with him all would be right for ever and the suspicion that, as usual, she was being silly. A silly empty-headed doll who went from the possession of one man to another. 'Oh Mickey, I feel like nobody's ever known me, but . . .'

'But what?'

'I'm alive for the first time in sixteen years.' He stroked her wounded hand and she felt her stomach churn with longing. Concentrate, she told herself. 'And the thing with being alive is that it brings up lots of other stuff. Sensible stuff. I can't just ride off in your gypsy caravan, because you coming back has allowed me to think. I haven't had a proper thought for years.' She laughed nervously. 'It's true. And now I'm filled with them.' Many of them lustful. Oh God, even in the strip lighting and chaos of the A&E department, she wanted to lie down with him or drag him off to the disabled toilets.

'I've waited sixteen years for you; I can wait a bit longer.'

'Oh I can't wait for *that*,' she said. With Mickey she'd always been so confident of herself sexually that it didn't seem at all odd to be propositioning him when with other men she'd been passive; sex being something done *to* her rather than with her. '*That* we do as soon as we can.' She paused to look at him, wanting to lick him all over, to relearn his body now that it was no longer filled with angles and ribs as it had once been. 'I mean everything else. My education, learning to live by myself, becoming a person.'

'One step at a time.' He smiled.

At last the nurse called her in, cleaned the wound, gave her a tetanus injection and a bandage.

'So,' Mickey said to her.

'So,' she replied. But where to go?

The hotel on the outskirts of town could not have been more different to the Nell. Where the Nell was rough, dirty, broken but somehow natural in all its asphalt splendour, this place was modern, characterless and neat. Tamsin sniffed it as she came in and it smelt of disinfectant. It smelt, she admitted to herself, not dissimilar to Mickey's car.

Their room was, apparently, the finest on offer. Tamsin had been to many hotels with John and they were always the best, with gyms in the basement and chocolates on the pillow. This small room with its chipboard wood-look headboard and thin curtains was very different.

'Cup of tea?' she asked Mickey, pointing towards the small kettle and UHT milk cartons in the corner.

He shook his head.

It felt like a now-or-never moment. If something didn't happen within the next sixty seconds then they might have to wait another decade and a half. It had never been hard to get going in the old days; quite the opposite, in fact: their bodies had ached with leg-crossing desire in every lesson they'd shared.

Mickey broke the silence. 'I remember how you liked to be stroked in a line from your belly button downwards.' To your cunt; that was what he used to call it then, with his Geordie accent.

'And I remember how you liked to be licked.' From underneath up the shaft of his cock, but she couldn't say it, not quite yet.

He walked towards her as she sat on the bed. She lifted herself up so he could shimmy her jeans down. 'Right here,' he said, touching her exactly where he had always done, his fingers still light, dancing down over her now flat stomach.

She shivered with desire. Although she was naïve, she was not stupid, whatever anyone else thought, and she knew there was every chance that sex that had been percolating for a decade and a half might be disappointing. She weighed up the two options: go straight for it, to get it out of the way quickly so they could take their time getting it right next time, or carry on delaying the moment as they were.

In a split second, she opted for the former, moving over to pull down his jeans and pants and then leaning backwards to drag him on top of her on the bed. He was hard – thank you, ghost of alfresco past sex, she thought – and she pulled him straight inside her, where she was wetter than she'd ever been with John, almost embarrassingly so.

He gasped, and the sound and feel of him seemed to fill her entirely. They paused for a moment to look at one another, and both grinned. Then he thrust inside her only a few times before coming noisily and joyfully.

'I'm sorry,' he said. 'I've been waiting so long.'

'Doesn't matter,' she said, smiling. 'We've got lots more time.' She throbbed with half satisfaction, which he sensed and dived down. With John she'd always been aware of his distaste for bodily fluids, which was why she was so careful to wash the sheets every time, but she knew, she just knew, that Mickey would have no such squeamishness about the taste of her mingling with the taste of him.

He was lapping at her, making really quite noisy slurping sounds, but she loved it, she was loving it. She wanted to come so much, but she wanted this to go on for ever, with her hands gripping his now dark auburn hair, which though less abundant than back then was still thick enough to feel substantial as she twirled her fingers through it.

Her body had changed so much over the years, but not where it counted. He seemed to understand exactly where she needed to be licked and at what speed, slowing and quickening in a way that she wouldn't have even known she wanted.

But then she suddenly knew exactly what she wanted. She pressed his face harder into her and rocked back and forth until she began to feel dizzy.

'Mickey, Mickey,' she shouted, then pushed him away and placed her hand hard against herself to calm down the almost painful throbbing. She leant back. 'Jesus, Mickey, I saw stars, I actually saw stars.'

He laughed, then took off her top and peeled off her jeans, which had been pinned painfully around her ankles. 'You're just as lovely as I could have hoped,' he said, visibly moved by the sight of her naked body.

More than a desire for his body in the same state, she felt an utter comfort and peace in the fact that she was lying there stripped down, emotionally and physically. She had laughed during sex. Now that was something she hadn't done for years – not with John or the random pile of men she'd bedded or straddled or been pinned in an alleyway by.

'I don't ever want to be apart from you again, Tammy,' Mickey whispered in her ear as he plunged inside her once again.

'Hmm,' she found herself saying without commitment.

Taking Rafa to the vet the next day gave the whole family some much-needed distraction. Emily and Matt from the question mark of the final bricks in the great wall of his accumulator bet and her uncertainty of which would be the greater gamble – winning or losing the bet. The children from the fact that they had become quite giddy with lack of sleep and the excitement of missing school for the day and possibly the next. Emily, again, from worrying that the children's manic behaviour was in fact a sign of the long-term damage sustained by the prolonged exposure to the gas. Emily, yet again, from Sue, her mother-in-law, wonderful woman that she was but who was driving her insane with her questions about what their plans were and when they would be returning to the house, 'not that you're not all very welcome to stay here for as long as you like. It's quite *lovely* to have you here.'

Rafa's behaviour wasn't getting any less odd. He alternated between running round in pointless circles, looking sleepy and worrying his bald patch ever more aggressively.

'It's called trichotillomania,' Emily said.

'What is?' said Matt.

'Rafa's compulsion to pull out his fur. Well that's what they call it in humans when they pull their hair out, anyway.'

In the end, they had to put him in a cage borrowed from the vet's reception, which led to much wailing and ranting from the children, who were quickly distracted by seeing what rude words Clem could read out to Zanna and Nate from the various pamphlets around the waiting room, with the one on threadworm yielding particularly giggle-worthy results.

'There's nothing funny about that word,' said Emily as they ran around the area shouting 'anus' over and over.

Matt raised his eyebrows at her as if to suggest that, well, yes, it was quite funny, especially when connected to dogs. She glowered back at him, both for the idiocy and for the earlier revelation. She was still trying to process the fact that while she'd been stuck out here in a cottage on the edge of a village, he'd been racking up debts that wiped out anything he'd been earning.

Finally, the family of five (six including the dog) trooped into the vet's office. While the doctor at the hospital had been reassuringly old-school, Jenny Naldrett, the vet recommended by Ben, looked as young as Sasha's daughter Bailey, her lithe body dressed in jeans and a T-shirt, her face glowing with wholesome good health.

Her good cheer soon waned as Rafa was brought out of his cage.

'Hmm,' she kept on saying, not giving anything away, sounding like a plumber appalled by his predecessor's work.

'What is it?' Emily finally demanded. At the sound of sharpness in her voice, the children stopped trying on the dog collar that a previous patient had left. 'Sorry, I mean, is there any damage from the gas? He saved our lives, you see.' Cue more tears from Clem and Nate.

'No, I don't think it's anything to do with the exposure to gas. Rafa's problems go back far longer than that.'

'Oh.' Could Bailey be right, that Rafa was the canine equivalent of one of those abused children who never learnt to talk or love because they'd had such a terrible start in life?

'What I'm about to say is going to sound strange, but my dissertation was on post-traumatic stress disorder in dogs.'

I knew it, thought Emily.

'It's often seen in animals that have been involved in conflict situations, just as it is in humans. Rafa's behaviour – his compulsive licking of this patch here,' she pointed at the most mangy bit of his black-and-grey-speckled fur, 'the turning in circles, the fear that he displayed in the cage – suggests to me that he didn't have the best start in life.'

Now Emily burst into tears, while the children looked at her with open-mouthed horror.

'Does that make sense to you?' asked Jenny.

She nodded and found she was unable to speak.

'What happened to him?'

Emily shook her head and at last managed to get some words out. 'I don't know exactly, but I think he may have come from a puppy farm, where he was locked up or something. That's what other people have suggested, and to be honest, I never saw where he was born or spent the first few weeks of his life.'

'Yes, that would make sense. Tell me, how did you come to get him?' Jenny's face was sympathetic rather than judgemental, but that didn't stop Emily from feeling ashamed.

She shook her head. 'The Internet, picked him up from a van,' she mumbled.

'What do you want to do about his issues?'

'I don't know, you tell me. Antidepressants for dogs? Cognitive behavioural therapy?'

'Dognitive behavioural therapy more like,' quipped Matt.

Emily rolled her eyes. 'What do people normally do in these situations?'

Jenny put her head on one side in the way that professionals did when they were delivering bad news. 'Often we recommend that when perhaps a dog is in a lot of pain, mental and physical, it's a good idea to end that pain.'

'No!' Emily surprised herself by shouting this. 'No.'

'What, Mummy?' asked Nate. 'What's she saying?'

'Nothing, sweetheart.' She turned to the vet. 'That is not an option.'

Jenny sighed. 'Well if you insist, but I'm ethically bound to explain to you that even to try to help Rafa with the physical signs of his inbreeding—'

'Inbreeding?' asked Matt. 'You mean our dog is the product of . . . of . . . ?'

'I think it highly likely,' Jenny continued. 'These puppy farms don't care about the end product so long as they're paid. What usually happens is that they mate their bitches far too frequently and with too much consanguinity. In layman's terms, the dogs they breed from are usually too closely related, so that any problems get exaggerated and more pronounced with each breeding.'

'Oh God,' said Matt. 'It's like one of those hillbilly tribes you read about in the paper.'

Emily stared at Rafa. She'd feared him, thought him deformed or deficient in some way. She had thought she was going mad when in fact it was the poor dog who was, as she'd suspected, mad in his own way. It wasn't his fault. None of it was. Like a grumpy teenager, he'd never asked to be born. And having been born, to parents who were probably related, he'd lived his poor little life in a state of neurotic confusion. Look at her: coming up to two years of dog ownership, she'd anthropomorphised him with the best of the mad animal-lovers that she'd once mocked, like a twisted Disney cartoon. 'So what are his problems, the physical ones to start with?'

'His malocclusion is the obvious one.'

'Sorry, his what?'

'His teeth.'

'You mean the cute little underbite?' She thought of what Bailey had already diagnosed.

'Yes. Probably one of the dogs had this issue and then it got bred and bred until it became worse and worse. He's in constant pain.'

'And is there anything we can do?' asked Emily.

'Perhaps she's right, perhaps it's kinder to . . .' Matt glanced at the children and mouthed, 'put him to sleep.'

'Why?' said Emily indignantly.

'Well, because he's a bit of a mess.'

'So what? If one of our children turns out to be autistic or schizophrenic or something, I suppose you're going to suggest we put them down?'

'Emily, don't be ridiculous, you know it's not the same. People put dogs down for all sorts of reasons, and this would be to end his suffering.'

'He saved our lives. We wouldn't be sitting here now if it weren't for Rafa.' She turned to the vet. 'What can we do?'

'I'm not an orthodontist,' Jenny said, 'nor will Rafa let me look at him in any detail.' Rafa chose this moment to bare his funny, misshapen, painful teeth at her. 'Ideally, I'd have monitored his transition from puppy teeth to adult teeth, which is when we spot any issues, just as we would with children. I'd have to refer him to a specialist in veterinary dentistry.'

'I've lost eight baby teeth,' said Clem, displaying the slightly discoloured set that had replaced the little pearls that had been there before.

Jenny gave a wan smile, as if Clem were an annoying talking animal. 'If I had been able to monitor this transition, then perhaps we'd have been able to remove teeth to prevent the later malocclusions, but this would probably have taken place when he was with his breeders.'

'So what can we do now?' asked Emily.

'I would imagine that we'd be looking at some extractions,

maybe some root canal work. The aim would be to decrease discomfort rather than give him a perfect smile, if you see what I mean. Every time he chews or bites, it's causing him pain. Even eating will be a discomforting experience for him.'

'Poor Rafa,' said Emily, feeling tearful once again.

'Indeed,' the vet said. 'Of course, I'm honour-bound to warn you that, even with pet insurance, the cost of such a course of treatment is likely to be very expensive, some would say prohibitive.'

Emily and Matt looked at each other, both thinking of the £12,000 debt and that accumulator with two more bets to come. Emily had felt that Matt had been gambling with their marriage, but now it seemed as if the stakes had been upped to Rafa's life.

14

Two out of Three Weekend Wives

Emily sat in the empty kitchen of the cottage at the end of the village. Gone were the jars filled with wild flowers and wooden spoons, Rafa's dog basket and the oversized clock on the wall. Gone were her husband, three children and the dog and with them the sounds of barking, bickering and laughter. The not-Aga Aga had been switched off for ever.

Strangely, it was Rafa's absence that she felt most keenly, above that of her children or husband. Matt had hardly ever been there, while the children had enjoyed their other life at school. She and Rafa were the ones who had spent hours together in the kitchen by the stove that almost killed them.

All that remained of the nearly two years they'd lived there were three cups, a pint of milk and the coffee machine. They were lined up in readiness for the last meeting of the weekend wives. She supposed they could carry on with their meetings – they had become good friends, after all – but at least two of them were no longer weekend wives.

As she looked around, she tried to absorb the significance of the fact that she hadn't been the legal owner of the house for the last three days; they'd just been lucky that their kindly buyer had allowed them that extra time to move out rather than insisting on the manic completion that usually happened at such times.

Completion was what estate agents called the day when contracts for buying and selling were signed off, and it seemed a good term for what had happened to her and her family. They were complete. They'd completed a circle that had sped around the city and a village before finally ending up in a town; hers a full-time job, unemployment and now part-time work. She'd had to go through moving here to get to where they were now, and she was grateful for it.

That morning she'd gone for a last walk across the fields that led to the Nell. With her ability to appreciate something only when she was about to lose it, she finally saw how beautiful the place was. Her eyes relished stretching to the horizon, taking in the morning mist that rippled its way across the crops and trees. She would miss life in the village, only now realising the many joys it offered along with the frustrations of patchy broadband and supermarkets you had to drive to.

Most of all, she would miss the friends she'd made but whom she was hoping to keep.

'Sasha,' she said as she opened the door to the first of them. 'Welcome to my home, which is neither welcoming nor my home for that matter.'

Sasha laughed as she looked round at the emptiness. 'You've got the coffee in, anyway.' She turned around to call to her companion. 'Come on, Rafa, say goodbye to your old home.' She ushered in that furry face once so familiar to Emily, but whose newly improved looks never failed to surprise her.

'Hello, gorgeous boy,' said Emily, leaning down to let him lick her face, like the mad dog woman she'd become. 'I've missed you, baby. Thanks so much for looking after him these last few days. I think his rehabilitation programme would have suffered a serious setback if we'd had to cart him around with all the boxes. As it is I'm worried about how he'll settle into the new place.'

'It was a pleasure, and good practice for the dog I've promised to get for the children. In a way, he's Bailey's therapy dog. She feels a kinship with him, especially now that they've both had successful orthodontic work.'

Emily looked at Rafa with some scepticism. 'Less successful and still ongoing in his case. Not exactly a Hollywood smile, but Jenny Naldrett says he should find eating a lot less painful now.' She shuddered at the memory of an anaesthetised Rafa with his mouth wired open for the extractions to take place. 'He certainly seems a lot calmer these days.' She hugged him close to her and he received her embrace with stiff acceptance. She'd only recently been able to forgive herself for all those months of resentment she'd felt towards him.

Rafa responded by jumping down and doing a few frenzied circles of the kitchen, as if searching for his missing basket.

'Not your home any longer, boy, but you'll like our new house. There's a street outside full of interesting messages left by other dogs. Clem calls them wee-mails.

Quite a lot of dog poo too, something I thought I'd left behind in London.'

'So was Rafa's dental work as expensive as Bailey's?' asked Sasha.

Emily grimaced. 'I can't imagine it was much cheaper.' She remembered the awful debates that she and Matt had had over whether they should save him or not, especially when Matt's accumulator bet failed at the very final fence, or should she say game, since it involved American football. It was hard to justify dog orthodontics with a £12,000 debt hanging over you. 'If you'd told me a year ago that I'd spend that much money on a mutt, I'd have thought you were mad. I still might be. I don't think I've ever agonised over anything as much as this, but, well, in the end, I don't really think we had much choice. Thank God we had such a good offer on this place, as otherwise we'd have had to bankrupt ourselves for the sake of his teeth. But I can't resent the money. Rafa saved our lives, didn't he? Can't put a price on that.'

'It's all worked out, hasn't it?' said Sasha.

'Yes, I think it has, though I'm sad about leaving here, however much I used to whine. I like our new place, I really do. Please come and see us there soon, it's only twenty miles away. I don't know why I didn't think of moving into a town in the first place. It didn't have to be all or nothing, I now realise, not so binary as rural versus urban. When we were in London, it seemed like it had to be me working full time and living in the city or me not working at all and living in the middle of nowhere.' She looked at Sasha. 'Sorry, I didn't mean that.'

'Don't worry, I like living in the middle of nowhere.'

'My old boss was great about me setting up a satellite branch, and in the office we've rented there's even space for Matt's business. We'll go from never seeing each other to seeing each other all the bloody time.' And it's good, thought Emily, it really is. There was more than enough patent work locally to give her a reasonable income and take some of the financial pressure off Matt, while seeing each other get on with their professional lives in such proximity was already leading to new respect. She hadn't quite forgiven him for the gambling debacle, but was surprised to find herself almost relieved when that last bet hadn't paid off. At least that meant it *was* the last bet, whereas she knew that if he'd won on it, she'd have been forced to monitor his Internet use on a permanent basis.

Moving out of the cottage when the gas leak happened, although only for a few days, broke the tenuous bond she felt with it. As soon as she had walked back through the door, she knew they'd be selling it. She had felt a joyful relief at the prospect. Of course, she had thought, we can move into a terraced house in the nearest university town. It will be bigger than the place we left in London, and I can work. Only that morning, she'd had another email from her old boss, asking her to consider taking on some freelance work. She was sorry to leave Sasha and Tamsin, but glad that she had at last found a way of bringing her family back together.

It had been fine, too; everyone else accepted the decision as soon as she announced it. 'I really thought the children would hate the move,' she said to Sasha, 'but it turns out they never really got into the whole tadpoles in jam jars thing that I'd fantasised about.'

'I'm so glad,' said Sasha.

'I'll miss you, though,' said Emily shyly, as she'd never quite felt she deserved Sasha's friendship. 'How are things?'

'Fine, fine. Bailey has had a terrible time at school, but she's through the worst of it, touch wood. She'll finish her exams there next summer and then go off to the sixth-form college for a fresh start.'

'What about you? Have you escaped the curse of the weekend wife?' Emily thought it was a rhetorical question, as of the three of them, Sasha seemed to be the only one who'd made it work for her.

'No, if you must know,' she said with a sigh. 'Ned and I have split up.'

'Oh, I'm sorry to hear that.'

'Don't be. It's fine. To be honest, we saw each other so irregularly that it doesn't make much difference. No, that's wrong, it's actually better now. He's made much more effort to find jobs over here now he knows he can't rely on me to keep the home fires burning constantly. The children see more of him, and they're closer to him without me always being some sort of UN interpreter standing between them.'

At first that had been the line she'd fed herself, the 'it's really much better this way, honestly, truly it is', but Sasha felt the truth of it now. Ned had been shocked, then angry, then resigned. The children seemed unfazed, as if they'd always known that somehow they weren't a real family and it was nice to have this formalised. Once she'd told Ned that their marriage was over, there was another person who needed to know he'd been punished.

Rosie had agreed to meet Sasha in an anonymous hotel halfway between them, like strangers hooking up over the Internet for extramarital sex. Sasha felt a kinship with the woman she'd once thought of as malign. Any anger she might have harboured towards the wreaker of such destruction was now replaced by gratitude that she had helped to bring Bailey back to her.

'I mean it,' she'd said to Rosie as they sat eating the hotel's special teatime offering of a cake stand laden with curling cucumber sandwiches and lurid pastries. 'I do believe you.' Anybody looking at them would think they were old friends having a happy reunion.

'I know you do,' Rosie replied.

'But I still don't really understand why you felt you needed to come into our lives after all these years.'

Rosie sighed. 'I'm not sure I know myself. What was it that Eddie said in his email to me? A mid-life crisis. It's the time of life when you start to take stock of things. I don't have children. I never wanted them, but it's still a shock when it's no longer your choice any more. And not having choices is a terrible thing.'

'I understand.' Sasha paused. She didn't want to give Rosie the next choice, but she knew she had to. For Bailey's sake, she wanted to both offer and deny Rosie this decision. 'It's up to you what you do next about what happened back then. If you feel you need to report it to the police, then you must.'

'I'd have your blessing?'

'Not exactly. I'm sorry, but it's not something I'd relish given what it would do to Bailey and Spike. But it's your choice, it really is. This time you get to choose, and I will not try to dissuade you.'

Rosie shrank into thought. After a pause she asked, 'You've really split up from him? For good?'

Sasha nodded. 'We're definitely over. It hadn't been great for a long time, but I suppose you helped me to realise that. Have you made up your mind what you're going to do?'

It seemed to Sasha that there was an agonising wait before Rosie finally spoke. 'I'm not going to the police. Even my best friends didn't believe me when I told them at the time. I won't go because I hope he's suffering enough now that you've left him. He doesn't like rejection, does he? But also because it would hurt people who don't deserve it.'

'Bailey,' said Sasha.

'And you. You don't deserve to be dragged through this.'

'Nor you.'

Sasha repeated the phrase once more, for it felt worth repeating. 'I believe you, Rosie.'

'So,' said Sasha to Emily in the empty kitchen, 'I was right about two out of three weekend wives. I'm glad I didn't take Matt up on his offer of a bet.'

Emily gave a little shudder.

'I'm glad it was you two that survived,' said Sasha. 'Really I am. Matt's always been a good man. Or boy, as I still think of him. And we're all right, Spike, Bailey and I, which I realise is all that matters to me. Them and my parents.' She smiled. 'But I'll miss you too, Emily. I'm someone who's quite happy in my own company, hence moving here from Los Angeles of all unusual relocations, but I liked the three of us meeting like we did.'

'Even though it ended up with a mad husband waving a penknife in a grotty agricultural building?' said Emily.

'Especially because it ended up with a mad husband and a penknife.' Sasha looked around the kitchen. 'After all, you did Tamsin a big favour.'

'Which ended up with her doing me a massive favour in return,' said Emily. They heard a knock. 'That'll be her now.'

They both went to the door to see Tamsin standing back on the road, leaning on a very cute aubergine-coloured Fiat Cinquecento.

'What do you think?' she said.

'Of what?' asked Emily.

'My new car, silly.' Tamsin actually stroked it, lovingly. 'Isn't it gorgeous?'

'Does that mean . . . ?' said Sasha.

'Yes! I passed. First time, and after just a week's intensive course. The examiner said my driving was perfect and that I was a natural. It turns out that driving is another thing I'm not rubbish at.'

'And picking cars,' said Emily with a sigh. 'I'm sure

there's some horrible correlation between the size of your car and your women's bits. I've got a very baggy people carrier. If you see what I mean.'

'I had to have a car, you see,' said Tamsin, 'to get to college every day. Those A levels aren't going to take themselves. My own car,' she said dreamily and dragged herself away from it reluctantly. She whirled into the kitchen with her shoulders back and an infectious energy. She was almost unrecognisable from the shrinking woman who'd been with John, having grown taller and a bit plumper in the six months since she'd left him. She sat down at the table and surveyed the room with pride.

'My car, and now my kitchen,' she said. 'It really is my kitchen, in my house, bought with my money.'

'Thank you,' said Emily. 'I don't know what we'd have done if you hadn't come in so quickly with the asking price and no chain.'

'No, thank you. I've always loved your house, and I can't believe it's now mine.'

'Did you not think of moving in with Mickey?' asked Sasha.

Tamsin shook her head. 'No. It's weird – being with Mickey gives me the strength not to live with him, if you see what I mean. I'd never have thought I'd be able to live without a man if I hadn't met up with the very man who always made me think I could do anything. Which is kind of sad, I know, but good too.'

'As is the fact that you've got the means to buy somewhere,' said Emily.

'Well that's sort of sad too,' said Tamsin, 'since all the

money comes from John so I'm still living off a man even if I'm not living with one. And the only reason I got so much money was because my father made him sign a pre-nup guaranteeing me a house and an income if we ever split up. I had no idea at the time, but it makes sense – Dad was sort of signing me away, getting me off his hands, so he wanted to make sure he was never going to have his mopey daughter living with him again. Of course, he knew I'd be too stupid to get any money myself, but I'm glad he did it. So there you go, money from a man organised by another man.'

'Yes, I suppose it is a bit sad,' said Emily, 'treating you like a chattel. But on the other hand, you're taking control of your own life in an amazing way. I'm so pleased for you.'

My kitchen, my house, my car. Tamsin couldn't stop saying the words to herself.

She'd been so afraid of John. Why, she'd never been quite sure, as she'd not thought he'd physically hurt her. It was more that he seemed to know her so well and so knew what a worthless, stupid person she was, just as her parents had always said. When she saw herself reflected in Mickey's eyes, she had realised at last that they were all wrong. Mickey was the most wonderful person in the world, he loved her, therefore she had to be OK. To put herself down was to question Mickey's judgement, and that she'd never do.

John was older, richer and stronger. The age thing she couldn't do anything about, especially since they had met when every month he had on her made him so much more powerful. Ditto the wealth – she had no money when they met and she wasn't about to get any without having a job. The strength he gained from all those grunting sessions at the gym and with weights at home.

Worse than that was his knowledge. He knew where she was, how many steps she walked, what she was wearing. He was God, all-seeing.

Rather belatedly, she had realised that technology had allowed him all this over her. He had no magic, only a phone and some apps. He tracked her not with some extraordinary telepathy but with a satellite that any old technically literate person could use.

And at the Nell, he'd been stripped of his technology and power and she'd seen him as a weeping, weak man. She thought he'd recover and rise up from his snivelling mess like the phantom in a horror film, but he didn't, instead only shrivelling further. It was as if he'd realised that Tamsin would never cower in front of him again and so he had no use for her. Last she'd heard, he was going out with a woman even younger than she was, though a little bit older than the girl she'd been.

Was it Mickey who'd unlocked her from her cage? He'd given her the key, yes, but she liked to believe that she'd used it herself. That was what he did for her: he gave her the confidence to make herself independent. So yes, perhaps she was only strong because of a man, but she *was* strong and that was what mattered, strong enough to have bought Emily's house, taught herself to drive and enrolled at a further education college.

Which wasn't to say that she wasn't enjoying Mickey. She swooned a little on thinking of him. The sex had picked up from where they'd left off all those years ago. It was a magic elixir that made her feel all-conquering every time she supped on it. They'd holed themselves up in the cheap hotel for a couple of days, having sex and talking and laughing. He was funny and clever, and he adored her. Most of all, his heart too had stopped when he'd had to leave her, so that Tamsin felt she was as much his reanimator as he was hers. This was almost what she loved most about him: that he had saved her, but more importantly, she'd saved him too.

Then she'd dared to go back to the house that had supposedly been her home. John had put it on the market and taken everything from it. Everything except her, his once most-treasured possession. And then came the good news that he wanted a divorce, and, what was more, a divorce where he had to give her enough money to make a new life for herself. A life that involved education and independence with a large dollop of Mickey on the side. She had managed to time-travel back to the Nell and come out the other side, into the present.

'I wanted to say thanks so much for buying our house and being so kind about everything with a small present,' said Emily. She gestured towards the coffee machine, as shiny and engineered as the car parked outside. She'd decorated it with a red ribbon. 'My beloved Gaggia, which I needed when I moved out here, but not now that I live within walking distance of a café selling artisan coffee in a cup with a lid on. Please think of me every time you make a cup of coffee.'

'Thank you so much. I will,' said Tamsin. 'And I'll make you a cup every time you come back here, which I hope will be often. I know you're busy with your proper job and everything, but please come and visit. It might not be your house any longer, but you'll always be welcome.'

'To the weekend wives,' said Sasha, and they clinked their coffee cups. 'Weekend no more.'

Acknowledgements

Writing is a solitary job and I'm lucky that all those who I do get to work with make up for the lonely hours. My wonderful agent Kate McLennan, Sandy Violette and everyone at Abner Stein have the best offices in London. Though no longer my agent, I'm thrilled to have kept Arabella Stein as a friend.

Thanks to all those at Hodder – especially Sara Kinsella, Carolyn Mays, Sharan Matharu, Emily Kitchin, Karen Geary, Becca Mundy and Lucy Upton. Francesca Best is a brilliant editor, enhancing the good bits and excising the bad. Jane Selley, like all great copy editors, leaves me awed by her talent and ashamed of my howlers. And queen of proofreading, Amber Burlinson, strikes again with her extraordinary eagle eyes.

I'm very grateful to Natalia and Greg Willmott, whose observations sparked the initial idea for couples spending their weeks apart. Bini Adams gave me lots of LA stories, while Lorna Hobbs helped explain to me what patent attorneys do (as well as both being ever-supportive friends). Ken Riddell helped with my building questions. There are many local dogs and their owners who've helped me with my canine queries – Rafa is not based on any of them.

Christina Hopkinson

Many thanks to Lucie McLaughlin for holding the fort and the children's hands.

Matilda Kentridge bought a character's name in an auction to raise money for our children's school, which was very generous of her and I hope she likes the result. Speaking of which, the witty and kind Kira Phillips makes toiling over school fairs and class rep lists (almost) a joy.

There are many friends who make me laugh and let me use their stories. I don't want to name check them individually for fear of missing anyone out through my own ineptitude, but I hope you know who are you. Special thanks to those who've moved to the country, all of who are living lives of genuine idyll – my characters are no reflection, but bliss doesn't make for a good story.

Lastly, always, my family, who put up with me not being as present as I'd like to be – sometimes distracted by thoughts of writing, more often by the phone.

Christina Hopkinson

THE A-LIST FAMILY

Imagine a world where your bikini body has to last *all year*.

Where *paparazzi* turn up for the school run.

Where EVERYBODY knows your name, and your eight-year-old daughter's.

Welcome to everyday life in an A-list family.

Newly employed to look after the daughter of a super-rich and famous power couple, Anna is about to find out what life is really like behind the closed doors of celebrity. And soon she starts to wonder: once you're in, can you get out?

Out now in paperback and ebook.

HODDER

Christina Hopkinson

THE PILE OF STUFF AT THE BOTTOM
OF THE STAIRS

Mary Gilmour feels as though her life is going down a plug hole clogged with cornflakes and Play-Doh. Her job is part time but housework is full time, and she has no time at all for her two young sons.

Mary is convinced that there is only thing standing between her and organised contentment: his name is Joel and she's married to him.

Since star charts have worked on improving the behaviour of their children, she designs an equivalent for her husband: a spreadsheet detailing every balled-up tissue, every sock on the floor, every wet towel on the bed.

Joel has six months to prove that his credits outweigh his debits. Or else . . .

Out now in paperback and ebook.

HODDER

Christina Hopkinson

JUST LIKE PROPER GROWN-UPS

'You don't really grow up until you either have a kid or one of your parents dies.'

Glamorously carefree and nearing forty, Tess shows no sign of settling down. That is, until she drops a bombshell on four of her friends: she's pregnant, and has chosen them as godparents.

Yet while they rally round the single mother, each one is struggling to face the realities of adulthood. Sierra may be only twenty-three but her mother is so irresponsible that she's had to grow up fast. Michael is too busy searching for Mrs Right to worry about collecting the essential accessories of spice racks or investment saucepans, while Owen eases the pain of a mid-life identity crisis with a string of unsuitable fiancées. Only Lucy has the trappings and offspring of a proper grown-up, but is terrified of ageing.

On a challenging and hilarious journey through birth, Botox, bad sex and beyond, all five friends must discover that while growing old is inevitable, growing up is optional . . .

Out now in paperback and ebook.

HODDER

In the best books, the ending often comes as a shock.
Not just because of that one last twist in the tale,
but because you have been so absorbed in their world,
that coming back to the harsh light of reality is a jolt.

If that describes you now, then perhaps you should track down
some new leads, and find new suspense in other worlds.

Join us at www.hodder.co.uk, or follow us on
Twitter @hodderbooks, and you can tap in to a
community of fellow thrill-seekers.

Whether you want to find out more about this book,
or a particular author, watch trailers and interviews, have
the chance to win early limited editions, or simply browse
our expert readers' selection of the very best books,
we think you'll find what you're looking for.

And if you don't, that's the place to tell us what's missing.

We love what we do, and we'd love you to be part of it.

www.hodder.co.uk

@hodderbooks

HodderBooks

HodderBooks